DOUG NAYLOR

Last Human

VIKING

VIKING

Published by the Penguin Group
Penguin Books Ltd, 27 Wrights Lane, London W8 5TZ, England
Penguin Books USA Inc., 375 Hudson Street, New York, New York 10014, USA
Penguin Books Australia Ltd, Ringwood, Victoria, Australia
Penguin Books Canada Ltd, 10 Alcorn Avenue, Toronto, Ontario, Canada M4V 3B2
Penguin Books (NZ) Ltd, 182–190 Wairau Road, Auckland 10, New Zealand

Penguin Books Ltd, Registered Offices: Harmondsworth, Middlesex, England

First published 1995
1 3 5 7 9 10 8 6 4 2
First edition

Set in 12/15 pt Monotype Bembo
Typeset by Datix International Limited, Bungay, Suffolk
Printed in Great Britain by Clays Ltd, St Ives plc

A CIP catalogue record for this book is available from the British Library

ISBN 0–670–85255–4

For Linda, Richard and Matthew

ACKNOWLEDGEMENTS

Thanks to Rob Grant

As many of you will know, the previous two Red Dwarf novels were written in collaboration with Rob Grant. In the summer of 1993 Rob expressed a desire to write a Red Dwarf novel on his own. I look forward to reading it and thank him for the sections in this book that are based on the TV scripts we wrote together.

Muchas gracias

Doug Naylor

London
February 1995

Special thanks to Tony Lacey for his support and patience. Special thanks also to Charles Armitage. Thanks also to Chris Barrie, Craig Charles, Danny John Jules, Robert Llewellyn and Hattie Hayridge. Also thanks to Helen Norman, Andy De Emmony, Justin Judd, Kerry Coldwell, Kate Cotton, Mel Bibby, Howard Burden, Graham Hutchins, Andria Pennell, John Pomphrey, Cate Williams, Peter Wragg and all the Red Dwarf backstage crew. Thanks also to BBC Northwest. Special thanks to Robin Bynoe. Thanks also to Judith Flanders. Also thanks to Christopher White for asking me to thank him in this special thanks section when he happened to wander into my office while I was writing it.

Also my undying gratitude to all the Penguin Reps who were told so many times a Red Dwarf book was coming, only to find it wasn't. Well, now it has. No, really – this time it's true. Thank you.

PROLOGUE

Something monumental was about to happen; possibly the most monumental thing ever to happen anywhere, ever.

Hunched against the spongy base of the baobab tree, under a strake of dyspeptic sky, she gazed across the lake towards the mountains as an endless flock of hooked-beaked birds migrated across the waters.

Why wasn't he here? Why wasn't he with her?

She knew the answer. He was unreachable, two, perhaps three days away – hunting. Molasses of sweat trickled down the ridges of her brow and dribbled on to the broadness of her jaw.

Then it happened again.

It came back.

The lasso of pain whipped around her hips and slowly began to tighten. She bared her teeth and a sound that seemed utterly alien to her small frame erupted into the night sky. For a second even the cicadas were silent. Alone, and as scared as she'd ever been in her entire life, she started to cry. Why had she continued to climb up-river looking for fruit? Why hadn't she turned back when the pains first started? But she'd been carrying the child so long she'd ignored them, not realizing that her time had finally come.

Now it was too late.

Another lasso.

Her brown nails dug huge crescents into the palms of her clenched fists as the garrotte squeezed and squeezed, until it felt as if her heart were being turned inside out. She pushed and grunted and screeched and screamed, and just when she thought she couldn't bear the pain any more her body parted, and a head thrust its way into existence.

She supported the child's head in her hands and pushed. First one shoulder wriggled free, followed by a second, then suddenly the child slithered out into her arms, trailing a trembling neon black umbilical cord. She took hold of the cord and wrapped a length of twine around it, a thumb's distance from the child's stomach, then carefully bit the cord in two, another thumb's distance from that.

She held the child up and peered at it critically. A whimper of delight staggered out of her exhausted body.

It was a girl.

She licked some of the ooze from its face. She could see it better now.

But wait.

There was something wrong. She felt it, instinctively,

The child's limbs were too short, its forehead was too high and its head — its head was so large. She held it, uncertain what to do.

But she was right — there was something wrong with the child. The child was going to be abnormal.

It wasn't going to be like its mother. It wasn't going to be like its father. It wasn't going to be like anyone.

Anyone ever.

She curled the savannah grass around her sun-gnarled fingers and looked across the clearing. Here, in a huge Y-shaped gorge, in a place later called the Serengeti plains, in northern Tanzania, she had given birth to the first. The first of a species that would later take the name Homo.

That would first become Homo habilis, *then* Homo erectus *and finally* Homo sapiens.

The first had been born.

The first human.

She fastened the tiny creature to her breast and it started to feed. After the child was nourished, the ape woman removed the child from her breast and placed it gently on a bed of red oat grass.

The child curled itself into a ball and slept.

PART ONE
Cyberia

CHAPTER 1

Six million years later, in a dilapidated class three transport ship, the last human being in the cosmos lay in the same foetal position as his long dead sister, murmuring remarks in the gibberish of Deep Sleep, until a poorly digested bowl of cabbage soup caused a noisy pocket of escaping air to flee his lower intestine and rouse him from his slumbers. For a brief nano-second he couldn't recall where he was. An inner voice, thick with spite, snickered quietly in his head. 'Embrace the moment,' it whispered. 'Hang on to the amnesia, because this tiny moment of zero recall is the best thing that's going to happen to you for some considerable time.'

Naturally Lister didn't much care for this inner voice, and was doing his best to ignore it. But nothing could stop the inner voice when it had bad news to impart, news as bad as this bad news. 'Whatever you do,' it continued to bait him, 'don't access reality – you're not going to like it one little bit.'

He struggled into a sitting position and peered through the grime of the porthole. He was on some kind of spacecraft that was preparing to land, swooping down over a series of huge canyons and ravines sculpted out of a barren sea of sandstone on a desert moon. He raised his handcuffed wrists and tried to massage a sensible expression on to his face with the balls of his palms.

Desert moon?

Why would he be landing on a desert moon? A desert moon with a complex of buildings surrounded by barbed-wire fences and tall sentry towers at each corner with huge swirling searchlights?

He pushed his face against the porthole and watched his reflection peer gormlessly back at him. He didn't recognize it at first. This hunched stranger with hooded brown eyes.

Was this him? This guy with the seven-day growth and hollow cheeks? This guy in the khaki jumpsuit and matching hat? This guy with the five rasta plaits of hair that usually slumped down his back, like slumbering snakes, but were now chained by a khaki hairband?

Where was his usually chirpy demeanour? Where was his lopsided smile, that amiable-slob grin that was as mischievous as the fourth wheel on a shopping trolley? Where were his biker's pants, and his leather jacket strewn with badges and hand-painted graffiti?

He was staring at a stiff in a jumpsuit with a number on his hat.

He shimmied across the bench and peered down the aisle. Fifty, perhaps sixty, bodies lined the craft's ugly gun-metal grey interior – a sorry bunch of rogue simulants, renegade droids, Axis-syndrome holograms and a bizarre mix of engineered life forms.

All handcuffed.

All reluctant guests of His Imperial Majesty F'hnhiujsrf Dernbvjukidhgd the Unpronounceable.

Then Lister remembered. He remembered everything. His face went whiter than a brand-new pair of trainers.

'Told you,' said the inner voice. 'Isn't this the worst situation you've ever been in in your entire life?'

The inner voice was wrong, but not by much.

Lister gazed out of the porthole and his facial muscles accessed the programme 'No One Home' as he began to catalogue the series of disasters that had led him to this point in Time and Space. He started to list the bad decisions, the poor career choices, the unreliable friend-ships that had led him here, to a prison ship bound for the most inhospitable penal colony in the outer reaches of the Cosmos. He'd never expected much from life. All he'd ever really wanted was to be a soft-metal guitar icon, thrashing out rock anthems all night to half a million fanatical hero-worshippers. Was that really too much to ask — to be mobbed nightly by hordes of emotion-ally unstable women who would feel compelled to smear his body with a wide range of dairy products and then remove said dairy products in a variety of interest-ing ways? A thin smile drove across his face and skidded to a halt at the corner of his mouth. Well, something had gone wrong somewhere. He'd never got within so much as a Whirlwind-amp-lead distance of fulfilling that particular dream.

Why? Was it bad luck? Had he just never had the breaks? Or was it simply that he'd never bothered to learn how to play the guitar?

Really play it.

Three chords.

What the hell — even four, maybe. If only he'd bought that damn book that taught you how to play in a day. One lousy day, and things could have worked out so differently. He wouldn't have wound up here, stuck in the middle of Deep Space, the last member of the human race, literally light years away from the woman he loved and a really hot curry.

Somewhere along the line he'd made a really poor career choice – he'd ignored the door that said 'Legend of Rock', instead opting for the one that said 'Useless Piece of Directionless Sputum Destined to Lose Big Time'.

Lister let out a sigh, like a newly opened bottle of chilli beer, and wondered when it had started to go wrong.

It was a mistake to wear the tie, he knew it the minute he entered the Forum of Justice. Major, major mistake. He should have worn his oil-spattered long johns with his black leathers over the top. That would have been far more suitable attire for a man on trial. Far more suitable for a man facing charges of serious crimes against the Gelf state. For a start he would have been comfortable. His one and only dress shirt was a good two collar sizes too small, and it made him feel as if all eight pints of blood had somehow been vacuumed up into his head and were trying to vacate his skull by forcing his eyeballs to catapult out of their sockets. Also, he could see now the tie itself was not a great choice. True, he had only one tie, so he wasn't exactly spoiled for choice, but on reflection a yellow kipper tie with a woman in birthing stirrups motif had probably been a mistake. Somehow it didn't give him that aura of respectability that he'd been aiming for. The wronged pillar of society number.

Silent curses chased around inside his head. If he hadn't tried so hard to look so damn distinguished he wouldn't have felt like such a schlub. He shouldn't have tried so hard to make a good impression, he should have worn his regular clothes.

It wasn't the first time he'd severely miscalculated in the ensemble department. His mind went back to the days before the radiation leak, before Red Dwarf had been sent hurtling out into the barren wastes of Deep Space while he slept, oblivious, in suspended animation.

He'd been invited to the summer party in the officers' mess.

Him, a lowly third technician.

The invitation had said the occasion was informal, so that was exactly how he'd gone – he'd worn a pair of zero-gee football shorts and a can of lager. Unbelievably, he'd been turned away by some officer in a beige summer suit. If they'd wanted him to go dressed as Noël Coward they should have said.

Now, as the mighty oak doors to the Forum of Justice hammered open and the Gelf security guards began to escort him down the aisle to his seat, he knew he'd done it again. He hush-puppied his way down the court room and took his place behind the smooth oak desk. He bowed his head in shame. *Hush-puppies?* He looked like a dentist.

From the rear of the Forum of Justice a door opened and the Gelf Regulator took his place on the podium. Like many of the Gelfs on Arranguu 12 he was an Alberog, a bizarre genetic cocktail of albatross, bear and frog. Seven and a half feet tall when standing upright, its body was covered in a black fur, with a crescent-shaped moon on its chest above giant frog legs. As with all Gelfs it had been programmed with slow-ageing genes, and its life expectancy was close to a thousand years.

The smooth white head with its long orange hooked bill and two eyes, colder than a doctor's hands, surveyed the courtroom then alighted on Lister. 'Do you have counsel?'

'I will conduct my own defence, my lord. During the months leading up to my trial I have made myself familiar with your legal system and I think you'll find me a pretty snazzy attorney.'

The Regulator nodded to the offence counsel. 'Let the case begin.'

Lister remained silent as the offence counsel outlined the charges against him. Finally, he sat down in a swirl of self-congratulation and Lister rose and stood before the six hooded figures of the jury. 'There is no case to answer and my defence is a simple one. I wish to take the fourth sand of D'Aquaarar and thus be protected from the breach of Xzeeertuiy by the Zalgon impeachment of Kjielomnon, as is permitted here on the asteroid settlement of Arranguu 12 during the third season of every fifth cycle.'

'What?'

A baby-sized smirk perched on Lister's face. 'I refer you to Mbazvmbbcxyy vs. Mbazvmbbcxyy. And I move for a mistrial.' He flopped into his chair, his head jutting back and forth in triumph. 'Nothing more.'

'But this is the northern sector of Arranguu 12.'

'So?'

'Not the southern sector.'

'So?'

The Regulator stared down at Lister, bewildered. 'We don't share the same outmoded, archaic, incomprehensibly bizarre legal system as they have in the south.'

'You don't?'

'Of course not. We adhere to the Jhjghjiuyhu system.'

'The what?'

'The Jhjghjiuyhu system, which is plain and straight-forward and can be understood by any Hniuplcxdewn or Tvcnkolphgkooq.'

'Any Hniuplcxdewn or Tvcnkolphgkoq?'

'Tvcnkolphgkooq,' the Regulator corrected. 'That's why we always celebrate Cvcbdekijhmnhuye's day – the day we won the right to be a self-governing state and were able to throw off the shackles of incomprehensible bureaucratic legal sludge. So what do you wish to do? Take the seventh branch of O'pphjytere or hurl your soul on the great fire of N'mjiuyhyes?'

'Uhhh,' said Lister, stalling. 'Give me the choices again?'

'Choose.'

'Uhhh . . .'

'Well?'

'I'll take the fourth twig of whatsit?'

'The seventh branch of O'pphjytere?'

'That's the fella.'

A tidal wave of shock reverberated around the Forum. Lister's eyebrows fossilized on his face as he craned round to gaze at the lines of disapproving Gelf faces sitting in the gallery.

'Is that bad?'

'If the Jury of Six find you guilty, then taking the seventh branch of O'pphjytere will mean tripling the length of your sentence.'

'In that case I'll . . .'

'You have chosen. Let us continue.'

Lister loosened his tie, unbuttoned his shirt and re-moved his nicely pressed cream slacks. He fished into his briefcase, pulled out a can of double-strength lager, crossed his hairy naked legs on the Regulator's podium and started noisily slurping his beer. Waiting to be found guilty.

CHAPTER 2

The craft's airlock door chu-chunged open and Lister and the rest of the prisoners began fighting their way down the disembarkation ramp and out on to the landing bay. A thousand minute dust particles scorched into his face, reminding him of the Moroccan after-shave Rimmer had once given him as a belated Christmas present.

Flanked by guards the prisoners straggled down the aeropad's promenade and into the domed interior of the Grand Hall. A thousand metres deep and over five hundred metres wide, it was constructed from steel, glass and reinforced concrete. Lister gazed around. It was an awesome testament to Gelf craftsmanship to have built a stadium as magnificent as this on a moon as hostile as Lotomi 5. Grandiose spiral motifs with dizzyingly high ceilings gave the hall a faint whiff of Fascist Rally, and, as with all Gelf settlements, huge green-and-black Gelf flags hung from every wall. On each was the giant double-helix of the nucleic acid DNA, and in a strange script, a sentence that read: 'The Key to Life – nothing should be denied'.

Suddenly, music started to blare into the hall through the massive PA system. Some kind of anthem. Lister hated anthems at the best of times. He was convinced they started wars. Especially ones like this, which was disturbingly rousing and spoke of conflict and strife and laying down your life for the cause of ultimate victory. When the anthem had finished the vast doors to the chamber yawned open and something that looked as if it had escaped from a really bad LSD trip entered the hall and took its place on the podium. A sickly warm tide of nausea slowly filled Lister's body from the stomach up. It had the legs of a giraffe, the body of a gargantuan slug and the earless head of a giant cobra; it also looked as if it had just had a bucket of mucus thrown at it.

He shuddered. He hadn't seen anything this hideous since he'd last cleared out the salad tray of his fridge.

The creature's huge, elongated head hovered over the assembled prisoners like a giant spent phallus, and its long pink tongue flitted in and out, dribbling a particularly unspeakable kind of unspeakable yellow mucus. The opening sentences of its speech were lost in a crescendo of retching and vomiting. But it was quite used to this. Very few life forms ever met the Snugiraffe without evacuating at least part of their bodily contents. As far as the Snugiraffe was concerned, 'Hello' and 'Yurrrghhhhhhh' were synonymous. Projectile vomit was a form of greeting. It was hardly the Snugiraffe's fault that it had been created from bits of leftover DNA grizzle. It had been given the opportunity of existence and it intended to grab it with all three moist and dribbly suction pads. OK, it was revolting. It was probably the most vile, graceless, deformed, distorted, asymmetrical, eye-wateringly unsightly organism that had ever had the good fortune to breathe oxygen – well, with the possible exception of George Formby. Besides, it wasn't all about looks. This was the new world, the new solar system, a galaxy of opportunity, where all creatures were equal and anyone could become chief of the United Republic of Engineered Life Forms no matter who they were or how they were born or even if they looked like a Snugiraffe and leaked unspeakable juices over the head of anyone it addressed. It was here to do a job and it was as good as anyone. In fact, here on Lotomi 5 it was a prized member of the community, much respected and valued, because it ate all the other life forms' body effluence and reconstituted it into much-needed smokeless fuel. Not everybody could do that. Also, it was the Colony commandant.

The Snugiraffe was halfway through its 'It may sound like a bit of a cliché, but no one has ever escaped from this penal colony and the reason for that is it's totally impossible' speech before any of what it was saying was in the slightest way audible. Those who weren't able to be sick, like the mechanoids and Holograms, were dry-retching. So the noise was substantial. The Snugiraffe continued unabashed; as far as it was concerned it was all just water off its deformed hump.

Finally Lister was able to hear the tail end of the speech.

'. . . however, if you attempt to escape and you are caught, you will be erased, but not before . . .' The Snugiraffe paused, and a fresh discharge, the colour of drowned frogs, leaked out of the corner of its mouth. 'But not before –' it repeated – 'you have shared my bed.'

A monsoon of fresh vomiting. An entire equatorial forest's rainy season of puke. A cacophony of chundering that lasted fully two minutes.

The Snugiraffe smiled coquettishly and continued to rain its ooze on the heads of its audience. 'You are here because you have all committed heinous acts against the United Republic of Engineered Life Forms. You have had fair trials on your home asteroids . . .'

'I haven't,' said a voice.

'No, neither have I,' said another.

'Nor me.'

The Snugiraffe tutted irritably. 'All right, most of you haven't had fair trials, but you *have* been found guilty. And you have been sent here to Lotomi 5 to be punished. In that department we will certainly not disappoint. After this assembly you will be escorted to the medi-floors where you will be washed, shaved and prepared. You will then be taken to the main chamber where you will each take your place in the artificial reality scenario deemed appropriate to your crime.' The Snugiraffe's tongue flitted in and out. 'Welcome to Cyberia.'

Cyberia, because each inmate was interfaced with a gigantic cybernetic network – the brain and nervous system attached to a vast machine-generated reality – where each inmate paid for his crimes by being forced to live out his sentence in his very own self-created hell.

He walked down the corridor phalanxed by six guards as a cold, tormenting air hissed out of the recyc vents, reminding him of his newly bald head.

They'd taken his hair. Lopped off his locks, the five rasta plaits he'd had since he was seventeen.

Two steel doors slid back and the party walked through into the main chamber. Its sickly-sweet smell was all too familiar.

He gazed at the gigantic matrix of heads: all bald, all bobbing on the surface of the giant cyberlake, all wearing Cyberia's regulation issue headsets.

Headsets that drilled needle-slim rods directly into their brains and transported them to Cyberhell.

He stood, helpless and sullen, while they made their preparations. A Gelf doctor, businesslike and unsmiling, injected him with an air syringe and he felt his body buckle and go limp.

Two assistants ripped off his flimsy white dressing-gown and hauled his naked body into a white-tiled cubicle and turned a hose on him. The hose spewed out a foul-smelling plastic liquid, which quickly cooled on his body and started to set. Soon he was covered with the gossamer-fine coating of cyberfoam that would control and manipulate his senses, obeying the commands of the giant mainframe that monitored the prisoners' scenarios. The two assistants hauled him to the edge of the vast pink cyberlake and gently lowered him into its warm, sweet waters.

They reminded him of his crimes, which he was too dejected and numb even to deny. Then they bent down and activated the headset. The rods were unleashed.

They burrowed into his skull like hungry rats that had been denied food for weeks. He felt the heat and smelt the stench of lasered skull as the rods punctured his brain and made a home in his mind.

Soon they had altered his whole perception of reality.

PART TWO
Time Fork

CHAPTER 1

Something was about to happen. Something almost imperceptible.

A click in the darkness. A click in the perfect silence of non-time. Then the click was followed by a second click.

And light.

Light that gradually filled the room with a shallow blue beam as the Deep Sleep unit flared into action and slowly began to drop from the ceiling. The unit landed softly on the deck and its hood hissed back, allowing tendrils of smoke to tumble out of the sleep chamber as the body of a slowly waking man sat upright, his face hidden behind a mad explosion of facial hair.

He scratched his chest with one of his six-inch-long fingernails and a groan crawled out of his body like a wounded bear. He swirled his tongue around his mouth and swallowed his saliva. It tasted like a cross between a stagnant canal and airline chicken Kiev.

He looked around. The cabin was familiar and unfamiliar in about equal parts. He knew it intimately and yet hardly knew it at all. An old star-shaped guitar with two missing strings leaned against a chair; framed posters of zero-gee football stars were propped against the walls and unpacked boxes and crates littered the floor.

His name was Retsil, he recollected. Retsil Evad. He picked up an empty tumbler resting on a stabilizer cabinet next to the Deep Sleep unit and tilted it to his lips, waiting for the water to gush out of his mouth and fill the glass up to the brim.

Nothing happened.

He cast his legs over the bed and waited for them to carry him into the bathroom where he would remove toothpaste from his teeth and brush it neatly back into the tube. After that he'd dab wetness on to his face from one of the bathroom towels before scooping the dripping water into the already full basin and watch as the liquid was sucked up into the two taps.

Strangely, none of this happened either.

Then Retsil realized what was weird.

Time was running forwards. No longer was he living in a backwards reality. No longer was he living in a dimension where time moved in reverse. That was why the room was both familiar and strange. These were his quarters, but he'd been away for so long living in a backwards reality – that was why it all felt so odd. In fact, come to think of it, Retsil Evad wasn't his name. His name wasn't backwards any more. His name was Dave Lister.

Dave Lister. At least he remembered something. In fact, that was the only thing he remembered.

He staggered to an uneasy balance and shuffled his way across the obs deck, walking on the outside of his feet to avoid standing on his six-inch-long toenails. Halfway across he caught his reflection in the Plexiglass of the view-screen. He looked like an arthritic penguin whose flippers were one size too small. After he'd completed the trek across the room and flopped into the leather swivel chair behind the flatbed scanner of the star-chart computer, he hauled his foot up and started to trim his nails in the table-top pencil sharpener.

A mechanoid head leaned in through the hatchway.

'Welcome back on-line, sir. How are you feeling?'

'Who am I? I don't know who I am. Apart from my name I don't remember a damn thing.'

A smile spread across Kryten's bald, angular pink face, like a stone skipping across a lake. 'Ah, you have a touch of amnesia, sir. That's quite common after such a long period in Deep Sleep.' The mechanoid carried his sharply chiselled matt-grey body into the room. In the middle of his chest plate a port-hole-shaped CPU housing glinted faintly in the soothing amber neons. 'You've been out for just over twenty years.'

'Twenty years?'

'Actually, I woke you last spring, but you absolutely insisted on another three months.'

Kryten handed him a breakfast tray. 'Here, you must be hungry.'

Lister thanked him with a nod of his head and peered down at his breakfast. 'These cornflakes have grated raw onions sprinkled over them.'

'That's how you like them, sir.'

'I do?' Lister shook his head in bemusement and took a large slug of orange juice. His expression petrified on his face and his eyes widened as if they were being inflated by an air pump. The liquid arced out of his mouth and sprayed across the floor. 'This orange juice is revolting!'

'That's not orange juice, sir. That's your early-morning pick-me-up; chilled vindaloo sauce.'

'I drink cold curry sauce for breakfast?'

'Depends on your mood. If you get up in the afternoon, you often prefer to start the day with a can of last night's flat lager. That's why you used to sleep with a tea strainer by your bed, so you could sieve out the cigar dimps.'

'I drink, I smoke, I have curry sauce for breakfast? Raw onions on my cereal? I sound like some barely human, grossed-out slime ball.'

'It's all flooding back,then?'

'No. None of it is.'

'Perhaps this will help.' Kryten turned and picked up the star-shaped guitar.

'I play the guitar?'

'Do I have a head shaped like an amusing ice cube? Why don't you chock out a few power chords? See if anything comes back.'

A wistful expression sat on Lister's face, his newly trimmed fingertips lovingly surfing across the strings, as he played a song that was stored deep inside his long-term memory. It was a love song he himself had written. Possibly his finest melody. The noise was appalling, an electric obscenity: music to emigrate to.

Kryten beamed. 'The Axeman is back!'

'Don't patronize me. I can't play the guitar. Anyone with half an ear can tell that.'

'Sir, when your personality's fully restored, you will firmly believe you can play the guitar like the ghost of Hendrix.'

'Isn't there anything good you can tell me about myself? Anything laudable?'

'Laudable ... Well, in the old days you frequently helped me with my laundry duties, by wearing your underpants inside out and extending their wear time by three weeks. Does that count?'

Lister's face deflated into a grimace. 'I'm an animal! I'm a tasteless, uncouth, tone deaf, mindless, revolting, randy, blokeish, semi-literate space bum.'

Kryten gave him a bear hug. 'Welcome back, sir. We've all missed you so much.'

Lister started to pick the onions out of his cornflakes. 'Why don't I remember anything? Why is none of it coming back?'

'Perhaps you need a little synaptic enhancer. I'll make some up.'

The Mechanoid ducked through the open hatchway and made his way up the steps to the small science room located in the ship's dome.

Lister pushed away the cornflakes and tugged off the metal lid protecting his cooked breakfast. He gazed down in revulsion at the triple-tiered fried-egg-and-chilli-chutney sandwich. This guy, this guy he was, was un-believable.

'Hey.' The girl walked into the cabin wearing a short cream dressing-gown and sipping a mug of warm milk and honey. 'How're you feeling?' Her lagoon-blue eyes speared him with a look, and something inside him buckled and fell like a stunned wildebeest. Her voice was educated, with a soupçon of something Scottish, or maybe even Irish, Lister wasn't quite sure – he'd never been great at spotting accents. From her posture and her almost haughty demeanour Lister guessed correctly that she was an officer.

Her lips split into a smile, lighting up her face like a pinball machine under a mop of uncombed pecan-pie brown hair. 'You feeling OK?'

Lister nodded a 'yes'.

'I've been out of Deep Sleep two months now. The medi-computer detected I needed an appendectomy, so it brought me out early so I'd be fully recovered by the time it revived the rest of the crew.'

'Oh, right,' said Lister and wondered if he should perhaps have addressed her as ma'am, or even sir.

'Kryten did the op with a laser scalpel. He did such a great job you can hardly see the scar.'

Lister laughed too loudly. This woman had the ability to shave twenty points off his IQ. What was wrong with him?

He looked at her. A distance short of gorgeous, she was still pretty special, and by the clear line of her body under the silk dressing-gown he was pretty certain she wasn't wearing a whole heap underneath. Just my damn luck, he thought, to have a superior officer who turns my insides into something that you'd expect to find in a half-eaten chicken burrito.

'Take a look,' she said. 'I bet you can't see the scar.'

Lister was only half paying attention as she tugged open her dressing-gown and let it slide off her back on to the floor. She stood naked in front of him.

'Can you see it?'

His whole body still-framed with shock. Was he imagining this? Was he insane? Or was this officer-type woman standing before him stark naked? His eyebrows climbed to the top of his head and clung on to one another for comfort.

'Can you see it?' she repeated.

'Huh?'

'You're not looking. Look properly.'

Lister glanced up fleetingly and mumbled incredulities.

'You're not looking. You're looking at the floor. Look.' She walked towards his chair and tugged his beard until his eyes were in line with the small mound of her belly. A tiny triangle of pubic hair flitted into his peripheral vision. 'Can you see the operation scar?'

'Pardon me?'

'Can you?'

Lister's eyes scanned her belly and found nothing.

'Look at me.'

His eyes travelled up her naked body and over her pouty breasts until they reached her eyes. As he arrived at her face he was aware her lips were spiced with mischief as she stared down at the tent that had suddenly set up camp halfway down his white sleep tunic.

Her hand stretched out and the hatchway door sighed closed. She pulled the tie-up at the top of his gown and tugged it open, then slowly lowered herself on top of him. Her arms draped around his neck and she bit him tenderly on his mouth as she started gently to sway back and forth on top of him.

'Ooh,' said Lister.

'Ooh,' said the woman with the invisible appendectomy scar.

'Aaaaaaah,' said Lister more enthusiastically.

29

'Aaaaaaah,' said the woman right back.

And so the conversation continued until a 'Aaaaaaaaaaaaaaaaaaaaaaaaaaaaaaaaaaaaaaaaahhhh' and a 'Ooooooooooooooooooooooooooooooooohhhhhhhhhhh' brought the exchange of dialogue to a satisfactory conclusion four and a half minutes later.

If you'd have asked him Lister would have said it was twenty minutes later. But he'd have been wrong.

They sat in one another's arms, coated in a fine rain of sweat, when a soft beep announced someone was at the door. She lifted herself off him, put on her dressing-gown and clicked the door-release mechanism. Kryten waddled in carrying a second breakfast tray.

'Ah, Kryten, I'm just going to take a shower. Just come to get a few things.' She opened one of the wooden crates and started rifling through its contents.

Lister caught Kryten's eye. 'Who is she?' he mouthed silently.

Kryten shrugged, not understanding. 'Sir?'

'Who is she?' he mimed as the girl with the lagoon-blue eyes pulled out a selection of clothes from the crate and piled them neatly on one side.

'Kochanski,' mouthed Kryten in dumb speak.

'Who?' said Lister silently.

'Kristine Kochanski.' he mouthed.

'Kristine Kochanski? Who's she, then?'

Kochanski turned and caught them in the middle of their silent conversation. 'He has got his memory back, hasn't he? I mean, he does actually know who I am?'

Lister and Kryten cackled simultaneously and assured her that of course he knew who she was. She raised an unconvinced eyebrow and disappeared through the hatchway. Kryten took out an air syringe and squeezed off a little jet into mid-air. 'Synaptic enhancer. We'll have that memory of yours back in no time.'

Lister's neck craned round the door as she jogged up the metal staircase. 'Kochanski, you say her name is? What a little raver. Tell me everything you know about her?'

'Sir, you've just spent the last fifty years of your life with her.'

A look of total incredulity spilled on to Lister's face. 'You mean, she's my girlfriend?'

Kryten nodded.

'Un-be-smegging-lievable. But why's she dating a jerk like me? What am I, the last human being alive or something?'

Kryten busied himself with the enhancer. 'The drug shouldn't take too long now, sir. Perhaps I could run you a nice hot bath.'

Lister shook his head. 'I mean, she's a touch of cut glass, no doubt about it. Educated, posh accent. I mean, she is somebody. Whereas what you've told me about me, man, well, quite honestly, I sound like scum. What's the attraction?'

'Oh, don't be so self-deprecating, sir.' Kryten smiled. 'You have your saving graces.'

'I do? Like what?'

Kryten uttered a little scoffing laugh that scudded across the room. 'I wouldn't dream of embarrassing you.'

'Embarrass me,' said Lister emphatically.

'Well, you have a certain amiability.'

'Amiability,' said Lister, unimpressed.

'Also, you have a streak of sentimentality that some people find attractive. And sometimes between curries you've been known to be quite romantic.'

'Amiable, sentimental, romantic curry-eater,' said Lister, in a voice close to monotone. 'Cut the crap, Kryten, what's the real reason?'

'I think she likes a bit of rough, sir.'

'Fair enough,' said Lister, finally convinced. 'How about that bath?'

'I'll just get Mr Rimmer on line, sir, and then I'll run it straight away. Follow me.'

Lister followed Kryten down the steps that led from the obs deck into the mid-section.

A man in a black stretch PVC body suit with a yellow flannel under-jacket and a coat made of acrylic zebra-print fur sat at the scanner table sipping a glass of milk. His black hair was swept up in a pompadour and he had two long eye-teeth that twinkled when he smiled. 'Who the hell's this?' he said, gesturing at Lister.

'This is Lister,' said Kryten. 'The other human one.'

'Ugle-e-e-e.'

'And you are?' said Lister.

'Apparently, I'm descended from cats,' said the Cat. 'And according to jello head, here, I'm incredibly vain, self-obsessed and only interested in myself. Boy,' he said, suddenly catching sight of his reflection in a spoon, 'I'm good-looking though, aren't I?'

Lister turned and addressed Kryten. 'How long is it going to be before I get full recall?'

Kryten typed a pass-code into the wall comp. 'Within the hour, sir.' A hatch cover flipped open and the mechanoid took out an object the size of a marble.

'Mr Rimmer, sir,' said Kryten in reply to Lister's look. 'He's a hologram, sir. This is his light bee.' He placed the bee on the floor.

'Rimmer?' said Lister. 'He's my best mate, isn't he?'

Kryten's face dissolved into a look of distaste, as if he'd just sampled his first goat kebab. 'You *are* sick, sir. Maybe you need another boost of synaptic enhancer.' He syringed Lister a second time, and then tapped the boot-up sequence into the computer and watched as the light bee gently lifted off the floor and hovered three feet from the ground.

'Download physical form,' he said to the voice-command unit and watched as Rimmer's black-and-white image crackled into existence rippled with white noise. Six feet tall and square-shouldered he stood, with a small embossed H imprinted across his forehead under a scoop of brown hair fastened down tighter than rigging in a storm; his face was pointy, his lips thin, his nostrils so cavernous that if they'd been bound in leather and turned upside down they could have been used by a leprechaun as a drum kit.

'Access personality banks,' Kryten murmured into the VC unit. A series of bar charts appeared on the screen. 'Download characteristics. Load arrogance.' The first bar, a tall one, was slowly filled with a green liquid, as if it were being poured from a vial to the accompaniment of a mounting scale sound effect. 'Load charisma.' A second bar, a very short one, was filled with a single blip. 'Load neuroses.' The next bar, by far the longest, slowly began to fill up.

'No point waiting, sir, loading the neuroses lasts longer than *Gone With the Wind*. I'll run that bath.'

'Oh, that Rimmer,' said Lister as the memory enhancer suddenly hit the spot. 'Oh, God. *That* Rimmer.'

The five crew members of the Jupiter Mining Corporation ship-to-transport vehicle sat around the scanner scope as Kryten began to outline the situation as best he could. He began by explaining why Starbug's computer had brought them out of Deep Sleep even though they were still some way from Red Dwarf. Obeying Space Corps directive 3211 it had spotted a crashed Star Fleet ship in a nearby asteroid belt and it recommended they go in and investigate. The reasons were two-fold: to rescue any surviving crew members and, almost more importantly, to scavenge for supplies.

'So, where are we exactly?' said Lister, now fully restored to normal working order and tucking into a second breakfast of black pudding and chips. 'Have we gone through the Omni-zone yet?'

'The Omni-zone?' said the Cat.

'The point in space time where all the different realities converge,' said Kochanski. 'Hit him with another memory booster.'

As Kryten discharged a third syringe into the Cat's neck, he explained how every decision in life creates a time fork; one line of reality goes down the pathway of the decision that was taken, while the other pathway – the rejected time line – is saved and stored in the Omni-zone. The Omni-zone is home to all the rejected time-lines and the entrance to all seven Universes.

'But,' the Cat insisted, 'what I'm asking is, what part of Deep Space are we in, and am I suitably dressed?'

'We successfully traversed the Omni-zone, sir, some time ago. In fact, according to my latest calculations we're only six or seven weeks away from rendezvousing with Red Dwarf.'

'So why all the heat to go into the asteroid belt?'

Kryten swivelled and addressed Lister. 'Sir, we've been away from Red Dwarf for many years now.'

Lister nodded. It was true. He and Kochanski had spent thirty-six years in Backwards World following his heart attack in his own reality. Buried there in his sixties, he'd un-died and de-aged until he'd reached his present age of twenty-five. Kochanski too had arrived in Backwards World in less than A1 shape; in fact, she had been nothing more than her own cremated ashes. Holly had performed some miracle to equalize their ages, and then reverse time had done the rest.

Kochanski continued. 'We don't know for sure that Red Dwarf will even be there, or, if it is, if the onboard supplies will be intact. So this derelict may be our last chance of stocking up with fresh supplies.'

'How long's it going to take? Two, three days?'

Kryten nodded.

'But we can't fly into an asteroid belt without deflectors,' said Rimmer. 'What about Space Corps directive 1742?'

'1742? "No member of the Corps should ever report for active duty in a ginger toupee"? Is that regulation really pertinent in this particular situation, sir?'

'1743, then.'

'Oh, I see. "No registered vessel should attempt to traverse an asteroid belt without deflectors."'

'Yes! God, you're pedantic.'

Lister shook his head. 'Rimmer, check out the supply situation. Your hologram's on battery back-up. We've only got oxygen for three months. Water, if we drink re-cyc, seven weeks. And, worst of all, we're down to our last two thousand popadoms. We can't rely on Red Dwarf. We've got to go in.'

'But you know how unstable those clusters are,' Rimmer whined. 'One direct hit on that Plexiglass view-screen and our innards will be turned inside-out quicker than a pair of your old underpants.'

'Look, man, this is maybe our last chance to stock up for months. I say we take her in.'

'For pity's sake, one breach in that hull and we're people pâté.'

'There's an old Cat proverb,' said the Cat, starting to feel more like himself. '"It's better to live one hour as a tiger, than a whole lifetime as a worm."'

'There's an old human saying,' said Rimmer. '"Who-ever heard of a worm-skin rug?"'

Kochanski poured herself a cup of water from the recyc dispenser. 'Perhaps this'll settle it,' she said, turning away from the bank of monitors. 'We've just logged on to the ship's ident computer.'

'And?' said Lister, getting to his feet. 'What have we got?'

She downed her cup of water and balled the paper cup into the recyc chute. 'That ship out there is Starbug.'

'Another Starbug?'

'No, this Starbug. We've just shaken hands with their mainframe and look what happened when we exchanged serial numbers.' She tapped the monitor. '"STA 7676–45–327–28V" – the exact same registration number.'

Lister squinted at the figures. 'How's that possible?'

She shook her head. 'It isn't.'

'Any sign of the crew?'

'Not so far.'

'That settles it. We'd better take a look.'

CHAPTER 2

The air-lock door purred open and the five figures stepped aboard the dead ship. Kochanski inhaled the heavy musk as the rash of torch beams swirled around the decom-chamber. Walking alongside Kryten she signalled with her torch and started wading through the knee-deep mix of oil and water that covered the floor.

If Kristine Kochanski's parents had still been alive, they would not have approved of the company she was presently keeping. They had not sent their eldest, most cherished and talented daughter to the finest schools money could buy so she could knock about the Universe with people like this. They had not paid for piano lessons from the age of four, or Esperanto classes from the age of six, they had not paid for jujitsu training at twelve or flying lessons and extra classes in quantum mechanics at sixteen; in fact, they had not done any of these things – which had finally contributed to her winning a place at the European Space Academy where she graduated with honours as flight coordinator first class – so that she could wind up in the far reaches of Deep Space with a bunch of degenerate half-wits and hardly any clean knickers. And her father – her poor, long-dead father – would have had more seizures than a ward of epileptics if he had ever clapped eyes on the object of her affections. The man she had spent the last half-century with, the man whose picture presently hung around her neck in a silver locket he'd given her to celebrate the anniversary of the first week they had been dating – the silver locket that always seemed to leave a purple tide-mark around her neck that was next to impossible to wash off without medicinal alcohol.

Lister waded to her side. 'Hey.'

'Hey.' She returned their ritual greeting.

'Want to show me some more of your scars?'

She looked at Lister's Grand Canyon grin. 'So, know who I am now?'

'Hey, I was still groggy and, hell, there you were, suddenly naked. It didn't seem right to ask you for your driver's licence.'

'So when did you remember?'

'Well, before it was over, let me tell you.'

'When exactly?'

'When?'

'Yes, when?'

Lister paused and looked at her seriously. 'Look, I remember who you are, Kublouski, OK? Relax, would ya?'

Kochanski kicked out with her foot and sent a torrent of water over Lister's snigger-hunched features.

Suddenly, the Cat's voice cut in. 'What's this?' His torch pointed to a matted fur island, about a foot across, floating on the water. He transferred the torch from his right hand to his left. 'What is it?' He started to pick it up. 'It's heavy.' The Cat hauled it out of the water and flipped it round to look at it. He stared into familiar brown eyes and his scream slammed around the chamber like a berserk squash ball.

It was a head. It was the head of a humanoid. The head of a humanoid who was identical to the Cat.

The head fell from his grasp and dropped back into the water with a splash.

Lister waded across to where the Cat was standing, his heart beating out a carioca on his ribs.

'You OK?'

'For a dude who's just picked his own head out of a swamp, I'm doing great,' falsettoed the Cat.

Kryten ran his psi-scan over the dismembered skull.

Kochanski waded across. 'Well?'

'It says, "Organism incomplete".'

'What a truly remarkable machine,' said Rimmer. 'And it knows all that from just seeing a dismembered head. Absolutely incredible.'

'Give it another minute, sir.' Kryten peered at the analysis machine as it birred and beeped, quietly processing all the variables.

Lister leaned in. 'Well, what does it think?'

'It thinks we should get the hell out of here in case the headless look is the fashion around here,' said the Cat.

'Here it comes now.' Kryten read the print-out. 'Head decapitated by laser. Victim possesses same DNA structure as the crew member known as the Cat. Advice: vacate ship immediately. Extreme danger.'

'Right, let's go,' said Rimmer.

'Maybe there're survivors, Mr Rimmer,' said Kochanski. 'We can't go until we've carried out a thorough search of the ship.'

'Says who?' Rimmer laughed softly.

'Says a flight coordinator in the Star Fleet, and your superior officer. Any other questions?'

There was a long pause.

'Wilful disobedience, Mr Rimmer? A full court martial if we ever make it back to Star Fleet? Is that what you want?'

Rimmer returned a reluctant salute. 'No, ma'am.'

The Cat's laugh echoed down the chamber. 'This bitch is good.'

Lister stood in front of the closed hatchway and jabbed the door-release button repeatedly with his index finger. 'No electrics.'

Kryten adjusted the medical bag under his arm. 'Suggest we go back to Starbug and return with the halogens and the mobile generator.'

Lister shrugged. 'I'm going to stick around here, take a look round the decom-chamber.'

Kochanski nodded. 'Mr Rimmer, stay with him.'

'Me?'

'Yes.'

'Why can't I come back with you guys?'

'You're a hologram. You can't help with the MG or the lamps. It's just a waste of your battery.'

Rimmer's eyelashes fluttered like a cartoon cow's. 'But I could still come back and help somehow, advise how best the lamps should be carried . . . what sort of grip to use . . . how many to . . .'

'Stay here.'

'You don't like me, do you? It's because I'm dead, isn't it? You living people hate us deadies.'

'Rimmer!'

'Right, OK, I'm staying. Just don't be long.'

He watched as Kryten, the Cat and Kochanski waded off back down the decom-chamber and disappeared through the outer hatchway. A hologram he might be, a computer-generated image of his former dead self he indeed was, but now he had a three-dimensional 'solido-gram' body that Kryten had ransacked from a derelict while the crew was in Deep Sleep, he intended to keep it in one piece. It was his proudest posession – his hard-light drive – and he wasn't going to risk it for anyone. For years he'd been soft light – unable to touch or interact properly because he lacked that all-important third dimension, but now, thanks to Kryten, it was different. His mind flicked back to the days following the mechanoid's discovery of the science on board the Lagos, a lost scout ship they'd come across frozen into the tundra of an arctic moon. As Kryten had pointed out, in terms of technology, the ship was genera-tions beyond anything they'd seen before: they even had yoghurt cartons that were easy to open. After several failed attempts Rimmer's personality was successfully siphoned into a new bee-housing with a hard-light capability. It was like taking delivery of his first car all over again. The joy, the glory, the unbridled ecstasy. While the others returned to Deep Sleep, Rimmer strut-ted around Starbug like a male model from a mail-order cardigan catalogue. For weeks no mirror was safe, and no sunbed could be passed without topping up his quiz-show-host tan, but gradually the novelty wore off, and after a while he found it difficult to remember what being 2D was like. Dead he still was, but now – in some respects at least – he was whole again.

Death had had a profound effect on Rimmer. In some ways he felt he was better for it. At first he'd been angry. No, more than angry, he'd been apoplectic with rage. A rage that roared through his being, like an out of control forest fire.

It wasn't fair. How could he have died? He'd never really lived. He knew goldfish who'd led more interesting lives. He'd met washing machines who'd had better sex lives. Then, next thing he knew, it was over. He was a hologram; a light-generated ghost, his personality stored on disc and revived by the ship computer to help keep Lister sane.

What had happened in his life? A miserable childhood was followed by a boring, sulky adolescence, which was then overtaken by his attempts to become an officer in the Space Corps. He'd spent eleven years of his adult life trying to achieve that goal; desperately trying to mimic his three brothers, who had each passed successfully through the ranks of the academy and had gone on to command their own vessels in the Star Fleet.

Frank, John and Howard. The blue-eyed boys. Bronzed and tall, with golden hair and coruscating smiles.

Rimmer had longed to be like them, had longed to be one of them, but that was something else that wasn't fair. Academically his brothers had never been more than average, but his parents, like many well-to-do families living on Io, had paid for them to have an Encyclo implant chip installed in their long-term memories. Suddenly a whole vista of knowledge was there just waiting to be accessed. What are molecular genetics? Ping! The answer would spring fully formed into the owner's mind.

When Rimmer was eighteen, when it was his turn to have his Encyclo implant chip, his father's business had gone bust. For him there was no short cut to the top. He was forced to enlist with the Space Corps as a menial technician, to work his way up the ranks to officerhood. If an officer he was ever to be.

And so countless evenings were spent grappling with the pages of mind-knotting incomprehensica that made up the engineering exam. And on no less than eleven occasions he had received that heart-scorching pink slip that informed him of his failure.

Meantime his brothers blazed their way up the ziggurat of command, leaving Rimmer, in his mind, with no choice. He had to cut himself loose from his family, never to see and rarely to hear from them ever again.

He had to, if he ever wanted to stem the torrent of pain and bitterness. Birthdays passed unmentioned. Christmases were spent alone. Valentine cards were self-addressed.

Then, finally, one day he died.

He died before he'd begun to live.

At least now the pain was over. At least now he could rest in peace, no longer fuelled by his incinerating jealousy and resentment.

Wrong.

His pain was just beginning.

Because in death, as in life, he allowed his failure to create something inside himself.

A creature.

A demon which prowled the plains of his soul, devouring his confidence, paralysing his initiative and poisoning his self-esteem.

It was a creature he longed to slay.

But it was a creature that could only be slain by one of two things. Love or success. And Rimmer attracted neither.

Lister sighed. He was bored and cold. For the last ten minutes he'd waded up and down the decom-chamber and had found nothing of interest; now he was beginning to wish he had gone back with the others. At least he could have a cup of hot coffee. Rimmer was talking about Kochanski and how they didn't have a structured ziggurat of command and how she shouldn't be so uptight. She should take a leaf out of his book. Lister nodded, not listening. Just for the hell of it he struck the door-release button with his index finger.

Slowly the door creaked open and revealed the interior of the ship. A mournful wail of metal yowled from somewhere deep within. 'It's opened.'

'How'd that happen? I thought the electrics were down.'

Lister peered into the ship through the open hatchway. 'I'm going to take a look around, OK?'

'In there? By yourself? Haven't you ever seen a schlock horror movie? That's what they always do – split up, then wander about in the dark by themselves, usually walking backwards. You're making the same mistake the girl in the tight top always makes.'

Lister grinned and walked backwards over the floor arch and stepped into the ship proper. 'If you need me, just scream.'

He flicked on a second torch, clicked the safety catch off his bazookoid and walked cautiously into the gloom.

For ten minutes he searched the control decks and

found nothing. Then he bounded softly up the stairs that led to the obs deck. Four steps in he heard a noise; a kind of low, wet, slurping sound that sounded like a feeding animal. It came from the far end of the cabin, behind a bank of bio-units that came out of the wall at right angles. There'd been flooding up here as well, he could feel the wetness beneath his feet. One match and this whole craft would go up in seconds. He stooped to check if it was the same oil-and-water mix as the decom-chamber. His finger drew a line on the floor and he tasted it. This time it wasn't oil and water, this time it was blood.

From his left a shadow angled towards him at great speed. He turned, lost his balance and fell headlong into a bank of hard disks before he scrabbled to his feet and nailed the shape with a single squeeze of his bazookoid. The rat splattered into the wall with a single squish.

Rimmer called from the decom-chamber, 'What is it?'

'Just a rat. It's OK.' As he finished speaking he saw the first body; slumped in a chair by the Hubble tele-scope. There were two bullet wounds, one in the back and one in the right shoulder between the two triangular scapula bones.

The body didn't have a head.

Lister looked down at the corpse wearing a pink wool barethea jacket edged in patent leather that was identical to one the Cat possessed. A little involuntary yelp leaked out of Lister's mouth.

Next he found Rimmer. His light bee had been shot in two; one half lay on the floor, its minute silicon boards spilling out on to the deck, the other half, like a burnt coffee bean, floated in a mug of cold tea. Peristaltic waves of nausea thrashed around in his gut.

After Rimmer he found Kryten. His right arm was missing and his head had been lasered from his body and placed on the geo-scanner with a cheap cigar in his mouth. He took the cigar from between his lips and gently closed his eyes.

'You found anything, Listy?' Rimmer called.

'No, not yet. Everything's fine, man.'

For the next twenty minutes Lister searched the entire ship: the obs deck, followed by the cockpit, the galley, the mid-section and finally the cargo bays. He went at speed, hoping to find his own body before the others returned so he could figure out what had happened and what he was going to tell them. To Lister it looked like maybe they'd wandered into a time loop. At some point they were destined to get wiped out by something. If that was the case there was very little they could do about it, so there didn't seem a whole heap of point in telling anyone. Better to say there was nothing here and hope to hell it was some time in the distant future. Although, judging from the age of the Cat's head, it didn't look like that far into the future.

Halfway through the cargo bays he found Kriss.

He'd first picked up a trail of blood as he wandered through the cargo bays. He'd followed it down the flight of stairs and through the sleeping quarters. Several times he lost it, as presumably she'd successfully stemmed the flow, but he picked it up again in the food hall as he was passing a row of empty freeze-dried fruit palettes. Now the flow was heavier. Much heavier. She wasn't able to walk any more, she was on all fours, dragging herself, slowly and painfully, across the cargo bay.

Lister wiped an oblong of sweat off his brow and

continued to follow the trail as it wended its way round the bay and down the steps which led to the spare Deep Sleep units on level two.

Then he saw her. Another Kristine Kochanski.

She was in Deep Sleep. And she wasn't dead.

Lister squeaked clean the Plexiglass covering and peered in at Kochanski's doppelgänger. Somehow she'd managed to crawl into one of the units and engage the mechanism to freeze herself. That's why all the electrics were down. The ship's drive computer had shut off all non-essentials to concentrate on this. He peered at the bio-readouts on the facia and wondered what to do. The life readings were dangerously low, their pointers barely bobbing above a red sea of danger. She was alive, but for how long? Lister remembered Kryten's explanation that the old stasis mechanism on Starbug didn't freeze time completely, it just slowed it down by 95 per cent. Kriss was still dying in there. Just dying very slowly.

What the hell was he to do?

He'd have to tell the others now. He knew next to nothing about medicine. That was one of the areas Kryten had specialized in since they'd worked out a way to override his limitation chip – the chip in his database that was designed to prevent him from becoming more than a sanitation droid. Kryten would know if it was safe to revive her and if it was possible to operate to save her life.

He took out his transmitter and flicked it on.

The Mechanoid 3000 series ran his medi-scan over the Plexiglass view-screen and waited for the results to slowly filter back into the machine and print out on the LED.

Kochanski stood by, her face tight with anxiety as she

watched the mechanoid collate the injuries of her other self.

Kryten looked up from the medi-scan. 'She has multiple wounds to the chest and left arm. She's lost a lot of blood, almost two pints, and she has a severe rupture to her stomach wall caused by laser fire. If she remains in Deep Sleep she could live for two, perhaps three, months. If we move her and try to save her life the medi-scan gives her a seven to four chance of survival. Under ordinary circumstances I would recommend we leave her in Deep Sleep until we are able to get her back to Red Dwarf. The medical facilities aboard Starbug are laughable.'

Lister nodded. 'Two bottles of anaesthetic, a roll of gauze, a nurse's hat, and that's about it.'

'Wait one minute,' said the Cat. 'I think I'm getting an idea.'

Rimmer looked impressed. 'It's not even May.'

'Red Dwarf's six weeks away,' the Cat began. 'Why don't we tow the ship back with us?'

Kochanski shook her head. 'Not enough power.'

Lister scratched the early-morning stubble that ran down his left cheek. 'How about we leave her in Deep Sleep and come back with Red Dwarf?'

'That would take close to twelve weeks, sir. She could have expired by the time we return.'

'Meaning?'

'I believe we should operate now.'

Exhaustion draped itself over Lister like a rain-sodden coat as he lined up the stretcher outside the Deep Sleep unit and Kochanski pressed the de-activate code. For the past four hours they'd made the required preparations: sterilizing the obs deck and converting it into a temporary operating theatre.

Now it was time.

The sleep unit's door swished open and Lister and Kryten gingerly lifted the dying Kochanski's body on to the stretcher and gently wheeled it towards the mid-section. As they passed through a hatchway leading to the cargo-bay lift she regained consciousness.

She stared up into a face identical to her own and a railway line of incomprehension wrinkled across her brow. Kochanski held her hand. 'Everything's going to be OK. Don't try and talk. Just rest.'

'Who are you?' said the dying girl.

Kochanski stroked the back of her hand. 'It's hard to say without knowing who you are.'

The stretchered Kochanski smiled, said something that no one was able to make out and then lost consciousness.

She came to again as they unclipped the stretcher from its carriage wheels and lifted her on to the temporary operating table.

'Lister? Where's Lister?'

'We couldn't find him,' said Kochanski. 'He's not here.'

'They took him.'

'Who took him?'

'Heard screams. His voice shouting. Went to look. Attacked from behind. Managed to . . .' She wasn't able to finish the sentence.

'You managed to get to a Deep Sleep unit?'

She nodded.

'Must have thought I was dead.'

'Where did they take him?'

She shook her head.

Kryten leaned in. 'Ma'am, please, no more questions.'

The girl took hold of Lister's shirt and pulled him towards her. 'Promise me you'll find him. He'll know who did this. Promise me.'

Kochanski stroked her brow. 'He promises. He'll find him, he'll –'

A single note piped around the room as the medi-computer suddenly started to flat-line. Kryten opened his medi-crate and hauled out the heart pads. Quickly he connected them to the MG then placed the pads on the girl's chest and pressed the release mechanism. A wave of electricity hurtled into her, making her body arc and fall.

Still the medi-computer maintained its sullen monotone. A second time Kryten released the pads, a second time she writhed and bucked as the volts raged into her body. A second time she fell motionless.

The third time the monotone was replaced with a heart-beat.

Lister's face looked like a squeezed orange. 'This is too risky. Get her back into Deep Sleep. We need more time to think about this.'

'What about the operation?'

'Not now. Later, when we're better prepared.'

Lister drank a cup of thick black coffee as Rimmer returned from a salvage operation of the cargo bays and entered the obs room. 'How is she?'

'Back in Deep Sleep and stable.'

'How long's that thing going to keep her alive? Four, five weeks?'

Lister shrugged.

'So how are you going to save her?'

Lister shook his head. 'We can't move her, we can't operate on her and we can't get her back to Red Dwarf in time.'

The Cat sat in front of the scanner scope. 'Perhaps this is the wrong question at the wrong time, but I got to ask it.'

'You're still the handsomest guy aboard, OK?' Rimmer snapped. 'How many times?'

'That's not the question. The question is this: who the hell is she?'

Lister took a slurp of coffee. 'I reckon we've wandered into some kind of parallel reality. We must have made an error with the navi-calcs when we were traversing the Omni-zone. We're in the wrong dimension.'

'A dimension where we all get wiped out?'

'Right.'

Kochanski peered into the dead navi-comp. 'Apart from Lister.' She wiped a coating of dust from the screen. 'He's out there somewhere. With whoever did this.'

Lister recognized the tight, determined smile that was presently in residence on her face.

'Kriss, we've got to get back to our own reality. What happens here is none of our business.'

'Did I utter a single word?'

'Look, right now, in our Universe, the human race no longer exists. Its last two members have gone AWOL, remember? If we don't get back they'll never exist.'

'Naturally.'

'What about Holly? We've got to get back, Kriss.'

'Eventually.'

'No, not eventually, now. We can't spend our time running around the wrong dimension looking for some other version of me and whoever wiped out the crew.'

'Since when the hell have you been so responsible? You've never worried about the future in your life.'

'Baby, c'mon, realistically, going back's the only sane point of view.'

'Don't call a senior officer "baby".'

'What? You're going to pull rank on me?'

Kochanski half smiled. 'David, you promised her.'

'Don't call me David. Or I'll call you baby again.'

'You said you'd help her.'

'No, *you* said I'd help her. *You* said I'd find whoever did this. Not me. You did.'

'Give it a week. One lousy week – then we'll head back to the Omni-zone.'

'And what happens if something happens to one of us? What happens to our Universe then?'

'Wear bullet-proof underwear, then, for God's sake. You can get killed crossing a hyper-way . . .'

Kryten walked in through the hatchway. His head slumped disconsolately on his chest.

Kochanski's eyes widened. 'What's happened?'

Kryten stared at the floor before finally he looked up. 'Moving was too much for her body to take, ma'am. I'm afraid Ms Kochanski died a few minutes ago.'

Lister's coffee cup slipped from his fingers and smashed on the floor.

'Request permission to give her a full Star Fleet funeral.'

'Granted,' said Kochanski quietly.

CHAPTER 3

Lister sat on a chair in his other self's quarters and scanned the room. His other self clearly didn't share these quarters with Kochanski. There was a rough bachelor feel to the whole room. Clothes and engine parts were scattered everywhere, cans of Swarfega jostled with after-shave, while stacks of cheap horror novels filled the bookshelves and a 2,000-disc Mental-metal hard-rock music collection was stacked in xylophonic piles. Skulls of all shapes and sizes, some ashtrays, some ornaments, some acting as storage jars littered the room. On the walls were framed posters of a variety of frightening rock bands, most of whom appeared to be eating a selection of cute furry animals.

He picked up a black Les Paul copy with two missing strings and plucked it tunelessly. 'Sweet as a nut.' He put the guitar down and opened the metal locker that doubled as a wardrobe. A pile of magazines slithered out from a top shelf, hitting him on the head and fanning out over the floor.

He stooped and picked one up. They were all different issues of the same title. Something called *Gore*. Lister idly flicked through their pages: murder, Nazis, Satan, Hell's Angels and lots of strange rambling letters and articles about subjects he wasn't familiar with; Lister wished he hadn't found them. So his other self had a morbid fascination with the lurid; it wasn't a big deal, but he'd rather not have known. He collected the magazines together and stacked them neatly back in the wardrobe.

Kryten stood behind him. 'Sir, I understand you want to head straight for the Omni-zone and back to our own Universe.'

Lister nodded.

'Don't you feel you have an obligation to your other self, sir? I mean, to help him.'

'Kriss has sent you, has she?'

'Engage lie mode,' said Kryten. 'No, sir.'

Lister smiled, then removed an elastic band around some photographs he'd found in the wardrobe's sock drawer and started flicking through them absently. 'We don't belong here, Krytie. This isn't our barney. Plus, if he isn't dead, which let's face it he probably is, I don't want to be the one to tell him he's lost everything. He's got smeg-all now: nothing to live for, nobody to live for. Zip.' Lister's eyes tightened and he blinked rapidly several times. 'For his sake I hope he *is* dead.'

'If you're worried about getting back to our dimension, sir, and your concern is that this could act as a dangerous interlude, then perhaps you should know there's an asteroid only two days from here, Blerios 15. According to the info-link it supports a substantial population.'

'What kind of population?'

'Pig-based Gelfs mostly. Some kind of drone-species, designed for manual labour. They've formed a society of no mean sophistication. And from what I can ascertain, they're not unfriendly.'

'So?'

'So they might well be able to shed some light on what happened here.'

'Kryten, man, we're not hanging around here, OK? We're heading back to our own Universe.'

'The point I'm trying to make, sir, is that finding him might well only take a day or so.' How could he tell Lister? How could he tell him he'd been sent to inform him that looking for his other self was precisely what they were doing by order of the senior officer on board, flight coordinator Kristine Kochanski? And if he refused, he risked court martial by his own girlfriend.

'Sir, I implore you . . .'

Lister nodded, not listening. Instead he'd paused at one of the photographs. Two figures were sitting in bed – semi-hysterical, their four pin-prick eyes peeked out of an avalanche of crazy foam that covered them both. Grinning, they posed arm in arm. He studied it hard. Kochanski and his other self. For the first time Lister felt a connection. It was impossible to say why he hadn't felt it before. The ship was identical, the furnishings were similar and yet, until now, until he'd seen this picture, he'd felt strangely alienated from his other self, in a way he couldn't articulate. But this picture changed everything. A smile tobogganed across his face. 'OK.' He looked up from the photograph. 'Let's find the son of a bitch and bring him home.'

The night shift passed without event as Starbug tacked its way through the asteroid belt. First watch was taken by Lister and Kryten, the second by the Cat and Rimmer. Meantime Kochanski started the laborious process of going through the navi-calcs looking for the computational error that had caused them to wind up in the wrong dimension. Shortly before five that morning, working by the eye-aching neon up in the obs room, she fell asleep on top of a pyramid of computer print-outs, and slept soundly for the next two and a half hours.

Rimmer passed her sleeping body, then clicked down the steps that led into the mid-section and turned into the galley.

'Seven o'clock change-over. Anything to report?'

Kryten looked up from his breakfast preparations. 'It's been a moderately quiet shift, sir, apart from one small scare a couple of hours ago, when we spotted an alien invasion fleet off the port bow. Thankfully, it turned out to be one of Mr Lister's old sneezes that had congealed on the radar screen.'

'How're things fuel-wise?'

'Reasonable for today, sir – only twelve course corrections. However, the supply situation is increasingly bleak. We've recycled the water so often it's beginning to taste like Dutch lager.'

'Food?'

'No meat, no pulses and hardly any grain. Worse still, the only liquorice allsorts left are those little black twisty ones that everyone hates. If that weren't bad enough, last night I discovered that space weevils have eaten the last of our corn supply.'

Rimmer's head jabbed towards the old galley cooker. 'So what are you cooking for Lister's breakfast then?'

'Space weevil.'

Rimmer watched as Kryten removed the grill tray. Lying on the mesh wire was a creature about eight inches long, yellowish in colour, with two horns and a pincer-shaped tail.

'You can't serve space weevil! Not even Lister, with his single remaining taste bud, will knowingly sit down and eat insectoid vermin. Let's face it, with him it's practically cannibalism.'

'Sir,' Kryten implored, 'it's incredibly nutritious. After all, it *is* corn-fed.'

'You'll never get him to eat it.'

'They say the first bite is with the eye. Trust me, sir, it's all down to presentation.'

Kryten took out a pair of serving tongs and placed the weevil on a dinner plate alongside a lettuce leaf and an elaborate carrot sculpture of a swan in repose. '*Et voilà*,' he smiled happily.

The Cat clambered up the steps and into the cockpit where Lister was snoozing under a copy of *A Demon Lurks*, one of his other self's horror novels.

'Change-over. Anything new?'

'Not much,' said Lister, waking quickly. 'Electrical storm. Couple of gas geysers. Usual stuff.'

'How far before we hit this asteroid?'

'Blerios 15? Go into orbit in about twenty minutes.'

The Cat stood in his black stretch PVC body suit and pink wool barathea jacket. 'Look at the state of this place. Why don't you ever clean up before we swap over?' The Cat swept a hand across the leather flight seat. 'What the hell's all this down the back of my chair? Peanuts?'

Lister shook his head solemnly. 'Nah. I've been trimming my verrucas.'

The Cat's expression iced on his face as he opened his hand and peered at the contents.

Lister grinned. 'You really think I'm psychotically disgusting, don't you? They're peanuts, OK?'

'Real peanuts?' asked the Cat, tasting one gingerly. 'Where'd you get 'em?'

'Remember that old derelict, ages ago? Found them in the dead captain's old donkey jacket.'

'You did what?'

'Don't look at me like that. You enjoyed that mint imperial didn't you?'

'That was in his pocket too?'

'No, he was sucking it when he got shot. I had to prise his jaws apart with a car jack.'

Enlightenment dawned on the Cat's features. 'You really think I'll buy anything you say, don't you? Well, wrong, buddy. Now get out of here, I've got to keep my eyes skinned for that asteroid shaped like a dancing moose you told me about yesterday.'

Kryten climbed up the steps into the cockpit and placed the supper tray in front of Lister's suspicious gaze. 'Supper, sir.'

'What's this?'

'Sir?'

Lister held up the carrot sculpture. 'Raw carrot? You know what I think of fresh vegetables – they're for health psychos. Vitamin freaks. People who exercise.' He shuddered in distaste, then flicked open a magazine and started to crunch into the weevil. He paused mid-chew.

'Is everything OK, sir?'

'No, it is not,' said Lister, tapping the magazine. 'Some smegger has filled in this "Have You Got a Good Memory?" quiz.'

'It was you, sir, don't you remember?'

'Was it?'

The Cat turned from the scanner screen. 'I hate to go all technical on you, but all hands on deck – Swirly Thing alert.'

'Where?' said Rimmer, taking his position.

'It's not on the radar yet, but I can smell it.'

Rimmer shook his head. 'Nothing here.'

'Nor on the long-range scan,' said Kryten. 'Sir, is it possible that you could have made a mis-smelling?'

'Listen, Butter-pat head: my nostril hairs are vibrating faster than the springs on a Spaniard's honeymoon bed. I'm telling you, there's something out there.'

'OK, don't get your double helix in a straight, no one's questioning your nasal integrity.'

Kochanski bounded down the steps from the obs room and into the cockpit. 'There's something on the Hubble.'

'Go to blue alert,' said Rimmer in a clipped tone.

'What for?' asked Lister. 'There's no one *to* alert. We're all here.'

'I would just feel more comfortable if I knew we're all on our toes because everyone is aware we're in a blue-alert situation.'

'We *are* all on our toes.'

'May I remind you of Space Corps directive 34124?'

'34124?' asked Kryten. '"No officer with false teeth should attempt oral sex in zero gravity"?'

'Damn you both, all the way to Hades! I want to go to blue alert!'

'OK, OK . . .' Lister soothed. He clicked a single switch and a small sad sign with 'Blue Alert' lit up over the rear facia.

Rimmer's head dipped in triumph. 'At last, a bit of professionalism.'

'Wait. I have something,' Kochanski said. 'Punch up long range.'

Rimmer massaged his knotted brow. 'My God, what is it?'

Lister squinted at the monitor bank. 'Too small for a vessel. Maybe some kind of missile?'

Kochanski studied a blur of read-outs. 'At this range, it's impossible to say.'

'Whatever it is, clearly they have a technology way in advance of our own.'

'So does the Albanian State Washing Machine Company,' Lister replied.

Rimmer swivelled round to face Kryten. 'Step up to red alert.'

'Are you absolutely sure, sir? It will mean changing the bulb.'

'There's always some excuse, isn't there? Always some reason why you can't carry out my orders.'

'Range: 15,000 gee-gooks and closing, guys.'

'Suggest evasive action, sir.'

'You got it,' said the Cat.

Starbug reared under the impact of the fuel injection and screamed off, tilting on its port side. The ship banked one way and then the other as the green streak tracked them effortlessly. It was some kind of heat-seeker. They couldn't outrun it.

'That's it,' sighed the Cat. 'We're deader than seersucker.'

Rimmer's head arched up from the monitor. 'Suggestions?'

'Sir, may I recommend I load myself into the reverse thrust tube and you use my body as decoy fodder? Of course, this would leave me splattered around Deep Space and unable to complete today's laundry, for which I apologize in advance.'

'Kryten, you're hysterical. Now stop your blathering and get in the damn tube,' Rimmer demanded.

Lister held up a hand. 'Don't move, Kryten, you're going nowhere. I'm not doing my own smegging ironing.'

Kochanski said, 'We'll have to reason with it. Open communication channels.'

'She's right,' said Rimmer. 'Broadcast on all known frequencies in all known languages. Including Welsh.'

Lister's fingers spun across the console as he opened the rusting com channel. Rimmer cleared his throat, leaned in and began broadcasting. 'This is Arnold J. Rimmer of the Jupiter Mining Corporation transport vehicle Star-bug. Now hear this, and hear it good, because it's only coming once.' He wiped his dry lips and then began. 'We surrender. Totally and without condition. Thank you for listening. Message ends. Oh, additional: sorry for taking up your time. Thank you so much. Sorry. 'Bye. Sorry.'

Lister hammered futilely at the control pads. 'God, Rimmer, you've got a longer yellow streak than a stampede of diarrhoetic camels.'

Rimmer flashed him an ironic smile. Who cared what

Lister thought. He didn't know. He didn't know that, like General George S. Patton, he, Arnold J. Rimmer, believed in reincarnation. In fact, it was his firm conviction that in previous lives he had been a soldier – a bold warrior soul who, tragically, in this particular incarnation, had been given the body of an abject coward. He bore it with dignity, knowing that in his next existence he would return once again as a hero, his dues fully paid. Until that glorious moment, he was lumbered. He excused himself in the most dignified manner possible and went off to have a panic attack under the scanner table.

'Here it comes!' shouted Kochanski. 'Five gee-gooks to impact.'

The green dart of light hit Starbug with a wet slurp, then started to wrap its glutinous matrix around the craft until the vessel was held in a pulsing bubble.

Lister watched as the cockpit filled with an unearthly glaucous mist, and a couple of minor explosions flared from the console.

'What the hell is this?'

'Some kind of suction beam,' replied Kochanski. 'We're being dragged down.' She grabbed a fire extinguisher and started to douse the flames.

'Fire up the retros,' said Lister.

'Dead,' said the Cat.

'Auxiliary power?'

'Dead.'

'Joystick?'

'Dead. The entire panel's deader than A-line flares with pockets in the knees.'

Kryten looked up from the navi-comp. 'Sirs, I've located the beam's source. It's coming from Blerios 15.'

The green cirrus cloud carried Starbug through the asteroid's atmosphere and down towards a city ringed by a river cut into the volcanic rock. For twenty minutes they flew over a range of flat stone-and-clay buildings, occasionally interrupted by vast golden-headed mushroom towers that stretched across the skyline, before being set down in an aeropad in the south of the city.

Lister loaded his fourth bazookoid and rested it with the others on the flatbed scanner.

'If anyone tries to get in, they'll come through that door,' he said, pointing at the bulkhead hatchway. 'Kryten, you in the cockpit, Kriss, top of the stairs, Cat, man, with me behind the scanner table.'

Suddenly, a face emerged out of a storm of white noise on the main monitor. It was a species of Gelf, mostly humanoid in appearance, with pig-like pink flesh, a low neanderthal brow and large, fleshy lips. 'My name is Leekiel. I am a Potent and a member of the Blerion High Council. You have flown across Blerios air space without authorization. As laid down by the Forum of Justice on Arranguu 12 and in keeping with the treaty signed by the United Republic of Gelf States, 876.3/16 you must now submit to our judiciary. What is your business here?'

'Well, the thing is . . .' Lister began.

'You will vacate your vessel within the next thirty seconds. If you resist, the Arre bubble will increase your cabin temperature to 75° Centigrade. We await your answer.'

'Uh, right, cheers, thanks, man,' said Lister pleasantly.

'Looks like Leekiel's got a problem. Might be wise to check it out.'

Lister led the group as they trudged down the disembarkation ramp and into a line of evil-looking rifle sights. The Blerions bound them with a thick rope made out of creepers, then bundled them into the back of a dirty brown open-topped transporter which fired up its engine and headed into the city.

CHAPTER 4

The midday sun lasered into the top of Lister's head as they powered through the streets in the crude diesel-driven transport vehicle.

Everything about the place was basic: the buildings held together by clay and mud, the potholed roadways, the stinking sewage system that caught in the back of his throat, even the simple one-piece grey cotton robes that all the Blerions seemed to wear; the only signs of culture were the hugely elaborate mushroom towers that arched over the city like giant sentries.

Lister sat in the back exchanging shrugs with the others as the transporter hooted its way through a route lined with open markets, selling fruit and carpets.

The sound came without warning.

From somewhere above.

Lister peered up to see what it was. High above, on one of the balconies that ringed the mushroom towers, a figure pulled on a massive black bell. The sound soon thickened as bells in towers all over the city started to join in too.

'Look,' Rimmer pointed to the nearest tower as two figures joined the bell ringer and started to cast rice seeds off the precipice. 'What's all this about?'

The transporter jolted to a halt by the side of a market stall selling papaya and mangoes. The guards grabbed a number of black hoods from under the seat and slipped them over the crew's heads and noosed them tight.

Lister stared into the blackness.

All he could hear were mumbled shouts as the Blerions ran around organizing something. It was impossible to see what, unless he could pull the cloth tightly over his face, somehow. He opened his mouth and tried to grab a piece of the hood in his teeth. The first three times it eluded him. The fourth his front tooth caught on the cloth and slowly he began to pull it in, like a fisherman who's just caught a hammerhead shark. Bit by bit, bite by bite, he reeled the cloth into his mouth, all the time stretching the material across his face.

Now he was able to make out vague shapes. Dark silhouettes of running figures. He swallowed a little more, storing some of it under his upper gum, and peered out again. The shapes took form.

The Gelfs were scampering back and forth and appeared to be dividing into groups of two – one male, one female. Some of them displayed coloured triangles on their tunics, which seemed to entitle them to choose the partner they desired; others, it seemed, had not found a partner and were frantically dashing around the remaining uglies, trying to choose the least objectionable.

Finally the bells stopped, and there was silence all over the city. Then a priest appeared on each of the mushroom towers and played a harp, while the entire population of

Blerios 15 started to copulate. Lister gawped through his black hood at the writhing mass of bored bodies as they went about their work.

Sixty seconds later the harp music built to a rousing finale and the ground shook as the entire population of Blerios 15 climaxed simultaneously – or pretended to, at least. Afterwards they split apart, quickly dressed and went about their day.

Soon Lister was shielding his eyes from the bright sunlight as a Blerion guard removed his black hood. Then the transporter started up in a coughing fit of petrol and they continued their journey through the streets of the city.

Lister hunched in the corner of the cell and watched as a rivulet of water dribbled down the wall and fell into the foul-smelling swamp that covered the floor. The Cat and Rimmer paced in unison on opposite sides of the cell while Kryten stood quietly in one corner as Kochanski repaired a faulty knee joint.

The cell door opened and four Blerion guards splayed out in a star formation. At the top of the formation was a Gelf they hadn't seen before. He wore an ornate face piece, like an Aztec priest, and a silver robe bedecked with jewels that covered his entire body from neck to feet; all except for a circle of material which was cut out of the cloth and allowed his genital organs to hang out of his costume. This was the only part of him they could see.

'You have strayed into Blerios 15 airspace without permission. This is a most serious charge.'

Lister began: 'We meant no disrespect, man. We're

looking for another version of me. We made a navi-calc error transversing the Omni-zone and . . .'

The Potent ignored him. 'You have two choices: go before the Forum of Justice on Arranguu 12 and protest your innocence, or pay the fine.'

'And how much is that, precisely?' asked Rimmer, staring steadfastly at the top of the priest's head.

'Two hundred barrels of oil . . .'

'Two hundred barrels of oil? We've hardly got forty.'

'Or five bars of Gatoo.'

'Gatoo? What is that?' He shook his head. 'Forget it, we don't have any, anyway.'

'Or if you wish you can pay in sperm. Four millilitres. What is it to be?'

Lister shared a look with Kochanski. 'So let's get this straight. Either we go before the Forum of Justice . . .'

'On Arranguu 12 . . .'

'Right. Or we pay the fine.'

'That is correct.'

'And we can pay the fine in one of three ways. First: oil – two hundred barrels, second Katoo . . .'

'Gatoo.'

'Right, Gatoo. Or third, we can pay in sperm.'

'That is correct.'

'Four millilitres.'

'Correct.'

'Which is about half a teaspoonful.'

'That is so.'

'May we ask what you would do with this sperm?'

'Our species was genetically engineered to help terra-form an inhospitable solar system. An ability to reproduce wasn't deemed necessary, because our life expectancy is in excess of a thousand years.'

'So you're all sterile?'

'Ninety-nine per cent of our male population is. All apart from we Potents.'

'But the women are fertile?'

'In most cases.'

'And that's why you have the towers with the bells and the call to . . . copulate? To ensure you achieve maximum fertility?'

'As a visitor you should have been blinded by the hood of darkness.'

A grin shimmied across the Cat's mouth. 'Healthy sperm is worth a fortune here?'

'On Blerios 15 there is nothing of greater value. But come, you do not pretend that you have any? We can tell from your craft that you are not rich. By your clothes and demeanour. You are not Emo-traders, you are not merchants. Where would people such as yourselves possibly get sperm?'

Lister and the Cat looked at the cell floor sheepishly. Finally, Lister looked up. 'We have a secret store.'

'Right,' said the Cat. 'Which we keep in a special place.'

'Back on your ship?'

Lister moved his hands about in mid-air, as if he were spinning plates. 'Uh, yes, obviously. In the safe. Back on our ship, right.'

'I will arrange for you to be returned to your craft.'

Lister bowed. 'We will be happy to pay any fine you deem appropriate. One last thing. For the appropriate fee would it be possible for us to spend some time here on Blerios 15?'

'For what reason?'

'We need to rest and refuel. Also, we'd like to stock up on supplies.'

The Blerion councillor nodded. 'Very well. But only after the fine is paid.'

Lister bowed a second time.

The news filtered quickly through the market place – merchants with substantial amounts of sperm to spend were making their way through the market. They had bought bread and cheeses, oil and guns, cloth and wine and a number of musty old volumes outlining the history of the belt that Kryten insisted would come in useful, and they weren't finished yet.

Chants of 'Grand sires, grand lady – over here' followed them through the market. They bought their goods, handed over the test tubes and continued to shop until darkness finally fell.

As they threaded their way back to Starbug it occurred to Kryten that a strange war of evolution was being fought in the belt. A war between the various Gelf species. What made it so strange was that throughout history no species had ever arrived in the Universe fully formed. They had battled through the evolutionary holocaust and adapted their form to survive and consequently deserved to be part of nature. They had earned their right to exist.

The Gelfs had not.

As far as he could ascertain, they had been created on Earth to help humankind terraform new galaxies and had wound up in this reality as a result of being sucked into the Omni-zone after some sort of mutiny with their human masters. Not only did they not deserve to exist, they had been created with genetic flaws to inhibit their long-term survival. The result, or so it seemed to the mechanoid, threw up a scenario which was unique in nature. No longer was it a case of each individual fighting to protect his genes over the genes of every other individual; it was now individual Gelf tribes fighting to overcome their genetic make-ups and multiply faster and become stronger than all the other tribes in the belt.

Out of this a strange kind of justice system had grown – where innocence was always related to behaviour that was in keeping with the further procreation of the species. Those who failed to copulate were imprisoned, polygamy was feted, adultery lauded.

As they trooped back through the market pushing their goods on a wooden rickshaw, Lister stopped at a stall that sold candles – he wondered if they might be more effective than the halogens the next time the electrics went down. He looked up to ask the price of the stallholder and stared straight into a pair of black eyes that dilated with fear.

For a second, Lister didn't understand the look. The Gelf was afraid of him. No, more than afraid – terrified. But how was that possible? They'd never met before.

Then he realized he was staring into the eyes of someone who knew his other self.

'You know him.'

The stallholder ducked under the stall's thin cotton back cover and started to sprint across the market place.

Lister pointed. 'He knows him. He knows my other self.'

The Cat removed his yellow flannel jacket, folded it neatly in two and held it out to Kryten as if it were the Turin shroud. 'Guard it with your life, bud. And I mean your life.'

'Sir, you can count on it.'

'If you get trapped in a burning building promise me the jacket leaves first.'

'Sir, protecting this jacket is my new reason to live.'

'That's all I wanted to hear.'

The Cat weaved past a group of onlookers and started to tail the stallholder as he fled through the market place. He leapt over two Gelfs carrying a roll of carpet, side-stepped an over-turned fruit stall and flung himself at the figure as he headed for a parked transporter. He brought him down in a skid of dust.

Lister ran up panting. 'How do you know me?'

The Gelf frowned, not understanding.

'How do you know me?'

'You know how I know you. What do you mean?'

'Just answer the question. How do you know me?'

'Is this some kind of . . .'

'How?'

'I gave you transport to Blerios 15. Your craft was irreparable. You were marooned.'

'And then?'

'We got picked up by the federal council. They knew I was an Emo-smuggler. I blamed you.'

'And?'

'They took you away for questioning. I never saw you again.'

'What about my crew mates? What happened to them?'

'I don't know. You didn't want to talk about them. I didn't press it.'

'How long ago was this?'

'Four months.'

'So if I wanted to find me, what would I do?'

'What the hell are you talking about?'

'Just answer the question.'

'Everything goes before the Forum of Justice on Arran-guu 12. Seek an audience with the Regulator.'

'Anything else?'

'If you were smart you'd send the mechanoid.'

'Because?'

'He's more lenient towards mechanicals. The 'noid's more likely to get information.'

Lister's right fist arced through the air and the stall-holder staggered backwards and collapsed into a box of plums.

'Thank you,' he said politely. 'You've been most helpful.'

CHAPTER 5

Kryten's strange gait, with its ludicrously high knee action on over-sized feet, carried him up the steps of the Forum of Justice and through the snarling knot of Gelf protestors who jabbed their placards up and down in the stifling evening heat. Kryten couldn't read the strange script scrawled across the placards – it was written in a machine code he didn't recognize, but whatever the Gelfs were protesting about, the mix of heat and injustice was driving them close to a frenzy. Seeing a mechanoid apologizing his way through the crowd, the mob immediately presumed Kryten was a member of the Justice Department and a monsoon of spittle and bad food poured down on him. As ever, Kryten was kind and courteous: he wished the baying mob good day and remarked on what a sumptuous evening it was and how absolutely splendid their placards looked and indeed how well and how far they could spit. A shiver of admiration shot through his whole being: Kryten loved anyone who bucked the system, who was able to stand up for themselves and disagree with the status quo, because it was a characteristic totally absent from his own programming.

He entered the low flat building made of yellow

sandstone, handed over his letter of appointment and was escorted down a series of corridors.

So this was it.

The big one.

Soon he'd know what had happened to Lister's other self and whether or not the Department of Justice would listen to his calls for leniency. He had to use all his powers of persuasion, all his oratorical skills and make them see sense. Almost immediately his CPU announced he was in Anxiety Mode – a stage four. He followed his escort as he made a left down a wide stone hallway and then a right up a short series of steps, all the time contemplating the task ahead. He found his CPU announcing an Anxiety Mode stage three, which rapidly turned into a stage two. Then a stage four Fear Mode clicked in, followed by a Serenity reading of 0.00000004321 – an all-year low.

The guide came to a halt outside a thick oak door covered in ornate brass edging, then waited patiently as Kryten practised a series of deep bows, huge, idiotically elaborate bows that dripped with false reverence. Finally, Kryten nodded to the guide to announce his presence. The guide knocked on the door, a bass voice barked 'Come in' and he was ushered into the oval chamber. Like the corridors, the walls were made of the same yellow sandstone and the floors had an elaborate marble mosaic depicting the Gelf's taming of the asteroid belt.

The Regulator sat behind a marble desk perusing a hand-written scroll. His eyes remained rooted to the page as he uttered a grunt-like greeting. Kryten bowed deeply, his right arm sweeping the floor and his knees bending into a semi-curtsey before he straightened and then bowed a second time, for good measure. Hesitantly and, at first, rather too quietly, he began to speak. 'My lord, it is a most extraordinary honour for a life-form as humble, and lowly, and worthless, as myself, a mere Mechanoid 4000 sanitation droid, to be allowed to meet you in your own chamber and partake of the very same oxygen molecules as your esteemed . . . uh . . . Esteemedness.'

The Regulator looked up from his scroll and peered at him through half open eyes. 'Yes, I suppose it is.'

'May I sit?'

The Regulator nodded.

'I am searching for a human who calls himself Lister. I understand he passed through your courtroom and you are willing to listen to my pleas for mercy.'

The Regulator nodded.

'I have been unable to discern the exact nature of his offences against the glorious Gelf state – and I wonder, my lord, if you might tell me?'

'His crime is a serious one. A very serious one indeed.'

'I see,' said Kryten humbly.

'He destroyed the entire asteroid of Cyrius 3 and looted and plundered his way across the entire belt. He destroyed a Starhopper which served Ariel 2 and he was responsible for many deaths, including my own.'

Kryten smiled meekly as he ordered his CPU to replay the last speech to check there wasn't a malfunction in his auditory system. 'He was responsible for many deaths, including your own?' Kryten repeated slowly.

'Yes.'

'He killed you, my lord?'

'I'm afraid he did.'

Kryten shook his head. 'I'm not sure I understand, sir.'

'Does anyone?' the Regulator snapped. 'What possesses a creature to go on such a wicked orgy of murder and mayhem?'

'No, sir, I mean I don't understand how he killed you and yet you are patently still alive, talking to me.'

'He hasn't killed me yet, you imbecilic droid,' the Regulator replied testily. 'He hasn't committed any crime yet. It's something he's destined to do in the future.'

'So at this precise moment he is innocent?'

'Well, of course he's innocent at the moment. He hasn't committed his crime yet.'

'Wouldn't it be fairer to . . .'

'What, you mean wait? Wait until he's actually committed the crime before we punish him?'

'Well, it's a slightly radical thought, I realize, but perhaps it's a more . . .' Kryten's voice trailed away into silence; then he looked up and said, 'I'm just being ridiculous, aren't I?'

A patronizing smile oozed on to the Regulator's humourless countenance, like old toothpaste being squeezed out of a tube. 'If you wait until the crime has been committed before you punish the guilty, then the perpetrators get away with it – the crime has been permitted to happen and what kind of absurd system of justice is that?'

'An absurd one indeed,' Kryten found himself saying.

'The stream of time may flow downhill but that doesn't mean we can't fish upriver.'

'So how do we know Lister will commit these crimes?'

'There is much evidence.'

'There is?'

'Oh, yes.'

'Like?'

The Regulator beckoned Kryten forward and then said softly, 'The mystics have seen it. They saw it in their dreams, they saw it in the great fire that celebrates the dawn of a new cycle and they saw it in the oils of C'fadeert – all six of them.'

'And they're certain it was Lister they saw?'

'They haven't seen a crime this clearly since they ordered the execution of the Gelf known as S'rtginjum for doing revolting things to a yak in three cycles' time.'

Kryten smiled warmly. 'Well, thank you, that's absolutely everything I need to know. You've been most helpful. Thank you. Oh, one last thing. Where is he serving his sentence?'

'He is prisoner in the penal colony known as Cyberia, on Lotomi 5.'

'Is he permitted visitors?'

'Not until he's completed five years of his sentence.'

Kryten excused himself and left. He now knew what the Gelfs outside were protesting about. They wanted an end to the Mystic system of Justice, where anyone could be thrown into Cyberia with no hope of defence. He also realized why the state wanted to keep the system in place – what better way of getting rid of dissidents and unbelievers? Chuck them in Cyberia and throw away the key.

Kryten walked down the steps of the Forum of Justice.

In a way, he was pleased – a tiny lacuna of doubt had tormented him since they had first come across the alternate Starbug; at the time he'd wondered if Lister had killed the crew himself. Now he knew the truth: he wasn't serving a life sentence for homicide, he was serving it for a crime he was going to commit in the future, something that was utterly preposterous.

Kryten started to formulate an escape plan.

CHAPTER 6

Lister floated to the surface of consciousness, but cowered behind closed eyes.

So this was it.

Cyberhell.

He lay there, his eyes clamped shut, his body rigid, as his heart beat out a funky up-tempo bass riff, while his mouth felt drier than a med student party at 11.45 on a Saturday night.

It seemed as if he were lying on some flat surface, well sprung, rather comfortable. His hand brushed the surface – cotton. Some kind of cotton bed.

Gingerly, he took in a series of little breaths, expecting to inhale the acrid sting of sulphur or some other obnoxious stench – but no, all he could smell were clean sheets and the sweet fragrance of the bark of a laurel tree.

A laurel tree?

He listened, waiting to catch the tortured screams and heart-freezing yowls from those bereft of hope wandering the cyberscape of his imagination. Nothing. Almost silence, apart from a gentle sound of lapping water.

Lapping water?

It was time. He had to face it. He opened his eyes.

The villa was stunning: white stucco walls, Spanish

colonial style with yellow-and-cream furnishings, terra-cotta vases and a massive C-shaped white leather sofa which could comfortably accommodate ten. The oval bed Lister was lying in was situated at the top of a raised section of flooring, looking down on the open-plan tessera-marble-floored sitting room.

It didn't make sense. He padded across to the white shuttered window and tugged open the newly painted woodwork.

What the hell was happening here?

A strip of white beach boomeranged round the bay, hung with palm trees lazily bowed towards the sea.

This was heaven.

An idea screeched into his brain. He unbuttoned his trousers, ripped down his underpants and gazed anxiously between his legs. He gasped, he couldn't believe it.

He had a penis. Thank God, thank God.

He'd been convinced he'd be hung like Action Man, but no – the same as always.

Belting his trousers, he wandered over to a white cane drinks cabinet and unscrewed a bottle of bourbon. He smelt it, gingerly. No, it was not rhinoceros urine, it was not some foul leakage from a rabid dog mixed with liquid sewage, it was Jim Daniels bourbon. He poured himself a double and dropped in two cubes of ice. He drank. The whiskey sluiced down his throat and for the first time in a while a smile stretched across his lips.

He hadn't felt this good for ages.

Taking his glass he clanked his ice cubes across to the sound system and started to browse through the library of discs. Again, he was wrong – no Neil Diamond, no brass bands, no twenty greatest drum solos, no flute music, no lift music, no accordion tunes and no James Last. Instead, the selection was pretty good. No, better than pretty good. Damn good. Great, in fact.

Lister put on some RBS, and poured himself a second bourbon. He was halfway through the second bourbon when he decided to wander into the kitchen, which was when he discovered the Welcome pack.

The Welcome pack was sitting on the kitchen table in a large straw hamper. On top of the hamper was a large bouquet of pink lilacs. Clipped to the flowers was a scented red letter. Cautiously, he pulled back the lid and peered inside. He stared down at a selection of food: a roast chicken, noisettes of pork and a joint of beef – all cooked; asparagus, stuffed olives, French bread, fresh strawberries; whipped cream, Belgian chocolates, a variety of cheeses and two bottle of chilled Marne Valley vintage champagne.

What was the deal here? Was Cyberhell a place where you got everything you wanted? Was that what made it hell? No censure or morality? No limits? Lister took the letter and slit it open with a kitchen knife.

Dear Mr Capote,

You have been found guilty of smuggling banned substances across Gelf territory. As a hologram, you have broken the agreement made by the Gelf state and all light-generated entities to keep the peace while in the jurisdiction of Gelf states. As a consequence, you have been sentenced to five years in a cyberscape scenario designed and created by your own guilt.

The letter continued, but Lister stopped reading.

He was in the wrong cyberscape. This was someone else's hell. Someone else's nightmare.

Suddenly, the figure of an Axis-syndrome hologram materialized in the middle of the room, together with a Gelf security guard. Capote, a short man with thinning grey hair and a plump face, looked horrified as he gazed around the room.

'Not meat, I'm a vegetarian. Champagne gives me heartburn.' He staggered into the sitting room. 'Spanish architecture – not Spanish architecture. It reminds me of my first wife. No, God, *nooooo*.'

The Gelf guard looked at Lister and spoke. 'There's been an error – you'll be transported to the correct cyber scenario as soon as possible.'

'Thanks,' said Lister numbly.

The room began to change and Lister blacked out.

The alarm clanged into life and Lister emerged from under sheets that looked and smelt as if they had been used by mating hippos, and started to grope around to silence the banshee wail that sliced through his head like a laser knife. He correctly performed all the clichés, groaning, knocking the clock off the bedside cabinet, banging his head as he stooped to pick it up, before finally surrendering to the inevitable. He flung his legs over the side of the bed, jacked open one eye and started to search for the 'off' button.

He turned the clock round and round, all the time its grotesque buzz burrowing through his eyes. It made his toothache worse and the boil on the inside of his left nostril throbbed more than ever. After what seemed an eternity, longer even than the time it used to take to get served in an electrical store on a Saturday afternoon, he arrived at the conclusion there was no 'off' button. He hurled the clock to the floor and smashed it to death with the heel of his shoe. Or thought he had. But no, just as he was climbing back into bed the clock lurched back into life and vibrated so furiously it appeared as if it were actually moving towards him across the matted green carpet that stuck to his feet like Velcro. He decided the only solution was to evacuate the room. He closed the door behind him and found himself in the kitchen.

The smell of dead gravy sodomized both his nostrils; leaning towers of dirty washing were piled on every available worktop; a metropolis of plate-squashed fossilized food leaked fresh vileness. He skated his way across the cooking-fat-splashed floor and opened the fridge. The smell of rotten warm cabbage and decomposing sprouts karate-chopped the back of his throat. Green milk pussed out of the top of bottles and something that looked dangerously close to an orang-utan foetus was in a bowl covered in Clingfilm.

'Well,' he thought, 'I've lived in worse places than this. In fact, by my standards, the fridge and kitchen are pretty tidy.'

He looked down at the Welcome hamper on the table and picked up the scented red letter which had been placed on the top. He slit it open with a rusty bottle opener he found in the sink.

Dear Mr Lister,
You have been found guilty of crimes against the Gelf state. As a consequence, you have been sentenced to eighteen

years in a cyberspace scenario designed and created by your own guilt.

Welcome to hell. Once you've settled in, we hope your stay with us here will be an excruciating nightmare of torment and revulsion and that your screams for mercy and redemption will be heard across the length and breadth of time itself. If for any reason you discover anything is comfortable or pleasant, or in any way to your liking, please do not hesitate to call us and one of our staff will be very happy to ensure that everything is extremely unpleasant and distressing again, as soon as possible.

Yours as ever.

the Cyberian Management.

Lister prised open the lid and peered in at the hamper's contents: sprout broth, sprout pâté, sprout wine, anchovy sandwich spread, a roast armadillo, two dozen rice cakes, four packs of herbal cigarettes, American coffee, Portuguese tea, a carton of dog's milk and a book called *Hamilton Academicals – The Glory Years*.

Lister closed the hamper, picked up a meat tenderizer, clicked open the door and made a beeline for the clock still raging on the floor. Four blows and it was an ex-alarm clock.

He peered through the grime-laden window and, as a mosquito whirred round his head, was aware of the constant drips of a psychotic tap filling an already overflowing basin in the bathroom. Suddenly, from the apartment above, the strains of a Neil Diamond song vibrated the dead lightbulb and its filthy orange shade, while from the apartment next door the bass thump of a demented drum solo began to pound into his skull.

He consulted the TV guide and scanned the listings. Sit-coms with cute five-year-old kids, documentaries on the history of Jacobean furniture, Syrian soaps and a ninety-minute live broadcast of a rectal examination.

He had to get out of here. Had to think. He decided to throw on some clothes and take a look around outside.

But did he have any clothes?

An old dilapidated wardrobe stood sombrely in one corner of the room. He knew what was in it before he even opened its horrifying, eye-piercing squeak of a door. Five traffic-light-coloured striped tank tops hung neatly on a row of hangers. Two pairs of orange dungarees hung on two more hangers and, alongside them, three shirts painted with newly cut hair. Underneath were three pairs of shoes that Lister guessed correctly were half a size too small.

He dressed in his ridiculous, itching clothes and decided to take a stroll around town. Take a look at Hell from the outside.

CHAPTER 7

The herd of short-haired yaks gazed up into the night sky and paid no attention whatsoever as the small green ship dropped its landing legs and prepared to touch down. As the retros spewed their jets of orange flame into the desert sand, whipping it into vicious little tornado twisters, the yaks continued to munch their hay and not think very much at all. They were not thinking very much at all, because, apart from having world-class bad breath, not thinking very much at all and looking stupid were the two features that singled out yaks as being perhaps the least appreciative species ever to witness one of the Cat's hand-brake landings.

Suddenly there was something else for the yaks not to be impressed about, as a panic of black-cowled figures hurried out of the half-moon of tents that were grouped around the watering hole and rushed past them, loading automatic rifles and unsheathing scimitars.

The small green ship landed on the crest of a surf of sand, its landing ramp concertinaed creakily to the ground in the baking desert heat and five figures stood in the open hatchway wearing fur-lined anoraks, ski goggles and snowshoes.

'Sorry, guys,' said Lister. 'My fault – didn't think ahead – should have checked the weather computer.'

'You didn't check the weather computer? But you said it was an ice planet.'

'It was a guess. It looked snowy to me when we were in orbit.'

'You never think ahead, you mookle,' said Kochanski without rancour. 'You're allergic to planning.'

They retreated back inside the craft and emerged some minutes later in beachwear.

Lister stood on the landing gantry and addressed the horseshoe of black-cloaked figures. He yelled through his cupped hands: 'Are you guys Kinitawowi? Nomads, badawi?'

No reply.

'We've been told you will help us.'

Silence.

'We have a friend in Cyberia. We need help: weapons, information, soldiers.'

Silence.

'We have much we can trade.'

'Sir, allow me.' Effortlessly, Kryten switched into Kinitawoweese: *'Kinitawowi, nekh nikhi nekh histan! Kanua watua nahoo.'*

The hooded figures stood impassively. Then they pulled back their cowls and revealed the lugubrious snouts of some form of hippopotamus that had been genetically mixed with gorillas. *'Yurarg eor dor degga!'*

Lister slid a trunk on to the top of the disembarkation steps and started hauling out some of the contents: 'Look, Levi jeans. Whisky. VCRs. Sperm. We need help? To rescue our comrade. *Comprendez?*'

89

Kryten translated: '*Aig gy gon banuu. Nilk tet kan ua nah oo yek ht!*'

The Kinitawowi nodded and started back towards their encampment.

Rimmer stared after them. According to some rogue droid they'd met in a bar back on Blerios 15, Kinitawowis were supposed to be friendlyish; they travelled in tribes, roaming the plains of the desert asteroids that made up most of the northern sector of the belt, and bartered with the various Gelf communities for emotions and memories which they sold on to Simulants for vast profit.

Rimmer didn't trust them.

In fact, he found it almost impossible to trust anyone; a characteristic which gave his face its fleshless lips and added sharp points to his nose and chin. His smile was like an iceberg, two-thirds of it remained under the surface, but nothing gave away his mistrust of life more than his eyes. When clouded by doubt, they would narrow to alley-cat slits beneath a clutch of paranoid hair.

'Suggest two of us stay back in case anything should go awry. Don't trust this lot one bit. Why don't you take Kryten? He's expendable.'

'Good point. I'm on my way, sir.' The mechanoid beamed happily and made to walk down the disembarkation steps.

Lister stopped him with a look. 'If anyone stays back it should be Kriss. These dudes are supposed to be pretty weird around attractive women. Plus, if anything goes wrong she can pilot Starbug and get help.'

'Ms Kochanski, ma'am.' Rimmer saluted smartly. 'Wish to volunteer to be your assistant, ma'am, on your extremely dangerous mission to stay behind and look after Starbug, ma'am.'

'No need. I'll be fine, Mr Rimmer.'

Rimmer gave her one of his icebergs.

A tent flap was flung back and the leader of the Kinita-wowi strode towards them wiping his brutish paws on a filthy apron before shaking Lister by the hand.

'*Hier bhju jnh dewj?*'

'He says do we want to trade, sir?' Kryten translated.

'Tell him we need aid to get our friend out of Cyberia. We understand for the right price he can help us.'

Kryten translated Lister's message and the chief spoke quickly in Kinitawoweese.

Kryten turned to Lister. 'Sir, he says it is true they can help, but the price will be steep.'

Lister nodded. 'Tell him we're loaded.'

The Cat's laugh roared around the encampment.

Kryten spoke: '*Grendee argenti nawagooty.*'

The chief nodded and gestured for them to follow him.

The dead rogue droids lay on their backs in rows of tens. In all there must have been close to a thousand. It was like a cross between an android burial ground and a car dump. Most of them were injured: one-eyed, one-armed, legless or with holes in their stomach showing daylight.

'*Ezenji.*'

'He's saying choose, sir.'

'But they're all dead,' said the Cat. 'What the hell is there to choose?'

The Kinitawowi chief held out a box of micro-boards and shook it.

'He says they're disarmed. Once the micro-boards are restored to their CPUs they'll be fully functional.'

Lister took Kryten's arm and led him off to a point where they were out of the Kinitawowi chief's earshot. 'Can we trust him? Is he the sort of guy you can buy a secondhand droid off?'

Kryten turned and peered at the chief as he leaned on one foot, beating his hands together shiftily.

'If the truth be known, sir, probably not. However if we want to get your other self out of Cyberia we need help. And at present this is the only help that's available to us.'

Lister nodded and wandered back to join the chief.

'We want to see some of them working.'

'*Hikmuie?*'

'He wants to know which ones, sir?'

Lister stepped into the matrix of droids and started to make his choices.

The twelve droids stood to a sloppy attention as Lister walked down the line to inspect them. The first three were in moderate condition – all limbs present and correct. After that the platoon went downhill fast. Rogue droids four and five had missing left arms, six and seven had ears and left legs missing and moved by using their arms like three-legged dogs; eight's eyes hung down his chest on their sensor wires; nine was complete but had a tendency to giggle and blow saliva bubbles; ten had no upper body whatsoever, being basically just a pair of legs; eleven's head was absent without leave; and twelve was just a hand.

'Atten-shun,' Lister barked. 'By the left, quick march – left, right, left, right.' The platoon slumped, slouched, limped, hopped, crawled and shuffled up and down the desert dune as Lister put them through their paces.

'*Juh utio as niug hui,*' said the chief.

'What's he saying?' asked Rimmer.

'He's saying Mr Lister has chosen well, sir.'

The Kinitawowi chief led them into the tent piled high with ammunition and computers and dome-shaped glass helmets patterned with lights, and invited them to sit on a row of strange-smelling cushions that were stacked around a dozing fire. Already seated around the fire were four other Kinitawowis, who stood, bowed, then reseated themselves. Two females, two males.

The chief flipped open a metal crate and took out a screw-top vacuum-sealed flask and emptied something into the palm of his hand. It was a tiny pink disk.

'What is it?' asked the Cat.

'A computer virus,' said Kryten.

'*Fth gy arf gt deh bji kio.*'

Kryten nodded. 'He says it is more powerful than the sun.'

'*Gt bb id lk aftrhe.*'

'It kills electricity.'

'*Hye ngh io deh vikm lpo seh.*'

'Extraordinary. He says with the powers of the disk we will be able to bring down the entire cyber-system.'

'Show us,' said Lister, gesturing with his hands.

Kryten translated. The chief dragged two computers from the pile of dead machinery and quickly connected them together and then inserted the disk into the first machine. '*Fgju grh erg nkiju.*'

'He's inviting you to modem the virus from one machine to the next.' The Cat pressed the keypad and watched the second computer explode in a plume of blue flame.

The laughter and smiles swirled around the tent.

'*Gfb hnu hul lks ain iifo do.*'

'Now he says he will insert the antidote disk.'

The chief inserted a blue disk into the second computer and it pinged jauntily back to life. Lister led the applause. 'OK, we'll take the virus and the antidote and the dirty dozen out there. Say half a test tube.' Lister rolled up his trouser leg and took out a single cigar tin that was tied around his ankle. He pulled the top off the tin and let a test tube fall into his hand. 'Deal?' He handed the test tube to the chief.

The chief rolled it around in his hand then pulled out the cork and smelled it. '*Rhy jio nkjh opoiu nmj?*'

'He says what is this?'

'What does he think it is?'

'*Gju ski gimj.*'

'He says it smells like sperm.'

'Tell him it's mine,' said Lister proudly. 'I can vouch for it.'

'*Hy bji,*' Kryten replied.

'*Nuj fer gimj?*'

'He says, "And you're giving it to me?"'

'You bet,' Lister twinkled.

'Sir, I . . .'

'*Proki, mgetm klif kzzen.*'

'He says this is an outrage . . .'

'He wants more,' said Lister, unrolling his left trouser leg. 'Well, I'll give him more.'

'That's mine,' said the Cat, pointing at himself.

Lister turned to Kryten. 'Is there a problem?'

'Listy, *mon frère*,' said Rimmer, wearing a grin the size of a billboard. 'Methinks the Kinitawowis aren't sterile and consequently don't have a spermatozoon-based monetary system. And if that's the case – imagine how it looks. Because to his eyes you've just given him a tube of your love custard, then looked mighty peeved when he wasn't thrilled to receive it.'

'*Hakh nik ikh han nab ekh! Pakh nij imh abe kh!*'

'What's he saying now?'

'He's saying to make up for this insult you must prove that you have respect for him and for his people.'

'Tell him I do respect him and his people.'

'*Fgb hn hm ojm ne im mkij mn djh nakjd pkij bgd be.*'

'He says you must prove it.'

'Yes, sure – anything. Well, anything except hand-to-hand combat with their strongest warrior wearing just skimpy leather thongs.'

The chief spat and jabbed his finger in the air and pointed at the group of Kinitawowis sitting around the fire.

'Sir, he says to prove you have respect for him and his people you must marry his daughter.'

'His daughter?'

The chief strode across the tent and gestured at the figure sitting in the middle of the group. She was six foot six and covered in matted brown fur, with a black hippo nose and encrusted saliva around her mouth.

'That's his daughter?'

'One of three, sir. Apparently she's the looker.'

'Hey, wait – what about Kriss? I'm taken.'

Rimmer's nostrils flared open. 'Come on, Listy, it's your duty – besides, you've dated worse.'

'Only due to very poor disco lighting.'

'Hann abe kh nik nitre khp.'

'He's saying, no wedding, no deal.'

The Kinitawowis rose and barked abuse at Lister, stabbing their dirty gorilla fingers into his chest and hurling the bangles and hats and jeans they'd accepted as presents on to the straw matting of the floor. Lister stood, shoulders slumped, trying to protect himself from their verbal savaging with his best idiotically winsome grin. They spat into the roaring fire, putting it out, and departed. He watched them go and then turned to look at the others, shaking his head.

Lister suddenly became aware that three pairs of eyes were staring at him with looks of barely concealed irritation.

'Hold on, let's get out the sheet music and play the Real Waltz. I am not going down to Moss Bros. for anyone who is less attractive than my own armpit after twenty games of table-tennis.'

Rimmer was incredulous. 'Are you going to blow the whole deal just because she doesn't hit your G-spot?'

'Rimmer, believe me, it would never work out. I'm a Pisces and she's part smegging hippopotamus – that, to my mind, makes us incompatible.'

'Sir, they're a proud people. They won't change their minds. The only possible way we are ever going to get our hands on the virus and the rogue droids is if you agree to marry Khakhakhakkhhakhakkkhakkkkkh.'

'That's her name?'

Kryten nodded.

'Man, I could never settle down with someone whose name sounds like a footballer clearing his nose.'

'Look, Listy, the plan is as plain as a Bulgarian pin-up. We do the trade, you go through with the wedding, and when everyone's asleep we come back and rescue you.'

Lister shook his head. 'Not a chance. No way. Wipe the idea from your minds. I'm telling you right now, guys. Forget it. OK? Forget it.'

CHAPTER 8

Lister stood in his Kinitawoweese wedding gown, a garland of flowers on his head, as the priest conducted the service. '*Kan kij giu nah tokha, han nah wok arghy.*'

Kryten leaned in and spoke in a confidential tone. 'Sir, you have to say, "*Kan kij giu nah tokha, han nah wok arghy*", which means you will love Khakhakhakkhha-khakkkhakkkkkh until a time when there is no sand in the desert and the sun is as cold as a yak's nipple on a winter's night.

'*Kan kij giu* . . .' Kryten prompted.

'*Kan kij giu* . . .'

'*Nah tokha* . . .'

'*Nah tokha* . . .' said Lister.

'*Han nah* . . .'

'*Han nah* . . .'

'*Wok arghy* . . .'

'*Wok arghy* . . .'

'*Hannah klahkhet,*' said the priest.

'Now what's he saying?'

'He's saying you may kiss the bride,'

'What, without a bag?'

'Everyone is watching,' said Rimmer through a mouth borrowed from a bad ventriloquist. 'Just gloody well giss her gefore they gegin to realize you're not gosher.'

Lister adjusted his garter and nodded. 'Kryten, man, give me a leg up.' Kryten linked his two hands together and Lister hoisted himself up and kissed his bride. She grabbed him gleefully around his tiny waist and bearhugged the air out of him. Then she tossed him over her shoulder and started to carry him off to their wedding hut. As he hung down her back, a maiden at the mercy of a Viking on the pillage, Lister called to his crew mates, 'See you soon, guys. Look in any time, don't be strangers!'

They waved their farewells and then Kryten addressed the chief: '*Hanna bekh yekh bhn knj ele njuh yekh.*' The chief nodded and handed the mechanoid the vacuum flask containing the two viruses, and some astro-strippers Kryten had taken a shine to. When there was time he intended to repaint the ship.

'Suggest we get the rogue droids aboard Starbug and leave at first light, sirs.'

Rimmer and the Cat nodded.

The door of the wedding hut creaked open and Lister's bride unceremoniously dumped him on the pile of yakskin cushions that made up their wedding bed.

'*Hegg onnen nikh hakken,*' said his bride, and started to take off her wedding gown.

'Well, what a day, darling. Boy, am I pooped. It's straight to sleep for me.'

Her gown dropped on to the straw matting and she started to clamber out of her sexy, honeymoon pantaloons; they could have sailed a forty-foot schooner across the Atlantic and back.

Lister pulled the blanket up around his chin and heehawed nervously. It was hard not to notice that her bikini line would probably have defeated all but the most powerful petrol-powered hedge trimmer. 'You've been looking forward to this, haven't you? You're not going to take no for an answer.'

'*Knakhenkh!*'

'How about a drink first?' Lister mimed drinking.

Khakhakhakkhhakhakkkhakkkh nodded and pointed to a clay jug with two goblets on a tray by the side of their bed. Lister filled her goblet up to the brim and took a small amount himself and then proposed a toast: 'To unconsummated wedding nights.'

'*Jhyg ge ni juk,*' she replied, and they started to drink.

Lister took a tiny, medicine-sized sip of the stuff and watched her devour hers and pour herself another. He remembered thinking everything was going to plan when suddenly he grimaced; his stomach felt as if there were a skipping pig inside it – a quite common reaction to those unaccustomed to Kinitawowi moonshine. The tent started to rotate like a crazed merry-go-round, while everything in it crash-zoomed in and out of focus and then his eyelids hammered shut like slamming vault doors and he pole-axed backwards on to his wedding bed.

Kinitawowi moonshine was strong. It was rumoured that once you were drunk on it you could stay drunk for weeks, sometimes even months. To Lister's way of thinking, this explained much of his subsequent behaviour over the next few weeks.

It was not unpleasant, but he couldn't remember what it was called. There was a name for it, it was very popular.

What the hell was it called? He dropped into unconsciousness again. Then that feeling again. If only he could remember what he was doing, everything would make sense. It was something you shouldn't forget. Yes, good, no one should forget this thing he was doing. Why had he forgotten? Because his head wasn't feeling well. That's right, someone or something had knocked him out. Good, very good, he was close now. He was so, so close to knowing what was happening to his body. This feeling that washed through him, that almost made him forget about the tympani bass throb that continued to drone on and on in his skull.

Concentrate.

He would get it this time. What was he doing? It was something he hadn't done a lot of recently. It was . . . He was . . . He was having sex.

That's what he was doing. He was having sex, but who with? He opened his eyes and saw her naked silhouette riding on top of him. Wait a minute. Sex? He was having sex? With a grizzly bear?

No, of course he wasn't. Crazy idea. It must be Kriss wearing an old gorilla-gram costume.

Why would she be doing that? Had she ever done anything like that before? Not really. So why now?

Damn his eyes, why couldn't he see properly? He tried to rub them back into focus but her mighty hands pulled them away from his face and placed them back on her large hairy breasts.

Hairy breasts?

Wait a minute.

He was being screwed by Khakhakhakkhhakhak-kkhakkkkkh.

His scream exploded into the cold night air. '*He-e-e-e-e-e-e-e-e-elp. Kryte-e-e-e-e-e-n. C-a-a-a-a-a-a-a-a-at.*' She placed a rough paw over his mouth and rode him, even faster. Oh, my God, he was close to climax. She really knew what she was doing. Oh, he was so disgusted. Did he have no self-control? She was descended from hippos, for God's sakes. 'Ooohhhhhh, aaaaaaaaahhhhh, oooohhh. Hel . . . m'mmmm . . . elp. Ooooohh, aaaahhh. Hel . . . aaaa . . .'

The two elders sat in front of the open fire frying celebratory catangu nuts to bless the wedding of Btrrn-fjhyjhnehgewydn's daughter when the naked figure of the human man dived out of the tent and started to run through the encampment towards the small green transport craft. He opened his mouth and hollered as he moved, 'Change of plan! *Le-e-e-e-e-e-e-g i-i-i-i-i-i-it!!!!!!*'

CHAPTER 9

The voice of the Cyberian flight controller crackled out of the com speaker in the midst of a supernova of blinking lights on the Starbug's instrument boards. It repeated its request for the craft's ident number and landing authorization code. For the third time in as many minutes the Cat ignored it. Instead, he yanked back the joystick and braced himself as a tornado twister hit Starbug's underbelly like an upper cut, and sent the ship temporarily out of control.

The voice was unrelenting. 'Kindly state craft ident number and landing authorization code.'

Kryten's eyes swept the scanner looking for signs of life. It didn't make sense. Lotomi 5 was only 500 miles across and they'd swept the planetoid twice, and somehow they still couldn't find Cyberia. Starbug banked along a giant drumlin of sand as he stabbed instructions into the navi-comp computer. 'Still nothing.'

'This is your final warning. Please state craft ident number, together with landing authorization code, otherwise a fleet of Cyberceptors will be launched to engage your craft in combat.'

Lister exchanged a look of frustration with Kochanski,

then jabbed a search instruction into the computer. Again it flashed a 'Sorry – nothing found' message. He mashed a styrofoam cup in anger. They had perhaps ten minutes before they would be attacked by the Cyberceptors and they couldn't drop either of the two landing parties until they'd got a fix on the penal colony. He was helpless. Frustrated and help-less. He moved past the group of rogue droids sitting in the mid-section, armed and ready to jump and wandered into the galley, where he started devouring a packet of breakfast cereal. What the hell were they to do if they were engaged in combat? Starbug was a ship-to-surface transport vehicle – the most lethal thing they had onboard was his secret recipe for chilli dogs.

'There. There it is!' The Cat flashed his famous forty-tooth smile and pointed to the scanner as a blinking yellow cross signalled a large power source. 'The scanners must have missed it through the storm. Hold on, buds and buddesses, I'm taking her down.'

Starbug dropped out of the dust storm and flew low over a meandering desert road that led away from the penal colony before veering off and making a vertical landing in the basin of a clump of dunes. The landing legs concertinaed into themselves and the craft flopped clumsily on to its belly, like a Bactrian camel preparing to lie down for the night. The engines wound down and the retros whinnied into silence.

A hatch opened in the fast-cooling desert evening, and three figures scrambled out of the top of the craft carrying a variety of equipment in backpacks. Once out, they closed the hatch door and started climbing out of the basin, looking for the desert road. As they trudged their way up the dune, Starbug blared off over their heads, in the direction of Cyberia.

Rimmer pulled down his bush hat to protect his eyes from the skin of fine sand the trade winds were peeling off the dunes and trudged down the desert road. The highway, built in a wide arroyo and pocked with pot-holes, ran the length of the asteroid, from the Gelf's quarters in the south all the way to Cyberia in the north-west. For half a mile the party of three walked in silence, preserving energy.

Rimmer normally enjoyed walking. In fact, he was a bit of a hiker in days gone by, climbing the fells and escarpments of Io, but the knot of tension that was slowly uncoiling in his belly was doing nothing for his current perambulation. Not for the first time, he asked himself why he was even here.

Why him?

He was not cut out for commando raids on enemy installations. He wasn't the macho type. He was someone who had needed a friendly hand to hold whenever he underwent dental surgery, a habit he hadn't kicked until he was twenty-eight. He was someone who had a medically authenticated fear of blood. That's why he had never become a famous brain surgeon. One tiny droplet of the stuff and he was on his back faster than his mother in the presence of a high-ranking officer.

What Rimmer was was a thinker, a plotter, a com-mander of men, not a fighter; he was someone who sat on top of the hill in the general's tent planning the campaign and drinking fine wines.

A common foot soldier he was not. He was too intelligent to be brave. That was why he never suffered the fool's rush of blood to the head that caused one man to fall across a grenade to save another. He was more likely to pick up a man and throw him over the grenade to protect himself.

He remembered an old girlfriend, Yvonne McGruder. They'd had a torrid fling back in the old days on Red Dwarf – it hadn't lasted much more than one long glorious weekend – but Rimmer thought about her still. She'd summed him up pretty well once. She'd said he was a brave man trapped inside the body of a coward. Rimmer liked that definition of himself.

'How about this?' Kochanski stopped under a telegraph pole positioned on the arc of a tight lefthand bend.

Kryten flipped his visual system on to long range and scanned the desert road. 'Excellent. It's well sheltered, and we can bury the hardware just behind that small hummock of sand.' He pointed to a site thirty feet from the road.

Rimmer watched as Kochanski shimmied up the pole's climbing rungs and Kryten started to strip the canvas covers off the computer and attach leads into the serial ports.

A real officer would not have shimmied up the pole. A real officer would have delegated. A real officer would have screamed, 'Rimmer, stop mooning about and get up that pole. You're a bloody maggot. What are you?' And he would have had to reply, 'I'm a bloody maggot, ma'am, on my way up the pole, ma'am. Thank you, ma'am.' Then she would have been a real officer, and maybe then she would have got a little of his respect.

Suddenly, he was aware that she was talking to him.

'. . . Rimmer . . . Rimmer?'

'Huh?'

'Are you listening?'

'What?'

'The leads. Hand the leads up.'

'Certainly.' A *trompe-l'œil* smile of affection painted itself across his lips. 'And we're still of the opinion that this is a good plan, are we? No second thoughts or anything?' She disembowelled him with a look and started connecting the leads to the glass fibres of the telegraph line with a Thurston J connector clip. Rimmer continued. 'If I recall my military history correctly, there was a most famous Japanese general called Kamikaze who made a name for himself by his rather original approach to battle. Comforting to know we're treading in the footsteps of one of the truly great military thinkers.'

Kryten clicked the computer on and jabbed a series of commands into its database. He spun the cylinder, took out the pink disk, which glinted slightly against his chest plate, then loaded the disk into the computer's hard drive and waited. After a few seconds a warning trilled across the screen.

You have just loaded the OBLIVION VIRUS into your database. The OBLIVION VIRUS destabilizes the electron/proton relationship of the electric charge as it passes through it. In effect, the OBLIVION VIRUS kills electricity.

Do you have the antidote disk? Press Y/N.

Kryten pressed 'Y' and waited for the next instruction.

Please enter antidote disk.

Kryten entered the antidote disk and received his authorization to enter his pass-code. He typed in Har Megiddo 46758976/Kry, the code number he had been given by the Kinitawowi, and set the alarm. In ten minutes, the oblivion virus would be released into the fibre optics of the telephone wire and would then hurtle on towards Cyberia. Five seconds after that there would be no electricity on Lotomi 5. Just enough time for Lister and the Cat to get into position for their drop into Cyberia.

There was a noise.

Overhead. A thundering, deafening, whooshing sound. Suddenly the sand was stirred into a swarm of tornado twisters. The Cyberceptors swept over the dune in a diamond formation, underbelly floodlights lighting up the desert as they loomed overhead.

'Down.' Kochanski hit Kryten at waist height and bundled him into the sand. They lay there for some moments as the crafts passed overhead.

Kochanski spat out a mouthful of desert. 'You think they saw us?'

'Of course they saw us – they're looking for us. The Kinitawowi have set us up,' said Rimmer, grim-faced.

'The dust storm won't help visibility, sir. I believe there's every good chance they missed us.' Suddenly, the jets rolled right and swept back towards them.

The Cyberceptors landed two hundred metres from where they were lying. Two cargo doors hinged open and ten six-wheeled buggies, with their huge rubber wheels, were lowered to the ground, each containing a squad of eight Cyberian guards. All armed and helmeted, ready for battle. The buggies screamed off in every compass direction.

Kryten's head appeared at the top of a ridge of sand and squinted down at the ten figures examining the roadway. Ten minutes before virus launch.

'What do we do?' Rimmer's brow wrinkled into an unintelligible signature of anxiety.

Kochanski thought about it. If the Gelfs found the oblivion virus they'd be finished. It was their one and only trump card. She brushed sand from her face. 'We've got to get the oblivion virus before they do and get out of here.'

'What about Mr Lister and the Cat, ma'am?'

'If we lose the oblivion virus we lose everything. We've got no choice.'

'Are you crazy?' said Rimmer. 'We didn't come all the way . . .'

'You want to end up in Cyberia too?' she shouted. There were five loud clicks behind them.

They turned and stared into the barrels of five clip-loading T 27 electron harpoons. 'Where is your craft?'

Kryten smiled benignly. 'We don't have a craft.'

The Gelf captain stepped forward. Like the other Cyberian guards, it was a Dolochimp. Kochanski shuddered – it possessed the matt-grey bottle-headed snout of the dolphin, the spindly legs of the locust and the arms and upper body parts of the chimp. Slowly it took a holo-whip from its belt. The orange lash of light hovered in the air, like a dancing snake.

'Where is your craft?' it said in a duck-like rasp.

'I promise you, sir, we don't . . .'

The lash swished through the desert night and sliced through Kryten's right leg as if it were soft ice-cream. Dumbstruck, Kryten watched his leg clang to the ground beside him.

'My God.' Rimmer covered his mouth with his hand.

'Please take us to your craft,' the Dolochimp said softly.

Kochanski picked up Kryten's leg and nodded.

The terra buggy pitched down the desert road. Kryten sat in the back between Kochanski and Rimmer, clutching his lasered leg. He doubted it was repairable – it would certainly require a massive operation to re-wire all the damaged tendons. He checked his trauma level – still high. He hadn't felt this stressed since his soufflé dropped back on the Nova 5. It was his first time in the kitchen and it was for the flight admiral's birthday too. Oh, the shame, the disgrace – it brought him out in over-heat flushes even now. He gazed down at his leg again. Who would want a mechanoid who was physically imperfect? There was no option: he would offer to terminate himself.

He checked his self-esteem level: it was absolute zero. Excellent. At least that was still normal.

Yes, when it was convenient he would wipe his hard drive and close down his programme. It was the only solution.

No. He was being absurd. Idiotic and ridiculous. How could he possibly terminate himself? Who on earth would tidy up his body parts? Terminating himself would just make the place untidy. Logically, therefore, he had to continue living. He couldn't think about this now. He glanced at his watch. Three minutes until the oblivion virus was launched.

Suddenly the vehicle slowed as they approached a tight righthand bend that was all too familiar. The telegraph pole was also familiar. Kryten held his breath. They passed it safely. The buggy changed gear and started to gun up the highway.

'Stop.' The buggy jolted to a halt.

The Gelf captain held up its paw and peered at a line of footsteps coming over the brow of a dune and hugging the roadway. He squinted at the tracks, then craned over his shoulder and peered back in the direction they had come.

'Reverse.'

The buggy reversed for three hundred feet before the Dolochimp ordered it to stop on the arc of the bend; right alongside the telegraph pole that housed the modem leads.

Kryten looked at his watch again. Two minutes. Tension level – close to blow-out.

'What is that?' The captain pointed to the black tape wrapped around the brown pole which held the leads in place.

Kryten watched as the Dolochimp jumped out of the buggy and walked slowly up to the pole. It ripped off the tape and the leads came free. Then it traced the leads to the bottom of the pole.

'What is this?'

It pulled at the lead which came up out of the desert. The Dolochimp fed it back to the buried computer in its lead box.

'What is this?'

The Dolochimp ran across to the telegraph pole and started to climb.

Kryten's watch. One minute.

It reached the top of the pole and stared at the connector clips feeding into the fibre optics of the main supply. 'They're feeding something into the electric supply.'

Two Dolochimp soldiers leapt out of the buggy and fired into the computer's lead box.

The electrons rebounded off the lead in a shower of sparks.

Thirty seconds.

The Dolochimp pulled out its holo-whip and clicked it on. The orange lash shimmered into life. It looked at Kochanski and tutted as it brought the plaited light swishing down on the modem leads that ran up the length of the telegraph pole.

CHAPTER 10

The Cat's face flicked to the wall monitor. 'Two minutes.'

'OK.' Lister slipped on his parachute and joined the line of rogue droids standing by the open bay doors. He stood behind the one who was just a waist and a pair of legs, whom they'd wittily nicknamed 'Legs', and looked down the line.

When Kochanski had first mooted the idea of rescuing his other self he'd expected it to be a bit more of a team affair. When it came to a straight commando drop into the penal colony itself he expected to have at least three members of the crew with him. Instead what he had was a platoon of partially limbed droids. Kryten, he accepted, couldn't come, on account of his programming. Kochanski, with her EI/Eng training, was their best bet to break into the optic lines, so she too had to be in the first landing party. But what was Rimmer's excuse? At the last minute he'd showed up and claimed he was allergic to parachutes.

'Allergic to parachutes?'

'Absolutely.'

'What the hell are you talking about, Rimmer?'

'It's the silk mix in the parachute material. It gives me

sinusitis. The first ten minutes after landing my eyes stream so badly I can't see a thing.'

Of course no one believed him, but he promised he'd provide documentary proof if they ever got back to Red Dwarf. There were no depths to which the man wasn't prepared to sink to save his own bony hide. So that left only the Cat, and although he had wanted to come, someone had to pilot.

So that left just Lister.

Just Lister and the Deformed Dozen. The Cat's voice crackled back on to the screen again. 'OK, buds, it's party time. T minus thirty seconds before lights out. We're in position – now!'

The first rogue droid flung itself out of the craft, quickly followed by the second. Lister checked his bazookoid, patted the belts of spare shells secreted about his flight suit and threw himself out into the warm night air.

Fifty feet above the colony's Plexiglass dome he fired off the first of the bazookoid mortars. The shell ripped into the dome and shattered the centre of the structure, in a muffled thud. The roof buckled, then sagged, as its support struts gave way and, to the accompaniment of a comical creaking noise, finally fell in on itself. One by one the droids dropped through the ex-roof and into the heart of the penal colony.

Lister made a perfect landing as he'd done so many times before on the artificial-reality simulator but, to his horror, when he twisted right to unclip his parachute he saw a battalion of Alberogs jogging down the hallway towards him. Almost in slow motion they raised their laser harpoons and fired at his defenceless body.

'Legs', 'Lefty' and 'Righty' skidded in from nowhere and formed a solid droid wall in front of him. The laser harpoons impacted on their bodies and exploded in a series of harmless flares. He scrambled out of his parachute and the three droids chaperoned him, crab-like, to the cover of an indented hatchway.

Lister's right eye snaked from out of the alcove as he peered down the hallway. The Gelfs were recharging their harpoons from a wall charger.

He looked at his watch. The virus should have hit by now. The laser harpoons should have been redundant, they weren't supposed to get a chance to recharge them.

That was the plan – withstand the early fire then, once the virus had hit, the whole colony would be defenceless.

A harpoon bolt bansheed into the wall just above Lister's head and he was showered by a fist of flying sparks. 'What are you doing, guys?' he sang quietly to himself. 'Why's there still electricity?'

The holo-whip skimmed effortlessly through the muggy desert night as the Dolochimp began his downward stroke to sever the oblivion virus from its modem.

Then something persuaded the Dolochimp not to.

It was Kryten. Well, Kryten's leg to be precise, which boomeranged through the air and caught him on the right side of his hairless snout. It arced sideways and plummeted on the hard desert road in a cringe of broken bones.

Kryten's watch. Zero seconds.

The oblivion virus erupted out of the computer, screamed up the telegraph pole, entered the mains supply and rocketed down the highway, destroying the electric

charge as it went. Three nano-seconds after it was released it hit Cyberia. It breached all its defences, and five
nano-seconds after that all power to the penal colony
had been extinguished. Then the oblivion virus made
its final slay. It bore down into the core of the asteroid
and knocked out the artificial gravity generator. Its
mission completed and all electricity on Lotomi 5 disarmed, the virus sizzled and sparked and finally burnt
itself out.

'Kill him.' The Dolochimp lay on the floor in a
gymnastic contortion of broken bones, mewling quietly
to himself. He raised his one good arm, pointed at Kryten
and repeated his order. 'Kill him.'

Kochanski stood up in the back of the terra buggy.
'Hey, look.' A pair of sand goggles had lifted up off the
seat of the vehicle and were floating in the air. The
goggles were soon followed by a pair of unoculars
which had been resting on the dashboard.

Rimmer's eyebrows dipped in fear, like two braking
cars in a head-on collision. 'We're losing gravity.'

His body lifted out of his seat and he started to
float through the open roof of the transporter and out
into the desert. 'I'm losing gravity. I'm . . .' Rimmer's
scream was partially lost as he floated out of the
truck.

Kryten staggered towards him and managed to grab
a hold of his ankle. 'Relax, sir, I've got you. No, wait a
minute, I'm going too . . .'

Kryten, still hanging on to to Rimmer's ankle, was
sucked out of the roof.

Kochanski fell across the truck, which was somehow
defying gravity, and threw herself at Kryten's disappear-

ing foot. She held on to his ankle until she too started to float skywards. As her feet passed the roof's support rail she tucked both her insteps under the rail. The chain of bodies shuddered to an uneasy halt.

'Good plan. Great plan,' Rimmer whined from the top. 'Knock out all the electricity on the asteroid, including the artificial gravity generator. We could win things for a plan this good – the General Custer Forward Thinking Award, for starters.'

'What do we do?' screeched Kryten.

'I can't hold on,' Kochanski moaned.

The two Dolochimp soldiers hugged the telegraph pole, uncertain what to do. Finally, the one nearer the vehicle hurled himself across the fifteen-foot gap between pole and transporter and was just able to catch the wheel arch with his outstretched chimp arm and haul himself back into the truck. He clicked on his harpoon. 'Out. Get out of the transporter.'

Kochanski said, 'Can we discuss this?'

He beat her ankles with the butt of his rifle and the chain of three took off out of the truck.

The Dolochimp fired up the transporter, paused to pick up the captain and the second soldier and took off down the road.

Rimmer, Kryten and Kochanski gently arced a 360° loop.

'Grab hold of the telegraph wires,' Kryten called from below and the three of them scrambled to a perching position on top of the wire.

They watched as the transporter accelerated down the highway, until it hit a hump in the middle of the road, lost gravity and spiralled through the air before it caught the ridge of a hogback dune and exploded in a Rorschach-ink-test-shaped blue flame.

Lister's rubber-soled flight boots squealed down the corridor as he pounded after Legs, Bader and Beethoven before he flung himself into a recess in the wall as a volley of flame scorched into an oxy-generation unit just above his head. He dipped on to his haunches and tried to catch his breath.

He pushed the flat of his cheek against the wall and peered out left; Cyberian guards were scurrying down the gently arcing corridor, dashing in and out of the power units that lined the wall. Fifteen, maybe twenty of them. His bazookoid craned out into the corridor and unloaded a round of fire into the ceiling. That wouldn't hold them for more than two seconds. Nothing else for it. He'd have to retreat. He peered out right – Cyberian guards were advancing in and out of the power-unit recesses from that direction too.

Oh, for a little help.

He looked across at Saliva, who was busy trying to create a massive six-inch spit bubble, his infectious giggle rocking his shoulders back and forth, while Headless was fumbling blindly with an ammo cartridge he was trying to insert into his bazookoid.

Lister sighed. 'Let me.' Headless gave him a thumbs-up sign.

'Guards on the left and guards on the right. Anybody got any bright ideas?'

Headless animatedly nodded his neck.

'You got an idea, Headless? Well, let's hear it.'

Headless pointed to the wall on the far side of the corridor.

'You want to know what's in that direction?'

Another nod.

'A wall.'

Headless held his thumb up again.

'What's your plan? Run through the wall?'

Another nod.

'Do you know what the wall is made of?'

Headless shook his neck.

'Do you care?'

Headless shook his neck.

'Well, if you think you can do it, you go for it, guy.'

Headless sank into the back of the recess and then catapulted himself across the corridor and towards the wall. Lister closed his eyes. There was a sound of smashing masonry. He looked up to see a haze of clearing smoke and a pile of broken bricks in front of a hole roughly the shape of Headless.

Lister unhooked a second bazookoid from around his neck and, firing with both hands, dashed across the corridor and dived through the hole, followed by Legs, Righty, Saliva, Van Gogh and Nelson.

He scrambled to his feet. A sea of head-setted skulls bobbled on the surface of a giant pink lake. Thousands upon thousands of heads, all prisoners of their own minds. Lister gawked at them incredulously. This was it.

He was here.

Cyberia.

Without warning everything was pitched into blackness. A thick, impenetrable cloak of rubied darkness.

The only sound was a slowly dying scale as the electrics whinnied to a halt.

Lister smiled. At last, something was going right. The electrics were finally out.

He felt his body suddenly leave the ground.

He was floating. Floating in mid-air. He kicked helplessly as he rose from the ground. Then he hit something; something hard travelling at speed. What, he never found out. The pain set off two explosive charges behind his eyes and he lost consciousness.

He rolled open his eyes, slowly, gingerly, like they were a pair of rattling grills protecting a store window.

Still black, still floating.

Groggily he groped for his bazookoid and flicked on the night-vision gun-sights. He was drifting above the cyberlake, spiralling head over heels as he gently jostled for position with the cyber prisoners who had been pulled free of the lake and their headsets. Below, Gelf guards hung on to sandstone columns and screamed for help.

His mind began to clear: asteroids aren't large enough to generate their own gravity; the gravity on Lotomi 5 must be artificially generated and they'd knocked out the AG unit.

He closed his eyes and tried to think.

It wasn't unpleasant here, floating in the blackness. Almost restful. Cooling balls of water, warm and sweet, bounced off his cheeks, blown up towards the chamber's dome by the last breaths of the oxy-generation blowers. He peered through his night-sights and looked down at the large empty basin on the ground below. Why had he never noticed it before?

Then he realized.

He'd never noticed it before because it hadn't been there before. This basin, this enormous dry dock, was what had held the cyberlake. Before the water had gone.

But gone where? Where the hell could it go?

He swivelled the night-sights skyward. Above him was the cyber lake. Twenty, maybe thirty feet deep and directly above his head. His body liberated from gravity and blown by the compressed air of the emptying oxy-generation unit was sucked up into the waters.

A deadly droplet of panic pipetted into him and began to spread its poison. He was drowning. And there was no way out. He started to hyper-ventilate.

The thought of drowning had terrified him since childhood, when he'd fallen in the local canal. Apart from being eaten alive by rats and gonad grilling it was his least favourite way of bidding the long 'so long'.

He had to do something. He was going in the wrong direction. The wrong direction too slowly. He had to find something solid, something he could use as a spring-board to power back out of the lake and back into what was left of the oxygen. He gazed around. There was nothing.

Nothing.

And all the time he was being pulled deeper and deeper up into the cyberlake's pink waters.

Thirty seconds passed.

Thirty-five. Forty.

A ball started to grow in his lungs. A red-hot ball, like a flaming coal inside of him. His ribs couldn't contain it. His chest wanted to explode. What could he do?

Then he saw him struggling past a renegade droid, holding on to the droid's arm and using it as a spring-board to push past him. Then he was floating in front of him. Looking at him.

His other self. His doppelgänger.

He'd found him. But it was too late, because now both of them were going to die. Before they'd properly met. Before they'd even spoken. His other self looked at him, expressionless, then clambered on to his shoulders and pushed himself off Lister's body and disappeared into the mix of threshing bodies and was gone.

Lister swam on. The coal in his chest was getting hotter and hotter. Bigger and bigger.

Up ahead he saw it – the domed roof of the cyber chamber. He squinted at it through the murk of the waters. Here was the something solid he could launch himself off; that could send his body back down into the air, back into the oxygen.

He flipped his body over and splayed his legs, frog-like, on the ceiling and pushed. Down he went towards the surface.

Down he went towards the oxygen.

Then he stopped and started to drift back up again. Hopeless. Not even six feet.

His lungs felt like white-hot medicine balls.

He was going to lose consciousness. No, not yet. One more try. One more.

For a second time he splayed his legs on the ceiling and pushed.

Down, down, down.

Ten feet. Twelve feet. He kicked with his feet and his hands pummelled the water as he stretched for the surface. Fourteen feet. Sixteen. Eighteen.

He was going to do it. He could see the light. He could see the air. The oxygen. Nineteen feet.

He opened his mouth ready to suck in an entire continent of air when something happened. Something that neutered his soul. Four inches from the surface he started to go up.

Four inches short. Four lousy inches.

Now what? Another go? He didn't have the strength. He didn't have the time. Maybe ten seconds. Ten seconds before he blacked out. Ten seconds to do something. What was that word that Kryten used to use? That special way of thinking? When you thought about the problem in a new way? Turned it upside down and took a look at it from there?

Six seconds.

Lack of oxygen had fogged his mind. The word?

What was the word?

What was it?

It didn't matter. He should do that word anyway. Do it. Do that word. Whatever it was.

What was it? Lateral thinking. That was the word. Think laterally. OK, that's what he would do. A head voice started to talk to him.

'*What do you need to survive?*'

'Oxygen.'

'*Where is the oxygen?*'

'On the surface.'

'*So what's the problem?*'

'No strength. Can't reach.'

'*So what's your only alternative then?*'

'There isn't one.'

'*Think.*'

'Can't think. Too tired.'

'*Think laterally.*'

'Laterally? Think laterally. OK, I've got it. Become a fish.'

'*Lateral but stupid. Again.*'

'An alternative to getting oxygen from the surface.'

'*C'mon.*'

'A solution.'

'*What is it?*'

'Find another source of oxygen, somewhere else.'

'*Good.*'

'Somewhere I CAN REACH.'

'*You're cooking with gas.*'

'Where?'

'*Where's the only place you can reach?*'

'The roof. Break the roof. The water will be sucked out through the hole. And the remaining oxygen will be able to float up to me.'

Lister sank to the bottom of the cyberlake and examined the surface of the ceiling. A filigree of cracks patterned its surface. The water pressure was rupturing the dome's outer surface. He brought his heel down hard on a cracked plate. A fresh filigree trilled across the pane. He brought his foot down a second time.

And a third, and a fourth.

Slowly, water started to seep up out of the cracks, as if it was being sucked out by a hugely powerful vacuum.

He leapt again – this time bringing both his heels down on to the plasti-plate. The plate smashed and water started to disappear through the hole and into the night sky outside.

The lake started to empty.

But his lungs had nothing left to give. Nothing left to keep him conscious. Not even the few seconds it took for the cyberlake to flood up into the asteroid's night sky.

He blacked out.

He saw faces. He heard voices. And then they faded away and there was nothing.

Just a peace and tranquillity that he had never experienced before and Lister knew more surely than he'd ever known anything in his life that he was about to die. He made a noise like a small child deprived of a favourite toy. A two-syllable moan of disappointment. 'Owwoo.'

Then he died.

CHAPTER 11

Kochanski perched on the wires of the telegraph pole and hung on to the insulated rubber cables as her eyes scanned the oranging sky for signs of Starbug.

For the past thirty-six years she and Lister had lived as man and wife in a reality where time ran backwards. They'd lived their lives in reverse, starting out in their dotage and gradually growing young together.

They'd had a good life. They'd owned their own Food Collection Depot – where members of the backwards society had dropped by and, in return for cash, had regurgitated meals on to the empty plates which Lister and Kochanski diligently laid out on the tables every day. Once the meals were regurgitated they were taken into the kitchen where they were un-cooked. Potatoes were returned to their peels, eggs to their shells, bread un-sliced and bananas from banana splits were carefully sealed in yellow skins. When the food was finally uncooked and packaged ready for collection, they paid to have it taken away. Trucks would then transport the food to huge warehouses where it would be stored until the meat was finally turned into living animals, which were set free on farms.

Life in a backwards reality wasn't easy. They'd

brought down two fine children together, Mij and Yelxeb; she thought about them often. They'd steered them through the anxieties of a backwards adolescence, a most confusing time, where pus hurled itself off mirrors into their faces, and they'd watched entranced as their children grew smaller until finally they'd become tiny babies and returned to Kochanski's womb.

For thirty-odd years they'd lived like that, thirty years of reverse-living and, at the time, Kochanski had been grateful; after all they'd both been killed in reality and transporting them to a backwards Universe was the only way to bring them back to life. But when they had rendezvoused at Niagara Falls, as agreed, on Lister's twenty-fourth birthday, and Kryten and the gang had transported them back to their own dimension, or so they thought, she'd believed at last the two of them could settle down and have a normal life together. She'd always pictured some kind of desert moon which they'd be able to irrigate; and some kind of farm and a family. A normal, forward-growing family. And then maybe they'd be able to ransack a bio-lab on a derelict star ship they'd come across one day and slowly start to rebuild the human race.

A normal life: that's all she wanted. And to her normal was a reality where time went forwards, and no one got marooned up telegraph poles in the wrong dimension of reality.

Out of the dawn sky a small green craft appeared, flying low over a series of dunes. The three figures on the telegraph wires started to shout and wave. Kochanski's mouth wrinkled into a smile of relief. At last they'd be able to get out of here and start searching for Lister.

Who cared about his other self? Not her, not any more, not if it meant endangering everyone's life.

She smiled. Now the Cat was here they'd be able to hover above the computer and insert the antidote disk and dispatch the healer virus into the system and resurrect the artificial gravity generator.

That'd be the first thing they'd do – return gravity to Lotomi 5.

Then they'd find Lister. And she'd say sorry for making him embark on this idiotic quest to find his other self. Then they'd get the hell back to their own dimension and find Red Dwarf and Holly and start looking for a planetoid to build a home.

That's what they'd do.

CHAPTER 12

Bang.

Pain. In his chest. Someone hitting him.

Bang.

Ribs aching.

Bang.

Must get them to stop.

Agony.

Bang.

His eyelids blinked open and he stared into the eyes of the perpetrator. The person who was doing press-ups on his chest, who was cudgelling his ribs with the ball of his right hand. He had brown eyes, the colour of mud.

He knew those eyes.

He'd seen them before, but he couldn't remember where. They were familiar, so familiar. Suddenly the eyes were gone and he could see nothing – only the blackness of a star-speckled night.

Then he felt a pair of lips fix themselves to his and fingers pinch his nose and air was hurled into his lungs. It made him cough. An arc of water jetted out off him, like he was a punctured water butt. He coughed and spluttered and gazed into the eyes again. Now he could see a mouth. Two lips, talking to him, shouting at him, then they were on him again and air was spewing into his lungs. Again, he was flipped on to his side and again a liquid arc cut a C through the air.

He coughed and sat upright – hunched and wheezing, unable to talk. He looked up and stared into the face of his lifesaver.

The face, the exact same face as his own, grinned back at him. 'You were dead. Heart stopped beating. Enough water in those lungs to irrigate the Mooli desert on Cyrius 3.' The face laughed, eyes twinkling. 'I saved your life. You know why?'

Lister shook his head.

'A guy as handsome as you? You gotta be kidding.' He laughed again. 'My curiosity was piqued, man. Who the hell *are* you?'

'I'm an alternative version of you.'

'Give me that one more time.'

'You've heard of the Omni-zone? The point in space time where all the . . .' A fresh strafe of coughing folded his body in two. He clutched his sides and it was some moments before he was able to continue. '. . . It's the point in space time where all the gazillions of possibilities of existence are played out. We screwed up the navi-calcs when we were traversing it and wound up in your dimension.'

'How'd you know how to find me?'

Lister shook his head not knowing how much his doppelgänger knew, and afraid to mention the dead ship and the bodies.

'Luck. Met some guy at a market on Blerios 15. Said he'd set you up.'

'Yeah, I remember him – son of a prosti-droid.' His

face, driven by the memory, twisted into ugliness. 'So you came to get me out of here, right?'

Lister nodded.

'And you wound up getting killed.' His other self laughed uproariously. 'You wound up getting killed for a guy like me.'

'I know we're going to be different, we have to be to justify existing, but I saw your quarters and I felt we were kinda similar too. I felt, I dunno, some kind of bond, y'know?'

His other self eyed him curiously and then his face corrugated into a savage grin. 'Well, I'm not entirely convinced I'd have done the same.'

'Where the hell are we, exactly?'

'The roof gave way about fifty seconds after you blacked out.' Lister looked down through his night-sights. They were eighty, perhaps ninety, feet above the empty cyberlake; both tied by the wrist to one of the dome's three foot wide support struts by lengths of torn clothing.

'Managed to tie us both to this support strut.' They both peered down. 'How do you s'pose we get out of here?'

The answer was almost immediate.

There was a spasm of light that spluttered and died and then spluttered again as the electrics fizzed back on.

'The electrics are back on . . .'

'That means gravity will be back on t –'

The sentence was never completed. Instead both Listers started to fall towards the empty cyber tank ninety feet below, before they both came to an arm-jarring halt as they reached the end of their cloth tethers.

Lister yelled out as a bolt of pain screamed through his body. He rocked back and forth, knocking into his other self as they hung from the roof strut.

He threw one arm above the other and had started to haul himself up the cloth rope when gravity finally reached the cyber-water in the domed roof and it began to flood over them in a torrential downpour.

Lister lost his grip, slithered down his cloth rope and hung there helplessly, until a staccato ripping sound announced that the rope had decided to resign as a rope. The material sheered in two and once more both Listers started to fall towards the ground.

As he tumbled through the air, Lister gazed through the sheets of falling water as bodies of other inmates hit the ground in a variety of bloody squishes. The precious moments he'd hung by his cloth tether had given him valuable seconds. With luck some of the water would be back in the lake when he hit the surface. Only one question remained – would there be enough to cushion his fall?

There was only one way to find out.

Both Listers hit the cyberlake feet first, and plunged through its pink waters towards the bottom. All too soon Lister felt the ground break beneath him and his left foot twisted savagely.

His scream was translated to the surface in a school of bubbles. Several seconds later his head broke the surface and he limped to the shore's edge. His other self rummaged through a drowned Cyber guard, removed his laser harpoon and started for the exit.

Lister hobbled after him. 'Hey, slow down, man, I've busted my ankle.'

Half limping, half skipping, Lister followed his other self up a switchback of corridors, passing knots of fleeing inmates and beleaguered guards refuelling their laser harpoons at the power units. They rounded a corner as a dazed rogue droid wandered towards them carrying a stolen laser harpoon.

'We've got to get a weapon for me somehow. If we get separated I'm finished.'

His other self nodded and unloaded his harpoon into the surprised droid, who buckled and fell to the floor. Lister's other self stopped and tossed him the droid's harpoon. 'No sooner said than done, O Master.'

'You killed him.'

'You said you wanted a weapon.'

'I didn't mean kill *him*. And I didn't mean *his* gun. I just meant *a* gun, at some point.'

'Well, why the hell didn't you say that then?'

'You killed him. It was pointless. There was no need. He was an inmate.'

'You told me to kill him.'

'What?'

'He was running towards us and you said you needed a weapon. Anyone would have presumed you meant kill him.'

'No, they wouldn't.'

'Of course they would.'

'Would they?'

'Yeah.'

Lister blanched as a biting wind of guilt howled through his being. Had he ordered the death of an innocent droid? Had his fear of capture driven him into a kind of temporary insanity? Was it his fault?

His other self shook him out of his reverie. 'We haven't got time for this. C'mon, we've got to get out of this dump.' They raced down the corridor and arrived at a set of crossroads.

Lister pointed. 'This is the way I came in.'

His other self shook his head. 'Look, man, don't tell me which way it is. I've been stuck inside of this stinking hole for four months. I know which way it is.' He took a right turn and started running down the corridor.

Lister paused at the crossroads, his face crinkled in confusion. 'No, it isn't. It's . . .'

Behind him he heard the sound of running guards. He stared after his other self as he powered down the white-tiled passage way. He began to follow his other self.

Although he was sure it was wrong.

They took a left and then a right, crossed two intersections and took another right before his other self opened a door on the arc of a bend and vanished inside.

Lister gazed at the machine code on the door, but was unable to read it. It didn't much matter. As soon as he entered the room it was immediately obvious where they were. Sick bay.

'What are you doing? Is this for me? For my ankle? I'm OK.'

His other self shot off the lock on the medical supply cupboard and grabbed a bottle of medicinal alcohol. He spun the top off the bottle and gulped down two big ones. 'Four months sober. Always vowed it'd be the first thing I'd do.'

Lister was dumbfounded. 'We came here so you could get a drink?'

His other self grinned and took another slug. 'Anyone ever told you you're a really uptight guy?'

Lister took in a series of deep breaths, trying to control his anger. 'We came here – you took a deliberate wrong turn – just so you could get a drink?'

His other self drained the bottle and grinned impishly. 'Aren't I a naughty boy? How can you ever forgive me?'

Suddenly there was the noise of guards searching the room next door. Lister held up his hand to silence his other self. He ignored him and started rifling through the medical stores, reading the labels on pill bottles and stuffing them in his pockets. 'OK, now, let's see what else we've got here.'

Lister hissed at him, 'For smeg's sake, shut up. They're next door.'

His other self turned and faced him, a fine sweat covering his forehead, like condensation on a damp wall. 'Don't tell me what to do, OK? No one tells me what to do.' He slipped his laser harpoon under his left arm, the wrong way round, and grabbed Lister by the throat, then started to bang his head against the wall in rhythm to the words of his speech: 'Do-not-tell-me-what-to-do. OK?'

The door creaked, open and two guards stood in the shadow of the doorway, holding harpoons.

'Understand? Do not ever, and I mean *ever*...'

A javelin of light flared out of the harpoon and exploded into both figures, killing them instantly. The Gelf guards slumped against the door frame, then staggered and fell to the floor.

Lister's other self grinned at him as he slipped his laser harpoon from under his arm and turned it the right way round. 'Sorry about that. I'll be a bit more careful next time, Dad. Come on,' he gestured with his head, 'we'll grab my stuff and get out of here.'

Lister's other self walked towards the back of the medical supply store and let himself into a room that led off at right angles. He activated the light switch and walked down the aisles of metal boxes. He looked at the code on his ID band – YT6564354 – and several minutes later located a box with the same number. Lister's doppelgänger lifted the box from the shelf and tucked it under his arm. 'My belongings,' he said in explanation.

The door opened and two identical heads peered into the car pound. The air was heavy with the smell of laser harpoons as a band of inmates pinned down a group of Cyberguards who were trying to crawl between the parked sand buggies and reach the lower floor exit. Off to the left Lister spotted a parked jeep with a swivel-mounted rocket-launcher in the rear. Crouching, they scurried across the car pound, ducking between oil drums and parked vehicles, until they arrived at the jeep. Lister short-circuited the ignition system and they screeched across the pound and out of the slide-back doors through a haze of gun-fire.

Lister sat in the back of the transporter as his other self gunned the jeep out into the desert heat. For several minutes they hugged the perimeter fence looking for an exit from the penal colony. He looked around the back of the vehicle: it was piled high with laser harpoons. He examined them – they were all loaded and fully charged. Could come in handy.

'You know how to fire a rocket-launcher?' his other self screamed from the front.

Lister shook his head.

'Well, now's a pretty good time to learn.' He indicated a group of thirty Cyberian guards running towards them. Lister pulled down a pair of unoculars fastened to the back of the seat and trained the sight on them. 'They're not armed.'

'Not armed?'

'Right.'

Lister's other self brought the jeep skidding to a halt alongside the battalion of Cyberguards. 'Are you guys not armed?'

The guards grouped together and backed off slightly.

Lister stood up. 'What the hell are you doing?'

'I'm just talking.'

'Drive the smegging jeep. Let's git.'

Lister's other self swivelled round and scooped up a handful of harpoons and tossed them to the guards.

'Are you out of your mind?'

'Well, if we're armed and they're not,' his other self grinned, 'that's not really fair. Now,' he said, throwing out another armful, 'we're a little more evenly matched.'

Slightly stunned, the guards picked up the harpoons and started to aim them at the two Listers.

The jeep took off in a swirl of dust, pursued by a hail of harpoon fire. Lister dived to the floor as one screamed over his head. 'You're out of your mind.'

His other self rocked with laughter. 'Hey, instead of

getting crabby with me, I suggest you work out how to fire that rocket-launcher.'

Lister watched as the group shrank into the distance as the jeep accelerated out of the Cyberguard's range of fire. He got to his feet and flung the unoculars on to the floor. 'You are certifiable! What the hell got in to you? Was that supposed to be some kind of joke? We came within about two feet of being flesh paint.'

'Learn how to work the rocket-launcher.'

'There's no need, we're out of range.'

The jeep arced round in a semi-circle. 'No, we're not because we're going back.'

Lister stood there smiling, refusing to accept what he had just heard.

'We're nearly there,' his other self taunted. 'Heading right for the middle of them. If you can't use that rocket-launcher in about twenty seconds we're in trouble – big time.'

Lister scrambled behind the rocket-launcher and furiously began pressing the control panel. A rocket whined out of the barrel and sizzled across the penal colony before it exploded into the electric chain-link perimeter fence, shattering the concrete posts. He peered through the sights and tried to pull them down to target the group of Cyberguards who were all lined up and ready for the jeep's kamikazi charge.

The sights wouldn't move, they were computer operated. He jabbed at the keypad frantically. It was useless: he needed the override code.

His other self cackled wildly. His eyes washed with mania as the jeep circled the guards on the periphery of their range of fire.

'Going in,' grinned his other self. 'Here we go!' Lister clambered into the front and started grappling with the wheel. His other self elbowed him hard in the shoulder and knocked him into the back. He scrambled to his feet, picked up a harpoon and slammed it into his other self's head. He slumped unconscious in the driving seat.

Laser harpoons whistled overhead as he hauled his doppelgänger out of the driving seat and powered the jeep towards the exploded perimeter fence. He bumped it through the mangled wires and revved it down the desert road away from Cyberia.

After almost five days and five mostly sleepless nights, he had done it. He had rescued his other self. He looked at the unconscious body, mouth angled in a deranged grin of slumber, and wondered if it would turn out to be the biggest mistake of his life.

CHAPTER 13

Lister dropped some brushwood on to the smouldering fire, then started peeling the red fruit from the saguaro cactus with the blade of his knife. His other self sat cross-legged in front of the camp fire, his hands bound by rope.

'Saguaro?'

His other self nodded, and Lister pushed the fruit in his mouth and helped him eat it.

'Look, it was the booze. It made me go off my head.' He held up his bound hands. 'There's no need for this.'

'You're staying like that until I know who you are, man.'

'I've been in Cyberia four months, man. Four long months. It does stuff to your head. It takes time to adjust to reality. Don't you see that?'

'What's in the box?' Lister pointed to the metal case sitting in the back of the jeep.

'Just personal stuff. Letters. Photographs. Clothes. Are you listening to me? I lost everyone – Rimmer, Cat, Kryten, Kochanski – everyone, then I wound up in Cyberia for some future crime and you're treating me like I'm some major nut because when I get out I let off some steam.'

'Mind if I open it?'

'Open what?'

'The box.'

'Yeah, I do.'

'Why?'

'Because it's personal. There's stuff in there that no one should know about.'

'That's why I want to see it.'

'Look, when they put you in Cyberia for a future crime, they also get the stochastic computer to evaluate what you're going to do for the rest of your life. When you're going to die, the whole works. That's what's in the box.'

'And you haven't read it?'

'Right.'

'And naturally you don't want anyone to read it before you do.'

His other self shot him a wan smile. 'I don't even know if I've got the guts to read it. Suppose I'll keep it till I've decided what to do.'

Lister stood up and shot the lock off the box and pulled back the lid. 'You really think I'm so dumb I'll buy a story like that?' He peered inside and brought out a bag of uncut Baquaii diamonds, a box of cheap cigars, an old rad pistol – which would one day come back to haunt him – and a handful of plastic bottles containing info pills. He read the labels – the pills were mostly factual: stuff about the layout of the belt. He placed them on the floor and looked in the box once more. 'What's this?'

'What does it look like?'

Lister pulled it out of the box. 'It looks like an arm.'

Lister's other self shrugged. 'Then that's what it is.'

'In fact, it looks like Kryten's arm.' He turned it over

in his hands. It was a right arm, the same as the one that was missing from the dead mechanoid on the derelict Starbug. It had been scythed off at the shoulder joint by some kind of light saw. He looked at the rad pistol to see if it had a laser setting – it had. Then he noticed the clenched fingers were holding a piece of paper. A piece of paper the mechanoid had given both his arm and his life to protect. Lister prised the hand open, and unscrolled the paper. 'Galactic coordinates.'

His other self remained silent.

'But galactic coordinates for what?'

His other self shrugged.

'You killed them, didn't you? You killed them for this. Why?'

Before he could answer Starbug appeared on the horizon, its distinctive pear-shaped searchlights sweeping low over the desert. Lister frantically fanned the flames of the campfire, then pounded up the nearest dune, rotating his jacket over his head, jumping and screaming. Unnoticed, his other self shuffled over to the fire and thrust his legs into the flames.

A scream, like a mournful prairie dog, spun Lister round. He watched, horrified, as his other self thrashed around in the fire, weeping and howling, until several seconds later he pulled his smouldering limbs from the flames, his rope binding burnt clean through.

Lister ran back down the dune as his other self fell to his knees and thrust his hands into the fire. His cold, saliva-sodden scream curdled the air. He took his charred hands out of the flames and pulled his bonds apart.

Then he rose to his feet and started to walk towards Lister.

CHAPTER 14

Kochanski placed the bowl of porridge on the breakfast tray beside a plate of bacon and eggs. She glanced at her watch – 2.30 p.m. ship time; he'd probably be awake now. She climbed the steps up to Starbug's sleeping quarters. 'Hey, Frog Prince, I've brought you some breakfast. Did you sleep?' She kissed him softly on the lips.

Lister grinned back at her impishly. 'Like Tutankhamun.' He struggled to sit up while she plumped up the pillows behind his back. 'God, I've got the strength of a new-born sloth.'

'No wonder, with what you've been through. Kryten says you have to have complete bed-rest for at least a week.'

'I'll go crazy.'

'Tough.' She poured milk over his porridge and drew a lazy spiral with a spoon of dripping honey. 'Listen, there's something I want to say to you,' she began. 'I'm . . . always, uh, ever since I was small, I've always had a big problem saying, y'know, well, apologizing and uh . . . and I just wanted to say, well, anyway, I am.'

'You are what?'

'Huh?'

'You are what?'

'I am . . . don't make me say it, you pig.'

'Say what?'

'Sorry, OK? There, I said it. Sorry, sorry, sorry.'

'What are you sorry for?'

'Besides having to say sorry, you mean?'

Lister grinned.

'For everything. For persuading you to go on this wild-goose chase.' She stirred the porridge round with the spoon and held some up for Lister to eat. 'How are your burns?'

Lister looked at his bandaged feet and hands. 'Hurt like hell. Probably be weeks before I can walk again.'

'I'll change the dressings after breakfast.'

'I was just standing there trying to get some sense out of him and the lousy bastard pushed me in the fire.'

She angled her head to one side sympathetically. 'It's over now. The poor crazy lunatic's dead.' She fed him another spoonful of porridge. He grimaced.

'Too hot?'

'No, it's just I'm not that crazy about honey in porridge.'

She looked at him, surprised. 'You love it.'

'What?'

'You love it.'

'Well, yeah, true, I used to love it. But, uh, I've kind of gone off it now.' She looked at him oddly, then smiled and started to cut up his bacon.

He watched her as she cut up his bacon. Did she know? No, he didn't think she did. But even if she did know, what could he do? His injuries were so bad he was practically an invalid. His body needed time to heal. His hands, especially, hurt like hell – picking up that spade in his burnt, blistered balls of smoking flesh and cracking Lister across the head hadn't really done them much good.

Neither had burying him alive, come to that.

He stared at Kochanski's breasts. Tasty. He'd get himself a piece of that later.

He smiled at her and she smiled back as she placed the bacon on the end of the fork and started to feed him. He felt kind of stupid, like a little boy again.

Small and helpless. He started to remember his foster parents.

Tom and Beth Thornton.

Tom with his round, sad spaniel face and terrible posture, and Beth with her ugly smile and sickly perfume. He could smell it now. It nauseated him. He could hear Old Prune Face's laugh; the terrible, terrible braying laugh that could have sawn down Canadian redwoods. And then he started to remember the beatings with the brown clothesbrush. Now he could see Old Prune Face's eyes and the darkness that descended over her when she was 'nettled'. He could feel the rips of pain that gouged through his body, ploughing furrows through his flesh. He could hear his own screams soaked in saliva, gurgling in his throat.

Why had he chosen the Thorntons?

He'd known instinctively there was something wrong the first time he'd spent the weekend when he was doing the rounds of possible foster parents and Old Prune Face lost her marbles because he didn't like her raspberry sponge cake.

'All little boys like raspberry sponge cake.'

'I don't like raspberries.'

'All little boys like MY raspberry sponge cake.'

'I don't like the seeds . . .'

Then she'd started to smash the crockery. Every single piece. Which was HIS FAULT because he didn't like her RASPBERRY SPONGE CAKE. And he was spoiling the PERFECT DAY she'd spent months planning.

HIS FAULT.

She'd sat in a sea of smashed crockery, sobbing quietly to herself.

'I'm sorry, Mrs Thornton.'

'Call me Mum-m-m-m-m-my,' Old Prune Face had screamed, her make-up smeared across her face like a road crash.

He was too scared to tell anyone. After all she was going to be HIS NEW MUMMY and it was HIS FAULT. And surely to hell he could learn to like raspberry sponge cake.

So he'd ignored the incident, pretended it had never happened. After all, the Thorntons were rich. Much, much richer than the Wilmots, the other couple who wanted to adopt him.

He'd liked the Wilmots better. He could use them easier, but Mr Wilmot was just some jerky clerk in an office, so they never had much money. They couldn't afford to get him the electric car the Thorntons had promised; they didn't have an indoor swimming pool with an inflatable starfish, they didn't have a computer library, with every wall lined with a different arcade game. And so he'd buried all his misgivings in a secret place, he'd shushed an inner voice that pleaded with him to make the 'right' choice and the seven-year-old Lister had chosen the Thorntons.

Cat and Rimmer ducked through the hatchway, exchanged greetings with the patient while Kryten swivelled the flatbed scanner on to its side.

'The navi-comp's just finished analysing the galactic coordinates, sir.' Kryten took hold of a hand-held remote unit and clicked it on. 'The results are most extraordinary.'

'Like?' he said, straining to sit up.

Kryten scrolled through a series of star charts. 'This is a map of the asteroid belt the navi-comp made during our crossing.' Kryten ringed a small area south-south-west. 'We are here, 3,000 miles past Lotomi 5 and approaching these clusters here. According to the navi-comp the coordinates are three-dimensional Cartesian coordinates and they intersect here, under this sea of molten lava on this volcanic moon.'

Kochanski peered at the flashing cursor on the map. 'Do we know what's there? Why're they so important?'

Kryten started to pace – at first a little hesitantly. So far his repaired leg had held up most encouragingly. He and Kochanski had spent the finer part of two days rewiring all the tendons and replacing some of the electrical synapses. Now he just needed to learn to trust the limb again – something he was finding harder than he had anticipated.

He continued: 'I've been doing some research, reading the volumes we purchased on Blerios 15 detailing the history of the belt. I believe these coordinates mark the spot of a derelict starship called the Mayflower. It was a

2 million ton space freighter that brought the Gelfs to the asteroid belt before it was forced to crash land. The ship's mission was to terraform a planet in the Andromeda galaxy. There was a mutiny *en route*, the navigation system got knocked out and the ship wound up getting pulled into Omni-zone, where it was ejected into this very dimension. Those who survived the splashdown grabbed what they could and took off in the escape pods.'

'And they're the creatures who presently occupy the belt?' asked Rimmer.

Kryten nodded. 'What they weren't able to take with them was much of the genetic-engineering technology that was onboard the ship; the technology that can create life and some of the key viruses required for terraforming planets.'

'So how come none of these Gelf dudes returned to this ship before?'

Kryten took out the scroll of paper that contained the Cartesian coordinates and unrolled it on the table. 'Notice anything strange?'

Rimmer peered at it for a few seconds. 'It's been cut in four and stuck together. And all four quarters are weathered in different ways.'

'The ship is marooned on the bottom of a vast ocean of molten lava. A salvage party would have to know its precise location to stand any chance of looting it and returning to the surface safely.'

'So what's this got to do with the coordinates being cut in four?'

'I believe the coordinates were split four ways by the four main Gelf species on board – some form of agreement so no single species would have sole access to it. Your other self, sir,' Kryten said, addressing Lister's other self, 'was somehow able to collate the four different pieces and with it he had access to unlimited power.'

Lister stared at him impassively. Kochanski patted his thigh. 'So what's aboard this ship? The power to create the human race?'

'They have the genome for all living things. The map, base by base, of all the DNA sequences of all potential life.'

Rimmer whistled. 'The genome of all known DNA?'

'Or, to use its acronym, G.O.D.'

'But when we left Earth, the World Council wouldn't let that out of its sight.'

'They must have considered the ship's mission outweighed those insecurities.'

'But why would he want this, bud?'

'Access to G.O.D. would make him God. He'd be able to rewrite his own genetic code – make himself immortal. He'd be able to use the technology to trade with the creatures of the belt. And, if he could get hold of terraforming viruses, maybe even sell them inhabitable planets. What would that be worth?'

Lister gazed at Kryten through immutable brown eyes. 'If what you say is true, then we should get this – what did you call it?'

'Genome, sir.'

'. . . we should get this genome for ourselves.'

Kryten stared at him for too long without smiling, then nodded. 'I agree, sir.'

PART THREE
The Rage

CHAPTER 1

At a different time, in a different location, in a quite different dimension, John Milhous Nixon, the third President of the World Council, stared at his ten ravaged fingers. He'd orgied on his digits in frenzied feasts of anxiety, and now as he gazed at their bloody cuticle-gnawed rawness he was filled with revulsion. He chewed on a pen-top, the nail biters' methadone, while a small-boned man with a putty-coloured face bathed the wounds with cotton balls soaked in isopropyl alcohol. Afterwards the manicurist clicked open a velvet-lined canteen that contained the president's new set of nails, and expertly started gluing them over the misshapen originals.

'Sir, I hope this isn't out of place,' the manicurist began, 'but I'd just like to say how sorry I am, and hope everything works out.' The man's voice suddenly rose half an octave and he started to weep. 'It's so damn tragic – I just can't believe it.'

The president's eyebrows glided up his head like two express lifts zooming up the outside of a skyscraper. 'Do you *know*? How do you know? It's supposed to be a state secret, for Christ's sake. Who told you?'

The manicurist was caught in the interrogatory headlights and froze with fear. 'Sir?'

'Who?'

'Ernie Simpson, sir, the doorman, sir.'

'The doorman knows about the situation?'

'All the staff know, sir.'

The door opened. 'Dr Sabinsky, Mr President,' an aide announced.

Sabinsky entered with his bodyguard, a rigid young marine with a clean, crisp face and short yellow hair, like an over-harvested field of wheat.

Sabinsky wiped his forehead with a handkerchief. 'Sorry we're late, sir. Delayed in traffic. Huge molecularization tailbacks at Washington Central. I've been waiting two hours to materialize. And then when I did I discovered they'd accidentally sent my legs to Tokyo.' He patted his thighs. 'Explained the situation – they managed to fix me up with some rentals.'

The President dismissed the manicurist and bayoneted Sabinsky with a look. 'Everyone knows, Bob. All the staff. Everyone. I've got to have an answer.'

'Mr President, we're simply not in any position to give you an accurate prognosis right now.'

'The word is out, Doctor. The economy is going to be crucified. I need an answer and I need an answer today. How long?'

'There's still a whole battery of tests, and mountains of data queuing up to be analysed and processed.'

'Then be approximate, dammit.'

A tight smile flashed on to Sabinsky's face, which he hoped would cushion the news. 'How long?'

'Yes, how long, damn you – how frigging long?'

'About four hundred thousand years, sir.'

Nixon slumped into his chair. 'Is that all?'

'It appears that exploding those thermonuclear devices so close to the sun –'

'Yeah, yeah, yeah,' Nixon said testily, 'almost certainly weakened the gravitational attraction of the hydrogen molecules. I made a mistake, OK? I'm sorry!'

'Slowly but surely the whole damn star is just going to come apart. It was a real blooper, sir.'

'But we were just trying to control the weather. And if we could have controlled the weather it would have helped the economy. It would have been good for the stock market. I would have got in for a second term. Now I'm going to be remembered as the president who wiped out the human race and killed the solar system.'

Two nails went pinging off in different directions across the Persian flat-weave carpet. 'How in God's sweet name am I ever going to recover from this? When a president kills a solar system, Bob, that's something the electorate doesn't forget in a hurry. The bastards hold that against you for your entire career. Not even my great-great-great-great-great-great-uncle got himself in this deep. What the hell am I going to do?'

'Follow me, sir.'

'Where are we going?'

'Hilo, sir, in Hawaii.'

'Hawaii?'

'If you recollect, sir, we have a bio-tech institute there. They've been doing some pretty exciting things just lately.'

Nixon shook hands with the series of scientists whose names he instantly committed to oblivion, then made his way along the aisle of the viewing theatre and sat down in one of the luxuriously upholstered leather seats.

McGruder, Sabinsky's wheat-haired bodyguard, clicked off the lights and a film started to play on the projector screen. At first it was a series of molecular profiles of some new type of virus that Sabinsky seemed inordinately excited about. Some virus that one of Sabinsky's bio-designers had created here at the institute. Most of the details eluded the president and his mind had started to wander when phrases such as 'plasmids', 'Avogadro's law' and 'nuclear magnetic resonance' started to reoccur regularly.

'Bob, start again and make it simple – remember, it's the president you're talking to.'

'Sorry, sir. Let me come at it from a new angle.'

'And no charts or graphs or those spirally-bally things on sticks – what are they called?' Sabinsky failed to capture an inner rebuke, which escaped on to his face.

'Let's review. We've killed the sun. In four hundred thousand years, maybe sooner, the lights go out. Unless we can find a cure to repair all those hydrogen molecules, the solar system will effectively be dead. So what do we do?' He paused for effect. 'As far as I can see, there is only one solution, and that is for the human race to call in the removal men and start packing the crockery.'

'Are you seriously suggesting we should move?'

'Not our generation, or even the generation after that, but moving has definitely got to be on the human race's agenda.'

'To another solar system?'

'I think we may have to move to a new galaxy.'

'A new galaxy?'

'Sir, whenever you move home you accrue a huge number of stress points. That's unavoidable. However, I think we can make this move as painless and as anxiety-free as possible. Just hear me out.'

A new slide appeared on the screen.

'I believe I've found a new solar system, in a new galaxy, that is absolutely perfect. Somewhere you'll be proud to invite the human race to stay. Take a look at this.'

A series of fuzzy slides were projected, one after the other, all involving a sprinkling of stars with a blurry blue spiral in the centre. 'Mr President, meet our new home. It's called the Andromeda galaxy.' There was a smattering of applause from the tweed of scientists.

Nixon peered at the screen. 'Where the hell is this?'

'Not far at all. In fact, in terms of galaxies, it's practically just around the corner.'

'How far?'

'Just 2.2 million light years. Also, there are other benefits.'

'Like?'

'Well, for a start it's bigger than the Milky Way, being 130,000 light years across, giving us an extra 30,000 light years to play with.' A snort of laughter trumpeted out of his nose. 'And if we have guests, that extra room might be real handy.' He ringed a small area, off to the right. 'I think this could well turn out to be our new solar system right here.'

The President peered at a smudgy blur. 'So does this solar system include a planet with a breathable atmosphere, with trees and lakes and sunsets and everything?

And has the atmosphere got all the required spirally-bally things on sticks?'

'No, sir. This particular planet, in fact, is awash with molten lava and volcanic ash, and its temperature is about 300° Centigrade, but that's why it's such a find.'

He was mad. It was quite clear to Nixon now: his senior scientific adviser was madder than one of those New York bag ladies who pull around stuffed dogs on leads.

'Which brings us back to the virus we were talking about earlier.'

'The virus that you created here?'

'Precisely.'

The door opened and three men wearing identical brown suits entered the viewing theatre. 'Mr President, meet the gentlemen who are responsible for a very remarkable discovery in the field of viral research.'

The president extended his hand as Sabinsky introduced them one by one.

'Professor Michael Longman.'

A man with watery brown eyes and a small black beard stepped forward and shook the president by the hand.

'Good to meet you, Professor.'

The second man stepped forward. He also had watery brown eyes and a small black beard.

'Professor Michael Longman's assistant; Professor Michael Longman.'

Nixon nodded. 'Good to meet you, Professor.'

'And thirdly, and by no means first, Professor Michael Longman's other assistant, Professor Michael Longman.'

A third man with watery brown eyes and a small beard stepped forward and shook Nixon by the hand.

'Good to meet you too, Professor.'

The first Longman spoke. 'Without my two clones working alongside me, I don't believe this breakthrough would have been possible in my lifetime.'

The other two Longmans nodded vigorously in agreement.

Sabinsky gestured for them to be seated, the lights dimmed and a film started to play of Kilauea, one of Hawaii's two active volcanoes. Sabinsky started to explain that the volcanoes had been a source of great consternation to everyone on the island. Over the last ten years their eruptions had become more frequent and their massive lava flows had got longer and longer, some extending as far as 120 miles from the summit all the way down to the edge of some of the villages. The footage, shot from a helicopter, suddenly cut to Kilauea's gigantic crater with its massive molten lava lakes.

'The three Professor Longmans have created a virus which is quite remarkable. Basically, it eats lava,' Sabinsky began. 'Or, rather more accurately, it corrupts its cell structure. Naturally we wanted to find out if this virus actually worked outside of the lab. So we injected the virus into a strain of self-replicating bacteria; then we sealed off the area and sent some crop-spraying planes over Kilauea. Obviously this act was completely illegal, and, uh, maybe even a little irresponsible, but, uh, we thought it was an illegal, irresponsible act worth taking. Take a look at this.'

Nixon watched as a fleet of bi-planes swooped over

Kilauea and dropped huge rain sheets of the virus into the volcano's crater.

Sabinsky pointed to the screen. 'Five and a half weeks later.'

The President stared, slack-jawed, at the screen as the film cut to new footage of the crater. Its lava lakes had gone, so had the eruptions and lava fountains. Instead all that remained was a dark, thick toxic sludge, like burnt treacle. Heavy black smoke spiralled off its surface.

'The virus eats the lava and reduces it to this kind of mulch, which, as you see, is pretty unpleasant stuff. But if we now introduce a second strain of genetically engineered viral bacteria, a strain which is programmed to eat the mulch – this happens.'

The film cut to new footage, again taken from a helicopter. The camera swooped up the side of the giant volcano. As it reached the top of the crater, the whole screen was suddenly awash with a mustard yellow.

The crater was a desert basin. Dunes of fine soft sand rippled and undulated across its entire breadth. It was almost unrecognizable as Kilauea. Only the shape of the basin itself distinguished it as the same location.

'The second virus turns the mulch into desert, and also secretes a mix of oxygen and nitrogen as a by-product. We also have a third virus which can turn the mulch into ocean. These viruses, working in harmony, can terraform planets for us.'

There was almost complete silence as the implications of the discovery percolated into the president's brain.

Nixon started to applaud. 'You sons of bitches, you clever sons of bitches!' He turned to the Longmans. 'How long before the new world is inhabitable?'

'After the planet has been terraformed . . .'

'The world will still be wild and inhospitable . . .'

'We will need creatures of great strength, resourceful-ness and durability to build our new civilization.'

'We will need to create life forms – creatures who will make our new home for us, whose lives are expend-able and who will be able to brave the forces of the New World.'

'And that's all possible?'

Sabinsky started to stammer. 'Wuh-wuh-we've already made quite some progress in that direction, actually, sir. Wuh-wuh-we didn't want to trouble you with the details until all the relevant . . .' He faded himself out.

Nixon eyed him narrowly. 'You mean, you've already created some new life forms?'

The three biodesigners stood in line, shame-faced. 'Nothing that we're really proud of . . .' they said, remembering the Snugiraffe.

'Permission to speak, sir?' McGruder, Sabinsky's body-guard, stood to an over-starched attention, his broad shoulder snapped into an enthusiastic salute.

'Permission granted.'

'I wish to volunteer, sir, to travel with the genetically engineered pioneers, sir. To sacrifice my life, if that is required, sir, to help save the human race, sir.'

The Longmans smiled benignly. 'The crew will cer-tainly need human supervisors.'

'Permission to speak again, sir?'

'Permission granted.'

'Graduated West Point, sir. Top of my year, sir. Fought on Hyperion, sir. Decorated, sir. Single, sir.'

Nixon spoke. 'Why so keen?'

'My mother, sir, told me many great stories of my father's feats of daring in the wastes of Deep Space, sir. They were never married, sir. He died before my mother was able to inform him she was pregnant. His ship, sir, Red Dwarf, sir, was lost to a radiation leak.'

Sabinsky nodded. 'Didn't the ship's black box touch down in the Pacific a couple of years back?'

'Confirmed everything my mother told me, sir. Details are sketchy, but it appears that out of the entire crew, my father was chosen by the on-board computer, sir, to be revived as a hologram. We believe he received that honour because he was such an awesome soldier, sir, and the computer deemed him the only crew member capable of steering the ship to a safe part of Deep Space and averting a major disaster.'

Nixon nodded. 'What was his name, son?'

'His name was Rimmer, sir.' McGruder beamed proudly. 'Arnold J. Rimmer, sir.'

'And a part of you believes he's still out there somewhere?'

'Yes, sir, I do, sir. But that won't interfere with my mission, sir.'

Nixon grinned. 'Although, if he is out there, you'd sure as hell love a chance to meet him.'

'You bet, sir, he's been an icon of mine since I was three years old, sir. If I hadn't had him as my role model I don't believe I would have amounted to anything, sir.'

The President's face cracked into a smile. 'Start preparing McGruder. You're on that ship.'

Michael R. McGruder cracked his arm into a perfect salute. 'Yes, sir. Thank you, sir. God bless you, sir.' He gazed through the window of the viewing theatre up into the sky. He'd always believed that somewhere out there was his old man. Old Iron-balls himself. The guy he'd looked up to his whole life. If only he were still around, and somehow they could meet.

What a day that would be.

CHAPTER 2

A dolorous rain sprinkled its melancholia over the strip of low-life neon which stretched into an infinity of billboards, movie houses and restaurants, as his shambling frame picked its way through the crowds. For the fifth time in as many minutes a speeding vehicle sluiced through a puddle of stinking rainwater and soaked him from the top of his sunburnt head to the bottom of his ill-fitting shoes. The hyena screeches of laughing passers-by spiralled into the night as he dripped past them, navigating his way through the minefield of garbage.

Cyberhell reminded Lister of 12th Street on Triton, with its ravaged sea of mournful faces and its choking air; it was like living inside the mouth of a senile dog after it had smoked a pack of Turkish cigarettes.

His mind went back twenty-nine weeks, to the night of the campfire in the desert, when his other self had burnt off his bonds and laid him out with a piece of desert rock. He'd come round to discover he was being buried alive as Starbug landed in a neighbouring dune basin. His other self had thrown a last spadeful of dirt over his struggling frame and run to the peak of the dune, twirling a jacket over his head. The craft touched down, took his other self on board and was gone in a belch of dust. For three hours he shivered under a blanket of sand until a buggy full of Cyberguards drove past later that morning.

He explained the situation. He was not Lister the inmate, he was from an alternative reality. He hadn't done anything wrong if you didn't count ringleading the break-out and helping half the inmates to escape from the penal colony, semi-destroying the complex and single-handedly setting out to destroy the system of justice that controlled the entire asteroid belt. If you didn't count any of that they had nothing on him. Sadly for Lister, they did count that. All of it. They shipped him to Arranguu 12 for trial, where he defended himself, and several weeks later, due to the incompetence of his legal team, he was sentenced to eighteen years hard thought in Cyberia, which, unhappily for him, they'd finished rebuilding.

So Lister had returned to Cyberia – this time on a dilapidated class three transport ship as a prisoner of the Gelf State.

He began to serve his sentence plagued by the thought that his other self had replaced him on board Starbug, knowing they were heading for the Omni-zone so they could return to their own Universe. In all likelihood he'd never see any of them again. His other self had stolen his girlfriend, his crew and his life.

He'd settled into hell as best he could, he'd cleaned and tidied his apartment, re-tailored his clothes and gone looking for work. But everything about this whole landscape was designed to sap his spirits, everything he saw, everything he smelt, everything he heard. On every block there seemed to be a Kochanski lookalike wrapped around some beefy sailor type. Billboards all over the city had pictures of him with taunting slogans, usually about how he had been abandoned as a newborn child and didn't know who his parents were or that he was the last human male of his Universe. And here he was incarcerated in Cyberia, watching the prime years of his life dribble away.

On the last day of the third week he'd got a job. It was a part-time evening job at a dentist's. The hours were lousy but at least it paid OK. He had to work from six until ten having his fillings replaced by student dentists who needed someone to practise on. It paid ten dollar-pounds a day, which was enough to buy a cup of sprout soup and the price of a ticket to one of the movie houses, which were usually playing *Chitty-Chitty Bang-Bang*. That killed time until his neighbours went to bed and turned off their drum solo music.

He trudged past the usual group of deadbeats who seemed to be on every street corner: hookers, pimps, drug dealers and, for some reason, here in his Cyberhell, encyclopedia salesmen. Why his imagination had chosen encyclopedia salesmen he wasn't quite sure, but they sure as hell were irritating – chasing him down the street waving introductory super-special offers and insisting that he signed now rather than going away and thinking about it.

He paused to peer into a TV shop, half watching a Czechoslovakian documentary about fifteenth-century cloud formations when he was suddenly plucked out of Cyberhell. The needles were removed from his skull, the cyberfoam washed off his body and he was dressed and strapped to a trolley which was wheeled to the commandant's office.

Lister lay strapped to the operating trolley. The Snugiraffe loomed over him, leaking its unspeakable juices. 'There's someone here to see you.'

Lister tried to sit upright, straining against the restraint straps.

A Dolochimp leaned over him too. Heavy-set, and glistening with the sweat of the overweight. 'I am Kazwa. I work for the Reco Programme.'

'No kidding.'

'You have been in Cyberhell now for five months. Your sentence is eighteen years. Eighteen years of the same kind of life-demeaning futility and anguish.'

'Yeah, but I'm up before the parole board in just twelve.'

'Are you familiar with the Reco Programme?'

'Aren't they a rock band? Big with teenage girls?.'

'Reco Programme. Recombinant DNA.'

Lister slouched his 'You got me' look.

'The same technique that created all the creatures of the belt,' the Snugiraffe interjected. 'Splicing gene cocktails into the host cell of a different species, then allowing them to replicate to create wholly original organisms.'

'What about it?'

'As you may know, this galaxy is being Hoovered clean by the Omni-zone. Stars, planets, asteroids – everything is destined to be devoured by the spiralling ring of black holes that surround its entrance. Only objects of great mass can survive the crossing.'

'And that's why you've quit your diet, right?'

The Dolochimp punched him hard on the top of the head. 'Like planets.'

'Oh, I see.'

'If we are to survive we need to terraform one of the planets, here in this galaxy, before they're all lost to the ring. Use it as a kind of ship to make the crossing to the other dimensions.'

Lister scratched his stubble. 'The planet may survive, but the guys on it are still going to wind up as ravioli.'

'Not if they're underground. If they're in the bowels of the planet when it passes through the ring we believe they will survive.'

Lister's head angled in semi-agreement. 'Maybe. But first you've got to find an inhabitable planet.'

'Or create one.'

'Which is what the Reco Programme is all about, right?'

'In years past we have pardoned Cyberian inmates if they agreed to donate their bodies for reco surgery and become part of the primordial soup of the new planet. A kind of protoplasmic broth from which all things evolve – the ecosystem, animal and marine life: everything.'

'And this has already happened?'

Kazwa nodded and unfastened Lister's straps and pointed at a chair for him to sit. 'The donors lost their individual personalities and became part of a gestalt intelligence that controlled the planet. A unified entity that speeded up the creation of the biosphere from millions of years to barely three. Creation was no longer in the hands of random chance. It was controlled by this intelligent gestalt which we believed would be under our control.'

'So why are you, uh, still here?'

The Dolochimp stroked its snout. 'We used DNA extracted from Cyberian inmates. After the gestalt had been created we discovered it was a malign entity.'

'Because?'

'Because it had been created from the scum of our society. It was a deceitful and bitter God who punished the just, rewarded the wicked and encouraged evil. The gestalt only allowed the dark side of our natures to prosper and soon the planet became inhabited by the cream of evil. Finally the Black Planet, as it became known, passed through the ring and now exists in some other dimension of reality.'

'So then you started again?'

'With a new gestalt on a new planet. But this time we didn't use the guilty inmates of a penal colony – we used the innocent.'

'The inmates of Cyberia are innocent?'

The Dolochimp paused and watched Lister's face blanch with shock. 'The mystics and the future-crime system of justice allow us to arrest the innocent and then coerce them into accepting the Reco deal.'

'But my other self was guilty. He wiped out his crew mates.'

'We didn't know that. He was tried for Emo-smuggling. Something of which we knew he was innocent.'

'So what do you want with me?'

'The planet is finished. The new "innocent" gestalt is complete. We need to test that it is safe. We want you to volunteer to be one of the first to set foot on the planet. We have already sent one ship. It did not return. You will be a member of the second ship. Or, if you prefer, you can return to Cyberhell.'

'If I said "yes" when would it happen?'

'Twenty-four hours.' The Dolochimp smiled. 'But we are extremely considerate of those who volunteer. You will be permitted to spend your last evening with a symbi-morph.'

'A what?'

'A symbiotic shape-shifter. Intuitively, they understand your needs and morph into the shape that most pleases you.' The Regulator pushed a typewritten statement across the desk and handed him a pen. 'Sign.'

Lister picked up the pen and looked down at the document in front of him. If he stayed in Cyberhell there was no chance of escape. If he agreed to test the gestalt then maybe, just maybe, there'd be an opportunity to pull something before they landed.

He signed his name.

CHAPTER 3

A series of hatchway doors slid back and slammed shut, as floor by floor, level by level, Lister and his party of guards journeyed through a dizzying labyrinth of corridors before they reached the symbi-morph quarters in the depths of the penal colony. They stepped out of the final lift and strode down a large white stone hallway, with rooms running off both sides patrolled by a series of guards with fearsome Gelf-engineered, four-foot-high security rats. Lister gazed at them in horror, his face contorted in revulsion like a scrunched up brown-paper bag. They stopped at a check-in desk.

'Name?'

'Lister,' said the Dingotang handcuffed to Lister's wrist.

The guard ran the index finger of his black paw down his intake list. 'Clearance number?'

The guard again. '3454H.'

'We can't take him in this batch. All the symbi-morphs are out.'

Lister's guard waved a grubby piece of brown paper in the other Gelf's face. 'Not my problem – he's yours.'

'But they're all out. We've got our full complement.'

'They want him in the next consignment.'

'But the only symbi-morph's that free is Reketrebn —
and it's not broken.'

The Guard fluttered the brown piece of paper again.
'Not my problem.'

The Gelf shrugged. 'Who the hell will know?'

'What do you mean?' asked Lister, being yanked off
down the corridor. 'It's not broken? Is that bad? It is
bad, isn't it? Look, I'm sorry, I want one that *is* broken.
Completely broken. As broken as they can possibly *be*.
You got that? Is anyone listening to me? What does
broken mean, anyway?'

The hatchway door slid open and Lister was encouraged to go inside. His nose hit stone and he slithered
down the cell wall like an undercooked piece of spag-
hetti. He got up and looked around the room. In fact it
wasn't a cell — it was more like a luxurious apartment,
tastefully decorated in cream and black. In the middle of
the room was a table set for a candle-lit supper for two:
a blue wine was chilling in an ice-cooler and some kind
of chicken-looking dish cooked quietly in a giant silver
salver.

Lister showered, helped himself to the change of
clothing that was laid out on the seven-foot four-poster
bed and harpooned his body with a series of vitamin
boosters that were available in the bathroom. All in all
he felt pretty good now; well, he would have felt good
if he'd been able to ignore the uneasy sea of nausea
swilling about in his guts — which he wasn't. He'd made
the wrong choice. He knew that now. There was no
way out of here. He'd panicked and instead of biding his
time and returning to Cyberhell and working out a
plan, he'd snatched at the Reco deal, hoping something

would turn up. He didn't think things through – he thought things halfway through and presumed the rest would work itself out. He didn't plan things properly. Kriss was right about that.

There was a commotion outside. Lister squinted through the grille and saw a female Dingotang being frog-marched down the corridor between two Dingotang guards. She was sobbing and dragging her feet as they hauled her towards Lister's suite. 'No, I don't want to, I want you, Deki. Just you. No . . .'

The Dingotang called Deki struck her forcibly across the face with his massive orang-utan arm and continued dragging her towards Lister's suite. There was a strange slurping noise and the female's form turned a metallic blue and started to fold in on itself.

Lister stepped back as the hatchway seal unlocked and two guards stood in the open doorway fighting with a huge sofa, trying to get it in through the door. One of the guards took out a baton and hit the sofa several times on its cushion, swearing at it savagely. The guards tried again, this time angling the sofa in on its end – all to no avail.

More swearing and more beating. Lister smiled. So this was his un-broken symbi-morph. It had turned itself into a sofa and it wasn't budging. Suddenly, both the Gelfs twisted the handles of their batons and spikes rose out of the heads and they started attacking the sofa's Dralon covers with these new, grisly-looking weapons. Lister watched, uncertain what to do – should he go to the aid of a Dralon suite in distress? He wasn't sure how he could help it, even if he did.

There was another slurping noise as the creature

weakened under the beating and started rippling into a multi-coloured liquid form as it prepared to metamorphose into a new shape to protect itself. Catching it in its malleable, viscous state the Dingotangs were able to push it into Lister's suite, where it turned back into the female Dingotang and started pleading with the Gelf called Deki again. 'I just want to be with you, Deki, to please you – I don't want to shape-shift for another. Deki, please.'

The Dingotang spat at her and told her if she didn't do what she was told she'd be sorry. She flopped on to the floor and started to weep.

Deki turned and addressed Lister. 'If it gives you any trouble, beat it; if that doesn't work, press the alarm and we'll try and get you another.' The Dingotang turned to the symbi-morph, who was still assuming the shape of his soul-mate, and screamed at it: 'Cast your hook!'

'No, Deki, please.'

'Cast it!'

'No.'

He raised his hand and the symbi-morph nodded in compliance. It morphed again, this time becoming a translucent spinning disc that changed colour as it spun. A tiny black dart shot out of the disc and hit Lister just above the right eyebrow. The initial pain was an agonizing surprise: an ice headache, worse – like someone had just ripped out all his nostril hair with a pair of rusty pliers. Gradually the pain spread out across the top of his skull and he staggered and fell.

He lay on the floor, curled in a ball, rocking himself back and forth. Over the next minute the pain gradually dissipated. Then suddenly it was gone. The dart of telepathic venom had been absorbed into his hypothalamus. He and the symbi-morph were bonded.

The Dingotang spoke. 'You have volunteered for the gestalt programme, and, in accordance with the Xion Treaty, amendment ii, you have the power to demand this symbi-morph fulfils your every desire, sexual or otherwise. For the next twenty-four hours, nothing is forbidden.' The Dingotang turned to the symbi-morph. 'Please him.'

There was a slurping noise and the symbi-morph started to morph again. Lister was suddenly aware of the most excruciating smell; an aroma that was so repugnant he had to clutch on to the table to keep his balance. He looked across at the steaming yellow mountain and saw the symbi-morph was now sitting there defiantly as a pile of yak dung.

The guard screamed at the excrement: 'Stop it. Change. Please him. You hear me? Change!'

The yak dung shook uncontrollably, almost as if it were sniggering. Lister grinned.

'I have never known a symbi-morph so wilful. All the others are broken. You will be too. We will return in half a cycle. If still you refuse to do his bidding then you will be spayed.'

Lister watched as the two defeated guards slammed out of the suite. He looked across at the dung and waved his right hand, amiably. 'How's it going?'

The dung did not reply.

'My name's Lister. That was quite a performance you just put on.'

Silence.

'Look, don't take this personally, man, or should I call

you YD, but isn't there something else you can be? Something that isn't quite so rank as yak dung? How about some moose dung?'

Silence.

'Look, you and me haven't got a barney. I'm just asking you to be something a tad more aromatic.'

The dung morphed into a bouquet of white roses.

'Thanks, man, I appreciate it.' Lister sat down at the table and started to serve the chicken dish on to the two plates. 'Have you got a name?'

Silence.

'I'm Lister. Did I say?'

Silence.

'Let's get one thing straight – I don't want you to fulfil my sexual desires, OK? If that's what's bothering you, you can relax. You're not my type.'

The bouquet of flowers turned in on itself and metamorphosed into Kochanski. She stood there wearing nothing but a tiny red G-string and smiled at him provocatively. Lister swallowed hard. 'OK, you are my type. Clearly, you're very much my type, but, uh, I'm still not interested.'

The Kochanski symbi-morph grinned. 'I only have one master – he's the Gelf called Deki.'

'You'd really be doing me a big, big favour if you put some clothes on, you know. We're going to wind up with all the food sliding down to your end of the table.'

A ripple of silver undulated across Kochanski's body like a wave being driven across a lake by a strong wind. When Lister looked again the symbi-morph stood before him, still as Kochanski, but now in an elegant ball gown. Lister couldn't help himself. He stared at this near perfect copy of the woman he loved and was suffocated by sadness. 'I can't function if you're going to stay like that. You see, I've lost her, she's in another Universe now. With someone else.'

The symbi-morph shape shifted once more and re-appeared as Rimmer. 'Listy, *bon appetit!*'

'I can't function if you're going to be him either.'

The symbi-morph nodded and then, like a second-rate impressionist, rotated its hands in front of its face and shape-shifted again, this time transposing into its neutral form – a black-and-white lightly matrixed humanoid shape. It sat down at the table.

'Is that the real you?'

The humanoid shape nodded. Lister pointed to the plate. 'You must be hungry. Don't you want to eat? Or don't you eat?'

The symbi-morph nodded again.

Lister poured them both some blue wine. 'So, who's that Deki guy?'

'He's my host – although he wants to share me with others. He has four of my hooks.'

'And me?'

'You are my co-host – you have just one, which I will remove when our time is over.'

'And the four hooks – they're four times more power-ful than one?'

'I am not able to interpret your thought patterns as accurately; our telepathic pathway has only one connec-tion; we are bonded only on one level only.'

'What happens when someone has all five of your hooks?'

'I am able to serve them completely, be whatever

they desire at any time. It is only then that I become fulfilled. When I am totally joined with another.'

They ate in silence for some minutes. Then Lister raised his glass. 'To prisoners.'

The telephone purred gently into life. Lister rose from the chair and picked it up before its third ring. It was Deki. Two hours had passed since the Dingotang had left and he wanted to know if the symbi-morph was performing. Lister looked at it curled fast asleep on the bed. He spoke into the mouthpiece. 'Yes,' he said. 'No problems.' He replaced the receiver.

The symbi-morph opened its eyes and sat up. 'Why did you lie for me?'

'He'd have spayed you. You'd have lost your ability to morph.'

The symbi-morph looked at him balefully. 'You want me to help you, don't you? Help you escape? Well, I can't. Deki is my master.'

'I know.'

'You believe that in time I will relent. I won't. Deki is my host.'

'He beats you. He treats you like a ... dog. No, worse, he treats you like a whore.'

'He's my host.'

'He doesn't deserve you.'

'Without him to serve, I'm nothing.'

'With him to serve, you're nothing. You're more of a prisoner here than I am.' Lister paced. 'Help me.'

'I cannot.'

'Just be Kryten, for ten minutes. Let me talk to him.'

The creature looked at him for some time.

'Come on, give me a break. Ten minutes, that's all I'm asking.'

Lister watched as the symbi-morph rippled into its morphing state, then reformed itself in front of him. Soon he was staring into the angular pink face of his favourite mechanoid.

'Mr Lister, sir. How can I be of service?'

'Kryten, man, is that you?' Lister beamed, idiotically.

'It is what the symbi-morph has created using all the available data from your mind, sir.'

'Will you be able to function like Kryten? Give me information and stuff about how to get out of here?'

'In many respects, sir, the information you seek from Kryten is often already known to you. Sometimes in the past you have requested Kryten's advice knowing perfectly well what to do but lacking confidence in your own opinion. Even this information about information is something you already know.'

'Kryts, I want to know about symbi-morphs. What they do, how they act, everything.'

Kryten shook his head. 'No, sir, what you want is confirmation of what you already know. What you have already deduced from observation and intuition. But putting these thoughts through my mouth will give you greater confidence and belief in what you already believe to be the case.'

Lister dismissed his pedantry in a shake of the hand. 'Symbi-morphs – let's talk.'

'Symbi-morphs are creatures who become totally devoted to one master. More dog than person, they possess the ability to mutate and redefine their molecular structure into practically anything, even objects made out of machine parts – but they can only maintain this for very short periods of time.'

'How do I know that?'

'You subconsciously overheard a conversation between two Gelfs in the bar you visited on Blerios 15.'

'Did I?'

'Yes, sir. You did.'

'Go on.'

'As their name implies, symbi-morphs are symbionts who have the ability to shape-shift into a form that will please their host. They are dependent on another organism, which is usually a member of a different species. With this host they form a relationship of great power and sophistication, which generally benefits both species.'

'I know all this?'

'Your subconscious picks up knowledge with all six of your senses. You'd be amazed what you know that your consciousness is not aware of.'

'Example?'

'Well, how about the statement I've just made?'

'Another one.'

'The photograph that you found on the derelict Starbug. The one of Kochanski and your other self covered in crazy foam.'

'What about it?'

'It wasn't your other self. It was Rimmer who was under all that crazy foam. In this alternative of reality it is he who was Kochanski's lover and not your other self.'

'And I knew that?'

'Your subconscious knew it. You told yourself there was a connection, but you never really felt right about the search for your other self.'

Lister nodded. 'So how do I get out of here?'

'You form a relationship with the symbi–morph and persuade it that you are a more deserving host than its present master. Then you ask it to help you escape by using its formidable abilities. You have to get it to empathize with your present predicament and explain how your other self has stolen your life and your ship.'

'How do I get it to empathize with me?'

'Surely that's obvious, sir.'

Lister nodded slowly. 'I just ask it to morph into me. Then it will feel what I feel.'

'Precisely. It will know your pain.'

CHAPTER 4

The Mayflower scythed its way through the meteor storm as it powered relentlessly towards the Andromeda galaxy, its giant ram scoop greedily snorting up the currents of space and driving it on. Its human crew of eight, together with nine new species – all genetically engineered back on Earth – a platoon of Simulants, assorted droids and a variety of bacteria and viral entities, slept soundly in the non-time of stasis, oblivious to the elements their ship was battling.

The lift door rattled open and all six foot two of Lieutenant-Colonel Michael R. McGruder ducked out. Forty-two years old, he looked closer to late twenties because, like all the Mayflower's human crew, he'd had the gene responsible for ageing removed from his genetic make-up. He ran his tongue around his mouth. It still had that dead aftertaste that always lingered after getting out of Deep Sleep. He spat into a paper tissue, folded it neatly in eight and deposited it in a garbage chute. Then he turned left and started down the corridor.

It was his tour of duty. Every ten thousand years each of the marines was assigned a tour of duty. This was his fifth. Generally, it took about two days. He'd check everything was running smoothly, fix anything that wasn't and then write up his report in his beautifully neat handwriting. He'd heard some of the guys took time out to wake up a symbi-morph, get drunk and play around. Not him. No, sir. He had sworn to serve his planet and that's precisely what he intended to do. True, he'd never be the man his father was, but damn it all to hell, no man could be.

He looked up at the corridor arches – odd, they were covered in cobwebs – where were the skutters? He walked along the metal grilling of the corridor and turned left at the T-junction where a sign read: 'Gelf Quarters.'

It was part of his tour of duty to check the 'passengers'. First on his check-list were the Dolochimps. McGruder strode between the sleep units and arrived at the first stasis pen. Six Dolochimps roamed up and down in their glass dome.

Something was wrong. They'd been de-animated. Must be some kind of temporary electrical fault.

He moved on towards the next pen to check out the Simulants.

Simulants were the most expensive and complex artificial human substitute ever created by *homo sapiens*. They were human with add-ons; they lived longer, were more intelligent and their bodies were stronger and hardier than anything with chromosomes. They'd been programmed to be ruthless, to be primarily concerned with their own survival, and the reason for this was simple: they'd been designed to be like humans, to replicate the characteristics of the species that had clambered to the top of the evolutionary ladder, but they had been programmed to be better than human, more single-minded, more driven, an even greater surviving machine. The theory was, make the individual look after itself and the species would thrive.

The segregation laws were simple.

Simulants had been programmed to 'survive', and incidents in the past had illustrated these droids wouldn't hesitate in killing their human masters if they believed it would best serve the survival of their species. Without remorse, without guilt, they would strike them down with scarcely a nano-second's thought. They had no choice, it was why they had been created: to survive and flourish in a distant land; to wage a war against the lava, and tame a planet in a new solar system in a foreign galaxy.

The segregation laws were long and complex, but the only law anyone ever had to remember was this: never trust a Simulant. Treat them like pit bulls: always be scared. Only then would you be safe. McGruder knew this.

He looked in at the pen. The Simulants were all de-animated too. They grinned and screeched and licked the inside of the glass domes with their long grey tongues. He moved on to the next pen – a batch of symbi-morphs. The next Dingotangs. The next a couple of Snugiraffes. They were all de-animated.

He peered in at the next pen. It was – empty.

He read the sign: 'Simulants/Batch 2'. All seven sleep chambers were vacant. Seven Simulants were free. A trickle of sweat trundled its way down his smooth, handsome face and trickled off the edge of a jaw an architect could have used to draw straight lines.

He must remain calm.

What would his father have done? He breathed deeply. Probably round them up single-handedly after some titanic bloodbath, then climb back into Deep Sleep and not even bother to mention the incident to anyone. But he wasn't his father. He was just a damned good soldier. And right now he was scared. He would get the crew out of Deep Sleep

Then a thought struck him. Where was the second batch of symbi-morphs? He'd seen the first batch, but according to his Itin. list there should be a second. Were they on the loose too? He doubled back to check.

He padded down the grilled deck. Passing the empty Simulant unit he peered in. It looked as if they'd pulled up the lead-lined grille covers and gone out through the ceiling. Maybe he should take a look. He unlocked the door and stepped inside. As soon as he was in he knew he'd been duped. This wasn't the Simulants Deep Sleep unit at all. This was the unbroken symbi-morphs assuming the shape of an empty Simulant unit to draw him inside. They shape-shifted out of the walls and overwhelmed him.

Twenty minutes later McGruder came round to discover he was now locked in the unit. He signalled the alarm from his transmitter.

Helpless and impotent, he watched as the mutiny raged for the next three days and nights. The electrical fault that had caused the temporary de-animation of the Gelf sleep units together with his own stupidity had allowed all the engineered life forms to escape. Now, led by the Simulants, they were engaged in a pitched battle with the human crew for control of the ship.

At the end of the third night the Mayflower's navigation

system was destroyed in the fighting and shortly afterwards the ship fell into a worm hole. The ship was carried through the lesion in space time and taken down the dimension hyperway to the Omni-zone, and ejected into a new dimension of reality.

The ship hurtled through the stratosphere of its new reality and finally fell into the orbit of a volcanic moon, where it splashed down into a sea of molten lava and glooped its way to the bottom of the sea bed.

On the fourth day the hapless McGruder was released from the sleep unit by a group of victorious Dingotangs, who promptly took him prisoner. It amused them to have a human slave, and he became part of their crew when they finally navigated their way to the surface in one of the Mayflower's escape pods.

As they soared out of the volcanic moon's orbit, looking for a desert asteroid to make their home, McGruder sat slumped in the hold. He knew he would never be the soldier his father had been. He would never even be a tenth of the man Arnold J. Rimmer was. He prayed now that they would never meet.

He couldn't bear the shame.

CHAPTER 5

The silver pool seeped under the bottom of the door frame, then sucked itself together and turned into a fly. The insect carefully walked up the hatchway surface before it inserted itself into the lock drive and became a computer key. The hatchway door purred open and Lister stepped out. By his side he was suddenly joined by a Gelf guard who walked with him down the hallway and up to the check-in desk.

They reached the counter and Lister's companion waved a note in front of the seated check-in guard. 'Transfer papers.'

'What transfer?'

'It's all on the form. Read it.'

Without breaking stride Lister and Reketrebn, still assuming the shape of the guard, dropped the note on the desk and strolled towards the exit.

'Hey, wait a minute!'

They quickened their pace.

'Hey! This isn't a release form.'

They reached a set of locked hatchway doors patrolled by two security guards. Reketrebn's hand turned into a key and they sauntered through.

'Hold that prisoner.'

As they ran down the long, wide hallway that stretched in front of them for almost 150 feet, Lister gradually became aware of Reketrebn's voice running by his side screaming at him: 'Jump on!'

He glanced across. By his side was a black-and-white mare.

'Jump on,' said the horse.

Lister leapt on, and Reketrebn galloped down the corridor. As they reached a T-junction they eased around the corner before powering down a second stretch of hallway and catching a lift as its doors were closing.

The lift doors squeaked open and Lister peered out. It appeared they were on some kind of maintenance floor. It was deserted. Lister trotted across the metal-grilled flooring, passing several rows of slowly rotating metal edifices three hundred feet long. Clearly this was some kind of oil generator that powered the asteroid. He peered over the edge and watched as a pump disappeared into the infinity of the drill hole.

Behind him he heard the lift door open and a pounding of feet signalled a small battalion of guards close behind. Reketrebn galloped down a series of grilled promenades that overlooked the abyss and finally came to a dead end. He looked down at the dizzying drop to the oil chamber below.

The running footsteps were getting louder. There was no way out. 'Damn it.'

Reketrebn shape-shifted back to its neutral shape. 'Hide behind that canister.'

Lister huddled behind the canister as the symbi-morph started to shape-shift once more. Minutes later twelve Gelf guards started to inspect the end of the promenade.

One of them barked that it didn't make sense. They couldn't have just disappeared into thin air. Then a second pointed to the lift that was positioned at the end of the promenade and plummeted down into the abyss below. They punched the 'door open' keypad and all twelve guards shuffled in. Reketrebn stopped pretending to be a lift and watched as the party of guards plummeted into the infinity of the drill hole.

Lister got up from behind the canister, grinning. 'Come on, I know where the aeropad is. Let's grab a shuttle and get the hell out of here.'

The human and the symbi-morph emerged from behind a wall of crates and watched as a party of Gelfs started loading the star ship ready for take-off. From its markings Lister was pretty sure it was one of the supply ships from Arranguu 12, one that brought food and water from the less arid asteroid on the perimeter of the belt.

They crept up to the end of the line. Reketrebn morphed into a wooden packing case identical to the ones they were loading and Lister climbed gleefully inside. Soon he was being lifted and carried up a gangway and deposited in the cargo bay of the ship. It was dark but warm, and he quickly fell asleep inside Reketrebn's latest shape.

He awoke several hours later. He was no longer in the crate. Reketrebn had shape-shifted into its neutral form and was prowling around the cargo bay trying to work out where they were. He opened his eyes and sat up. 'What are you doing?'

'Where did you say this ship was going?'

'Arranguu 12. It's a supply ship.'

Reketrebn shook its head. 'Wrong. Look.' It pointed through the Plexiglass viewing window into the ship proper. The seats were filled with prisoners braced by ankle and wrist to their seats.

'This is the gestalt volunteer ship. This is the ship you were trying to escape from. Somehow we've wound up on it.'

Lister's face mixed to grey. 'Not possible.'

'Know something else?'

'What?'

'I don't think we can even jump the crew.'

'Why?'

'There isn't one. The ship's on auto-pilot.'

'Out of the frying pan and into the very same, identical frying pan. Smegging great.' Lister prised open a nearby crate. 'Food and supplies for the volunteers.' He kicked one of the crates with the toe cap of his boot and then started to beat up one of the walls.

CHAPTER 6

The Deep Sleep unit hissed slowly to the ground from its nesting position high in the ceiling. Kryten sat upright while his optical system adjusted itself to the light. After a few seconds he stumbled groggily out of his slumber bay and waddled across to check out the other units.

He always liked to get out of Deep Sleep a week or so before the rest of the crew. It gave him time to catch up with his duties and deal with any problems that may have arisen during their time in suspended animation.

His eyes flicked over the array of bio-data. The rest of the crew were soundly asleep. All was well. He glanced down at the medi-computer that was spewing out endless data about the four sleepers: heart rate, blood pressure, cholesterol; info on ears, nose and throat; even up-to-date dental charts.

Strange.

Kryten looked at Lister's dental chart. It was wrong. The machine was declaring that he had twenty-six teeth, when Kryten knew he had twenty-seven and one cap. He asked the machine to run a secondary check on the data, which it did. Still it declared Lister had twenty-six teeth. Kryten asked the computer to delve into the medi-log and confirm that two winters ago he had replaced Lister's central incisor with a cap and at the same time removed all four of his third molars. The computer flashed up an old X-ray of Lister's teeth – no third molars and one cap. Kryten asked the computer to show him the present dental chart of the sleeping Lister – all third molars present, no cap, and two missing second pre-molars, three missing first molars and one missing first pre-molar.

Extraordinary.

Some of Lister's teeth had grown back.

Unlikely.

Kryten checked through the medi-computer for Lister's scar history. He had four scars in all – two appendix scars (due to a freak of nature which had bequeathed him with a double helping of the body's most unnecessary organ), a scar on the top of his right shoulder which had been caused by a childhood accident, and an artificial earlobe due to a run-in with some acid rain.

Kryten compared the scars with the scar history of the presently slumbering Lister – three scars; right thigh, left arm, right knee. He looked in at the body presently sleeping soundly in the safety of decelerated time.

He was not Lister.

Or rather, he was not their Lister.

Here they were about to go into orbit around the lava planet, twenty-odd weeks away from Cyberia, and they were carrying the wrong Lister. Thank goodness he'd come out of Deep Sleep early. At least now he'd have some time to evaluate the situation and compute the most advantageous course of action. This was the Lister who'd been a prisoner in Cyberia. Why would he pretend to be their Lister?

Kryten needed more information. He scuttled through the hatchway and stumbled up the steps to the ops room and turned on the com channel. Minutes later a beeping noise announced he'd successfully logged on to the derelict Starbug's on-board computer. An hour after that he'd outwitted the security system and gained access to the crew's personal files, confidential reports that had been written before the nuclear leak that had wiped out Red Dwarf's crew. Kryten downloaded the file marked 'Lister, David' and started to read.

Confidential

Personnel evaluation on crew member: Lister, David.
Technician, third class.
Report completed by
  Flight Commander Dr Alice Kellerman.

Lister first came to my attention when Dr Nicholas Thompson told me he had a particularly difficult patient and asked if I would see him. In Dr Thompson's opinion, Lister was a grade two sociopath and he requested my view. My only previous knowledge of Lister was that he'd been a constant offender during his time in Deep Space and had spent most of his passage either in the brig or confined to his own quarters for a range of misdemeanours ranging from shoplifting to beating up an officer. Naturally I was curious as to how a personality such as Lister's was able to have passed the initial intake committee and been accepted into the Star Fleet.

In all I had six meetings with Lister, who was happy to talk to me about his life and history.

In keeping with the model for sociopathic behaviour, I found him to be a man of immense charm, a trait he used frequently to manipulate and exploit others. Indeed, he used this ability and his ability to project absolute sincerity to extricate himself from many of the predicaments he found himself in. We talked about his schooldays, which were littered with examples of truancy, suspension and expulsion. Before joining the Space Corps at the age of twenty-three, he had spent his time in and out of work; he told me that after a few weeks of employment he became restless and discontented and he found it impossible to hold down a job for more than a few months. During this time there were also two periods of imprisonment; the first for burglary and the second for drunken driving. He boasted to me that he had committed several robberies and had escaped scot-free.

Throughout his life, he explained, he had found it close to impossible to form lasting relationships with either sex. He claimed he had never been in love and doubted whether the concept even existed. In total, he has fathered three children, all to different mothers, but at the time of writing has lost contact with them all.

He exhibited no remorse about his life or his predicament and had no guilt feelings about his behaviour or his actions which had led to any of his crimes; most of which were spur of the moment and totally unplanned. He found his failure to plan ahead almost always got him into trouble, but his impulsiveness and general recklessness prevented him from overcoming this trait.

I agree with Dr Thompson that his personality disorder is caused by both genetic and environmental influences.

Orphaned from birth, his adoptive father was sentenced to a ten-year prison term for embezzling funds from the Miranda Insurance Company when Lister was nine years old. He was then reared by his adopted mother, Beth Thornton, who had a history of manic-depression, a fact withheld from the authorities to allow the Thorntons to adopt Lister.

Lister's case follows a classic pattern. Children born to parents with criminal backgrounds who are then adopted by middle-class parents with similar law-breaking tendencies have a greatly increased chance of developing sociopathy. Also, from a genetic point of view –

'What are you reading?'

Kryten wheeled round, looking for the source of the voice. Lister stood under the arc lights of the hatchway sipping a cup of coffee, darkly serious and unsmiling.

Kryten fumbled together the sheaf of papers in his hand. 'You're out of Deep Sleep, sir,' he said, unnecessarily.

The pause was long and sinister. 'And so are you.'

Kryten stood frozen, as immobilizing swathes of terror wrapped themselves around his body. 'I always de-animate a few days early, sir. It, uh, allows me to catch up on any little tasks that may need doing.'

'What are the papers? You seemed very engrossed.'

'Oh, just some files, sir. Nothing special.'

Lister started unwrapping the bandages from his hands. 'Should be healed by now – five months in Deep Sleep I may have been, but I adjusted the programme to keep my hands and feet in real time.' He dropped the bandages on the floor and held up his pale hands to show Kryten. 'Good as new.' He picked up a spray can used to keep reflections off the compu-screens and squeezed the life out of it. 'Give me the pages.'

'Sir?'

'Give me the pages.'

'Sir, I think you should hear my explanation, I . . .'

Lister tore the sheets from Kryten's grasp and read the cover page. 'Nothing special, you say?' He started towards him as Kryten backed off towards the wall. 'My confidential report, that's nothing special, right?'

'Sir, I . . .'

'You lied to me.'

Kryten's elbow smashed the glass case to his right and he hauled out the fire axe. Lister stopped his advance.

Kryten started his. 'Where's Lister? What have you done with him?'

Now Lister started backing off. He waved the papers. 'This stuff isn't true. I can prove it.'

'Where's Lister?'

'Kellerman had a grudge against me. I can prove it.'

'Where's Lister?'

'Are you listening to me? I'm not out to lunch, OK? None of this is true.'

'Where's Lister?'

Lister shook his head. 'He's dead.'

The news cut through Kryten like a cheese garrotte through ripe brie. 'Explain.'

'He died in Cyberia when we lost gravity. He was sucked up into the cyberlake and drowned.'

Kryten grimaced. 'Not possible, the water molecules wouldn't form a lake – they'd all be disparate.'

'The oxy-generation unit had enough left in it to act as a fan and blow the water up into the ceiling.'

Kryten nodded. 'I see.'

'I didn't know how to tell you – and when I saw how much Kriss loved him I thought I'd try and take his place and no one would get hurt. Was that so terrible?'

Kryten didn't reply.

'Look, let me prove this report's not true. Call up Kellerman's CR and you'll see that everything I say is true.'

Kryten nodded. 'Very well.' He half-turned in front of the Info-link and started to log on to the derelict Starbug's computer. The metal flight seat hit him across the back of his cranial dome, followed by a second mighty blow from an oxy-wrench that struck him on the top of his right shoulder; as he swivelled round a punch hit him on the bridge of his nose and he slithered on to the floor. Lister dropped on top of his body and started prising off his chest plate to get at his CPU.

The alert siren howled out of the com speakers. At first Lister's doppelgänger thought Kryten had somehow turned it on, but seconds later a laser cannon exploded off the starboard bow and the ship rocked back and forth in its wake. Kryten's optical system blinked its way back into focus. Lister sat on top of him, smashing his chest plate in with the fire axe. The mechanoid swivelled left and tipped his attacker to one side as he scrambled to his feet. 'Sir, we're being attacked.'

Lister threw himself at his legs and started clawing at his chest plate once again. Kryten began to curse in machine code. Why wasn't he allowed to harm human beings? Clearly his programmer had never seen the need for dealing with homicidal alternative versions of your crew whilst simultaneously being attacked by a foreign space craft. An oversight he couldn't forgive.

A second laser cannon rocked the ship, this one shaving Starbug's nose cone and starting a series of small fires in the cockpit. Lister held Kryten across the bank of data read-outs and started pummelling him to death with the back of the fire-axe as a face faded up on the com screen.

It was the face of a woman. Not by any means an unwelcome face. In fact, it was the face of Khakha-khakkhhakhakkkhakkkkkh – Lister's bride.

'*Ig negga bu nilk nju mnhe njki njh.*'

Lister's other self glowered at the face uncomprehendingly. 'What the hell is that?'

'That,' said Kryten, dodging one blow and opening the com channel with his free left hand, 'is an old friend of a friend. You'll forgive me if I do a little match-making, won't you, sir?'

Kryten opened com frequencies and began conversing in Kinitawoweese. '*Ji nju nbv mnkl negga nhw rthy njki.*'

'What are you saying?'

'They're Kinitawowis – a tribe of nomads who journey across the deserts of the asteroid belt – selling emotions and hunting for oil. We made a deal with them for supplies.'

'And?'

'We left without settling the bill. They're saying if we don't settle it right now, they're going to reduce this craft and everything on it to something smaller than a weight-lifter's winkie.'

'So give them what they want.'

'Very good, sir.'

The Kinitawowi ship docked on to Starbug and four Kinitawowi tribe members marched through the decom chamber and into the mid-section.

Khakhakhakkhakhakkkhakkkkkh gazed around the room as Kryten and Lister stepped down from the cockpit.

Lister's other self held his arms open in supplication. 'Your barney's with him. Grab what you need and get out of here.'

Khakhakhakkhhakhakkkhakkkkkh's right jab hit his chin with a wince-making crunch. A puzzled expression rippled across his face and he fell like a toppled water tower.

Khakhakhakkhhakhakkkhakkkkkh sat on his groin, grabbed him by his collar and hauled him into a sitting position. She kissed him greedily, her green tongue exploring every nook and cranny of his mouth; then, her lust temporarily sated, she lifted his limp body into the air and draped it over her left shoulder.

She made a violent gesture with her right hand and spoke in Kinitawoweese. 'No one cheats the Kinitawowis. No one.' She spat on Kryten's right boot and signalled it was time to leave. She settled Lister's other self more firmly on to her shoulder and the Kinitawowis marched back through the mid-section door and headed for the decom chamber.

Kryten watched them leave, his face saturated in smiles. He knew there was no innate sense of justice in the Universe, which was why it was all the more pleasing when, quite by chance, justice was actually achieved. A small machine-gun staccato of laughter echoed round the mid-section, his shoulder blade housings rocking back and forth. They'd taken him. He could just imagine his face, waking up on the Kinitawowi ship and discovering Khakhakhakkhhakhakkkhakkkkkh bouncing up and down on top of him in 'full welly' mode.

Kryten was just thinking how being on-line could be so good sometimes when his olfactory system detected the fire. The fire caused by the laser cannons that was now in the cockpit and sending hacking black plumes of smoke into the mid-section.

The fire that was now impossible to put out.

CHAPTER 7

Starbug bansheed through the lava planet's atmosphere. Its madly vibrating nose cone sliced through layer after layer of advert-white cloud before finally the clouds gave way to a massive expanse of sky. The sky looked like Van Gogh's palette on a bad day: furious hues of reds, oranges and yellows, all whipped to the point of frenzy. Beneath the sky a sea of molten lava was in an equally irascible mood. A single sound bellowed from the engine housings – death dive.

The three Deep Sleep units hinged quietly open and the three figures sat up in the sleep bays and started to rouse themselves.

Kryten stood over them, smiling happily. 'Welcome back on line, sirs, ma'am.' He emitted this greeting without a trace of panic. At no point did his voice hint at the fact that the ship was out of control and caroming towards a planet whose ground temperature was hotter than a gigantic chicken phal. He gave them a few moments to acclimatize. 'Is everyone awake?'

'Have we reached the lava planet yet?'

'Yes, ma'am,' he soothed.

'Have we gone into orbit?'

'Yes, ma'am, we certainly have.'

'When will we touch down?'

Kryten's eyes flicked upwards to a wall clock. 'About thirty-two seconds. I'm afraid we're in the middle of a bit of a death dive.'

'Death dive?' said Rimmer.

'That's not all. I'm afraid the ship's on fire, too.'

'Fire? What kind of fire?'

'A hot one.'

'Well, put it out.'

'It's not possible to put out. At least, not by myself. If no one has any objections I suggest we skip morning tea and engage panic circuits forthwith.'

'God, what a way to be woken up,' said Rimmer. 'Any other bad news? I mean, let's hear it all if there is any.'

'Oh, there is some about Mr Lister, sir.'

'What about him?'

'He's not here. We left him behind in Cyberia. The other gentleman was the alternative version. I've shown him the door, ma'am.'

A tic of anger thinned Kochanski's lips. 'I knew there was something wrong. I knew it.'

'It probably don't matter now,' Rimmer grimaced. 'Chances are we're all going to be chargrilled in about thirty seconds anyway. If we have to abandon ship, my suits go with the women and children.'

Kochanski, Cat and Rimmer scrambled up the steps into the cockpit, spraying fire foam out of large orange canisters while Kryten's fingers jitterbugged over the command keyboards ordering the craft to abort its death dive.

Rimmer ran through some breathing exercises from

the first two chapters of *Relaxation: A Beginner's Guide*, then finally conceded he couldn't stand the tension any more. 'How long?'

Kryten screamed above the engine wail: 'Five seconds.'

'How long before we regain control?'

'Just a matter of . . .'

Starbug bulleted into the broiling heat of the ocean of lava and glooped its way downwards into the cloying currents.

Ten fathoms.

Twenty fathoms.

Forty fathoms.

The glass covering the cabin temperature monitors shattered with the searing heat and the plastic arrows on the gauges drooped into surreal poses.

The Cat grappled with the joystick. 'Give me manual, bud.'

'I'm trying,' Kochanski croaked. 'How about now?'

'Nothing. Everything's out.'

The Cat hammered redundantly at the control panels. 'It's deader than penny round collars.'

Rimmer's hologramic image wavered like a heat haze as the sweltering temperature began corrupting his light bee transmission. 'It appears, peeeeoooppppplllle, we've got about twe-e-e-e-e-nty seco-o-o-o-o-onds bef-u-u-u-u-u-u-or-r-r-r-re we beco-o-o-o-o-o-o-o-o-me a micro-o-o-o-owa-a-a-a-a-ve dinne-e-e-e-e-er.'

Kryten looked up at the blur of lights above his head. 'That's it, sir. You should have manual now.'

'You're right, bud. I got it.' The Cat snapped back the joystick. The engine sound transposed into an agonized hum as it fought against the currents of lava. It whined, it whinnied, but the craft was unable to change direction; it was impossible to break the lava's embrace.

Kochanski's fingers spun across the command keyboard. 'Launching scouter. Let's see if there's any other way out of here.'

The remote-control search probe screamed out of its launch chute as Starbug continued its downward spiral.

Kochanski ripped off her flight suit and used it as a makeshift towel to mop up the blinding monsoons of sweat that ran off her head in stinging gullies. 'It's nearly 95° Fahrenheit in here,' she brayed. 'Can we get those sprinklers on?'

'You got it, ma'am.'

The brief respite of a fine, cooling rain hit the interior of the cabin. Rimmer's image unwarped as his light bee cooled and he sighed with relief. At least now he would be able to help them get out of this mess. At least now he would be able to think clearly and calmly and logically. 'Please, God, someone save me, I don't want to die,' he sobbed shamelessly.

The Cat put his hand into the centre of Rimmer's image and took hold of his light bee. He rapped it three times on the scanner and released it again.

'Sorry,' Rimmer apologized. 'The heat must have got into my programme and corrupted my character traits.' He tutted. 'Almost made me look like a gutless flapper with the spine of a freshly filleted haddock.'

Jets of ice-cold water continued to knife out of the sprinklers, causing steam clouds to hiss and pop off the deck and consoles. Half-blinded by sweat, Kochanski slugged back some sprinkler water that had collected in a disk holder. She was thirty, perhaps forty seconds from passing out.

The Cat maintained his one-arm wrestling competition with the joystick. 'We can't manoeuvre in this stuff. It's thicker than me. It's like driving through a double-thick banana milkshake. There's no way out of here.'

Scouter remote-link bleeped into life, and the white noise of the relay monitor suddenly gave way to a murky brown picture. At first it was impossible to make out.

'It's found something?' Rimmer squinted into the monitor.

Kochanski hammered the transmission screen. 'What?'

After several seconds, feed-back data started gushing on to the console in machine code.

Kryten translated. 'It's found an ocean. Beneath the lava. It appears the lava only covers the first 500 fathoms. Underneath that there's a normal sea-bed with a degree of underwater life.'

Kochanski squinted in semi-comprehension. 'Meaning, we can't get back out, but at least if we can make it to the ocean we won't be boiled in a bug?'

'Not glad tidings of the first order, I'll grant you, but at least our demise has been postponed long enough for me to complete this week's ironing.' Kryten shook his head in relief. 'I'd hate to have gone knowing your panties were still crinkled.'

Starbug slithered free of the lava's cloying grip and hit the cooling waters of the ocean.

The craft stabilized and the steel-and-metal framework

screamed out in agony as the dropping temperature twisted and buckled the ship beyond all recognition.

They examined the damage via the monitor. The hull was intact but hugely misshapen. It looked like a cheap plastic toy that had been held in front of a flame.

The Cat tapped in the commands to transfer the engines to marine propulsion and Starbug banked to its starboard bow and started to explore the world under the molten lava.

Travelling just beneath the lava ceiling, the craft covered almost 400 miles in a four-day period, looking for some kind of blow-hole that could act as an escape route. They found nothing. Meantime the oxygen and fuel supplies continued to run down.

The yellow alert signal peeped from the cockpit.

Rimmer looked down at the read-out. 'Scouter's found something. Something big.' He jabbed enlarge instructions into the remote link and a picture slowly jump-framed into focus.

A corkscrew-shaped ship the size of a three-day music festival lay half-buried in a giant bank of sand. A hundred thousand portholes pocked one side of the vessel.

Scouter tracked down the craft's hull, passing the empty moorings where the evacuation pods had once been, passing the labyrinthine engine housings that held the ship's negative gravity drive, until finally it came to rest on the ship's name, browned by seaweed and moss. It was scarcely readable. Scouter's optic system zoomed into the name and magnified the image several times.

The ship was the Mayflower.

CHAPTER 8

The air-lock hissed open and three figures dripped sea-water into the Mayflower's reception chamber. Kryten removed Rimmer's light bee from its waterproof pouch, and launched him into being.

Rimmer nodded courteously. 'Thanks, Krytie.'

Kochanski threw the Cat a torch. 'OK. Let's split up. Rimmer, you go with the Cat, I'll go with Kryten.'

Rimmer's eyes darted down the maze of darkened corridors. 'Why? Why should we split up?

'We'll do the search quicker.'

'What's the hurry? You've got a major luncheon appointment you've got to rush off to?' Rimmer jabbed his nose at the Cat. 'I'm not teaming up with him.'

'Me? What's wrong with me?' asked the Cat.

Rimmer brayed with contempt. 'You're totally ego-centric, you only look after number one, you flee at the first sign of trouble, you're vain, selfish, narcissistic and self-obsessed.'

'You just listed all my best features,' said the Cat, confused.

Kochanski bundled Kryten down the corridor with a single jerk of the head. 'Rimmer, you're going with the Cat.'

Rimmer's nostrils flared mutinously before he won control of his face. 'Yes, ma'am,' he said through lips that scarcely moved.

A safety door hissed open and Kochanski and Kryten stepped into a gallery lined with Deep Sleep units. Six hundred feet deep, sixty feet wide, perhaps one hundred and twenty compartments in all. Kryten's feet scrunched across the shards of glass that littered the floor; the units had been ransacked, their contents looted. A strange orange fungus with yellow pustules dripped down from the ceiling. The psi-scan informed them it was totally harmless. They took a quick vote and decided to ignore the psi-scan's advice. Stupid damn cheap Martian power-packed multi-analysis machines – Kryten vowed to write a letter of complaint to the manufacturers. Quite honestly he didn't care that they almost certainly no longer existed.

They unscrewed a floor square and took a time-consuming and hazardous detour down the under-floor air-vent shafts. When they surfaced they found themselves in some kind of research lab. Kryten paused in front of an impressive-looking bank of computer terminals. 'Hubba-hubba, what have we here?'

He flicked a switch on his chest plate and pulled out a stretchable computer lead which he attached to one of the terminals. 'Just downloading the black box, ma'am.' The pupils in his eyes suddenly disappeared and were replaced by two small clock faces. A hand whizzed round each of the dials until finally the information transfer was complete. Kryten searched through the data muttering incredulities. 'Extraordinary!'

'What is it?'

'This ship has two new strains of bacteria that have the capability to terraform planets.'

'Designer viruses?'

'Created at the Hilo Institute in Hawaii, they have the ability to make certain lava-active planets inhabitable for a certain oxygen-breathing species.'

Kochanski grinned, understanding.

'I think it's these two viruses in combination that have created this very ocean, ma'am. Shortly after the Mayflower crash-landed into the sea of molten lava, one of the survivors must have released the terraforming viruses and produced this world under the lava ceiling.'

'Presumably as a means of enduring the lava's searing heat.'

'Precisely. But why would they only partly terraform the planet?"

'Perhaps the lava cover gave them a defence from Simulants or Gelfs who'd have come back and ransacked the ship.'

'But if this is true, ma'am, where are they? According to the psi-scan, the ship's deserted.'

'On occasion the psi-scan has been known to be wrong.'

Kryten nodded.

'The important point is this: if we can find some vials of the terraforming viruses, we may be able to use them to eat our way through the rest of the lava crust.'

'According to the mainframe, all viral strains should be located in the next ante-chamber.'

The hatchway door arced open and they stepped inside. The whole of the chamber had been pointlessly wrecked, vandalized, in the blood-rush of mutiny; a sea of ampoules, thousands and thousands of virus-carrying vials, covered the floor to a depth of several feet in places. All the racks where the vials had once been stored and labelled lay in pieces.

Kryten stooped and picked up a handful of the pencil-thin tubes of glass. He switched his vision from normal to micro and honed into the contents of the vial. Hundreds of thousands of virions writhed around inside, clambering over and under one another, vainly searching for an escape route out of their glass prison.

Kryten ordered his optic system to access 'maximum magnification' and zoomed in on one particular virion; it had a large head and a long thin tail that tapered to nothing. Inside the vial it was totally harmless, just a single molecule of DNA nucleic acid, unable to replicate until it came into contact with a host cell.

But what was it?

What kind of virion was this?

What did it do?

Identifying the different viruses was going to be close to impossible. Floodwater had washed away most of the ident codes and without them they couldn't cross-check with the mainframe to discover the nature of any of the strains. They simply had to find tubes with ident codes intact.

After almost an hour Kryten finally found a vial that did have an ident number. He returned to the gallery and searched through the data banks on the Mayflower's mainframe. There was a brief description of the virus's structure and what it did; it was intended to be used in the tenth year of the terraforming programme to help create a giant, fast-growing super-wheat. The virus re-wrote the wheat's growth instructions. Fascinating but ultimately useless.

Kochanski pulled on her earlobe. 'There are hundreds of thousands of vials in there. It's taken over an hour to identify one, and we've got barely five hours left. We're never going to find it in time. It's a billion-to-one shot.'

Kryten started back into the ante-chamber. 'It's the only shot we've got, ma'am. We just have to keep looking.'

The twin beams of light zigzagged down the corridor and paused at a heavy-looking lead archway. A soft machine hum which leaked from the Cat's backpack was the only sound they made. They reached a T-junction and turned left, following a sign that read 'Gelf Quarters'. They walked in silence, past a series of sleeping domes – Dolochimps, Dingotangs, symbi-morphs – all empty. Rimmer peered into the fifth one; it contained something. Something slumped in the corner. He breathed on the glass and tried to wipe it clean. It was still unclear. 'You see that? What is it?'

The Cat peered into the dome. 'Not sure, and I can't smell much either.' He pressed the keypad and the glass window yawned upwards. The Cat walked into the dome, stooped and picked it up. It was a jacket, belong-ing to a marine named McGruder. Rimmer hated marines. They all thought they were God's gift to soldiering. The Cat tossed it to one side and they contin-ued their walk through the crashed ship.

As they walked, Rimmer smiled. He'd dated a girl called McGruder once. Had a bit of a fling with her.

He started to remember how they'd met back on Red Dwarf. They were only a few months out into space, and he'd just finished his duties with Z-shift and was making his way back to the sleeping quarters when they caught the same lift together. She was pretty. Dark-haired, with computer-blue eyes. Normally shy around attractive women, unusually for him he'd opened the conversation when he'd inquired why she was wearing a white bandage around her head – was she a Buddhist or something? She'd smiled and said she'd just been released from the concussion ward: a large piece of machinery had fallen on her from a great height, but she'd made a complete recovery.

They'd got on like a house on fire. She found him amusing and attractive and told him so, even asking him to come round to her quarters that evening for supper. Of course Lister had taken the smeg out of him, saying she was only dating him because she thought he was someone called Simon.

He'd ignored him.

For two and a half days everything was fantastic. This was the real McCoy. Then, quite suddenly, and for no reason he could work out, Lister's remarks had got to him; so he'd set out to prove to himself that Lister was wrong.

He decided not to phone her. He would wait for her to phone him. It was only a little thing, but in some small way it would prove to him that she really did care.

Yvonne never phoned. They never dated again. And although they shared nods when they passed in the ship's corridors, they never really spoke ever again.

Why had he let it slip? What a schlub.

What he didn't know was this: twenty minutes after he'd left her quarters McGruder had fainted in the bath. She was kept in the medi-quarters overnight, where she became convinced that her 'relationship' with him had been a fantasy; something she'd wanted so desperately her concussed mind had convinced her it had actually taken place – she'd been hung up on him long before their meeting in the lift.

The solution was simple: she would wait for Arnold to phone. If he did, she would know it had happened, if not she would know her mind had played the cruellest of tricks.

He never phoned. They never dated again. And although they shared nods when they passed in the ship's corridors, they never really spoke ever again.

Rimmer and the Cat turned on to a new corridor and walked under an archway which detected their presence and slid open, revealing a large, horseshoe-shaped crypt. They ducked inside.

Computer terminals carpeted in a shag-pile-thick layer of dust lined three walls. At the end of the chamber a giant multi-coloured matrix covered in a strange notation dominated the room. It was as if it were some kind of keyboard, but the hieroglyphics on the giant keypads were chilling in their bizarreness.

Rimmer's torch beam turned left and started to explore the left bank of computer terminals; the Cat's beam made a bee-line for the matrix of coloured squares. He jabbed one, as much to discover the depth of the dust as anything else. A soft humming sound kicked in, then the chamber came to life, as line after line of multi-coloured neons clicked on and advanced around the horseshoe of machinery like a forest fire.

Rimmer turned. 'Don't mess with that. We don't know what it does.'

The Cat poked at a second square. 'I'm just taking a look.'

'Well, don't take a look, and that's an order.'

The Cat hissed at him quietly, then went back to pressing the keypads.

Suddenly there was a noise from above and, as Rimmer looked up, a glass cylinder slid from the ceiling and dropped neatly over him with a satisfying squish. Rimmer's eyes scrolled up inside his head. 'Why me? Why is it always me? How many times did I tell you to leave it alone?'

'I'm a cat, I'm curious. Sue me.'

Rimmer hammered on the inside of the glass cylinder. 'If I'm not out of here pronto you're in trouble big time. Got that?'

'Stay slinky. I remember the sequence.' The Cat went back to jabbing the keypads.

'Get Kryten.'

A flashing red light triangled into the chamber, accompanied by a stern bass throb. The sound made the dust dance off the machinery and pattern the light shafts with shimmering hazes.

The Cat was transfixed. 'Wow, that's beautiful.'

'Forget the light show. Go and get Kryten.'

'Wait – I'm getting something.'

A computer throbbed into being. 'Transmogrification sequence initiated.'

'Transmogrification? What the hell's that?

'Hey, maybe it's something nice. Stop thinking loser.'

'Gene sample accepted and cloned,' the computer burred. 'Please key in new genetic structure.'

'Do nothing! Press nothing! Go and get Kryten.'

'Hey, you think I can't handle this on my own? I have to rush off and get novelty condom-head to bail you out? I got you in this mess, I'll get you out. OK?'

'Get Kryten,' repeated Rimmer in precisely the same steadfast tone.

'Relax, would you, I know what I'm doing.' The Cat started pummelling the keyboard with the ends of his clenched fists.

'New genetic structure accepted. Metamorphosis in ten seconds and counting.'

The Cat twinkled winningly. 'Hey, I've got an absolutely terrific idea. Why don't I go and get Kryten?'

'Forget Kryten. Press the pads. Any pads. Keep pressing!'

Without warning the cylinder whited out and cut Rimmer off in mid-rant. The Cat stepped over and peered through the glass. A thick, swirling smoke rotated inside the cylinder, making vision practically impossible. Gradually, agonizingly, the vapour twirls began to dissipate. The Cat's face suddenly looked as if a large question-mark had been branded on it. His eyes darted around, looking for some sign of Rimmer. He wasn't there. Nothing was there apart from a chicken. A chicken that was glowering at him furiously.

'Sequence complete,' the computer said coyly.

The Cat fled out of the chamber and off down the corridor calling for Kochanski and Kryten.

★

Kochanski peered into the cylinder and watched trans-fixed as the chicken pecked furiously at the glass.

'That's Rimmer?'

The Cat nodded. 'What can I say except "whoops"?'

Kryten gazed at the array of hardware. 'What is this machine?'

Kochanski stretched upright. 'Must be some kind of DNA modifier to help the terraformers.'

The Cat gazed around at the vast network of compu-ter banks. 'They really must have liked chicken a whole hell of a lot to go to all this trouble though, bud.'

Kochanski peered at one of the hard-drive facias. 'Looks like its hard disk is loaded in some sort of digitized form with a kind of fossilized DNA from an incredible variety of life forms. A kind of library of life – well, potential life. Presumably you just summon up whatever combination of genes that you need and put together the resulting life form.'

'But Rimmer's a hard-light hologram, ma'am. He hasn't got any DNA.'

'The computer must have managed to do a transposi-tion – swapping hard light for genes. I don't understand how.'

Kryten made comforting clucking noises as the chicken circled angrily inside the cylinder. 'The question is, can we turn him back again?'

The Cat shook his head. 'The question is, do we want to?'

Kryten moved across and gazed up at the matrix. 'Hypothetically, there shouldn't be any problem recalling Mr Rimmer's original form. It's simply a matter of decoding the keypad. Seems a fairly straightforward hexadecimal layout. Logically, this should be the recall sequence.'

Kryten tapped expertly into the keypad. 'Let's try that.'

For a second time the cylinders whited out and three sets of eyes gazed in through the smoke.

A white-bellied brown-backed Mongolian gerbil, with unnecessarily ridiculous ears, returned their stares with a look of seething ill-humour. It lassoed in its long tail and furiously set about cleaning its whiskers, trying to take its mind off the fact that a group of so-called crew-mates were seriously screwing around with its molecular structure.

'That's not it, is it?' Kryten exchanged a look with Kochanski and they both started to study the DNA modifier as if they were only seconds away from the solution.

It took four hours. Four hours where Rimmer under-went nearly three hundred genetic reshapings, involving most of the animal kingdom. They ranged in size from a rimmerphant, which plodded around the chamber and made rather a mess, all the way down to a small buzzing rimmeroo, which had the legs of the Australian marsu-pial and the head and upper body of Red Dwarf's finest.

Finally Kryten deciphered the hieroglyphics, tapped in the correct override sequence and the glass cylinder retreated back into the ceiling. An ashen-faced Rimmer stepped out of the plumes of smoke and shakily staggered through the hatchway.

As the others left, Kryten hung back in the chamber and stared wistfully at the huge multi-coloured matrix. Here in this room was a machine that could fulfil his greatest desire: it could make him human. No longer would he be second class, no longer would he be a prisoner of his ridiculously shaped angular face and absurd body. This machine could make him human.

When the time was right he would return.

CHAPTER 9

The ship swooped through a nest of cloud and the auto-pilot landing procedure light clicked on on the facia of the drive monitor. Lister hammered impotently at the controls.

Useless.

They were landing on this planet with its Gelf-created gestalt whether he liked it or not. He glanced down at the ship's navi-comp and couldn't help noticing something rather large north-north-west. It was like a huge tornado half a mile wide powering across the planet's surface.

'What is that?' he said to no one in particular. 'Is that a storm? What the hell is it?'

The ship stabilized and the retros furied into life and started to lower the craft gently to the ground. Behind him the volunteers' restraint-cuffs clicked open and gave them their freedom. Simultaneously, the ship's controls whinnied and died. Lister jabbed hopelessly at the key-pads. Some kind of electrical interference had killed the ship. No option now. This ship was going nowhere; they had to get off.

The craft's airlock door chu-chunged open and the volunteers began fighting their way down the disembarkation ramp. The heat hit Lister like a punch in the face.

He reeled backwards and steadied himself. Suddenly his all-in-one flight suit felt bulky and absurd. The planet's thin air made his heart hammer around in his ribcage like a demented pinball.

He huddled behind Reketrebn, blinking back tears of sweat as he battled his way down the steps. Halfway down a particularly vicious sand swirl smacked into his back and sent him careening forwards. His hand grabbed for the rope rail, missed and he flipped over the edge and started to plummet towards the ground twenty feet below. Reketrebn's hand rubbered down and grabbed him expertly in mid-fall before setting him back upright on the ramp.

'Nice place,' Reketrebn remarked.

Lister nodded. 'As Godforsaken hell holes go, this is definitely one of my favourites.'

'Now what?'

'Kill some time before we die, I guess.'

Lister and Reketrebn splintered off from the rest of the volunteers and headed along a pass between two sand mountains, looking for shelter. The planet seemed unremarkable: almost total desert, with only the occasional straining patch of light vegetation. As they reached the end of the pass they climbed the eastern of the two sand mountains and stared down at the land below.

Rich greens of grass and trees, vivid yellows of wheat. Lister swivelled to look at the desert pass they had navigated. From his vantage point it looked quite different. It was almost as if a huge lawnmower had been driven across a whole strip of land, incinerating every single piece of vegetation as it went.

Was this the planet's gestalt? He asked Reketrebn to form Kryten and they started discussing it as they headed back for the ship.

But then, without warning, darkness fell. They stopped and made camp for the night. Reketrebn became a fire and Lister hunched in front of it and was soon asleep.

He felt her body nuzzle next to his. Still drugged by sleep, he turned and wrapped his arms around her and they started to kiss. Soon they were clawing at one another's clothes, in a tangle of naked limbs. He opened his eyes and stared into the eyes of Kristine Kochanski. 'Reketrebn, uh, what're you doing?'

'Making love to you. I am being Kristine Kochanski.'

'Why?'

'It's what you need. I can read your libido.'

'Don't read my libido again, OK?'

'Not if you don't desire it.'

'I don't, no.'

'It is because we are bonded with only one hook. I misread your desires.'

''Night.'

''Night.'

Lister stood on the crest of the hill and stared down at the valley below. It was as if someone had taken a gigantic razor and cut a swathe across the land. He followed the twisting but perfectly mown pathway of obliteration as it dipped and rolled before it finally disappeared over the horizon. In the middle of the carnage was the carcass of what was left of the ship. The skeletal outline of the craft was just about recognizable, but the outer walls had been devoured, the inner furnishings ravaged. All that remained was the pathetic squeaking of the hideously contorted metalwork.

Silent and numb, Lister and Reketrebn searched through the wreckage. They found the bodies of many of the volunteers. Oddly, they hadn't been devoured; they were perfectly normal apart from the fact that they were dead. Many of them were holding makeshift weapons of wood and metal. Several were locked together in combat. A bitter wind of fear howled through Lister's guts. 'It's almost as if they killed one another.'

Then suddenly a cliché happened: a handful of small rocks rolled down the gully and scattered around their feet; a ring of figures surrounded them. Partially blinded by the sunlight, all Lister could see were eight silhouettes, who barked something in machine code.

Lister and Reketrebn exchanged looks. Then a spear, seven feet long, sheathed in fur and tassels, buried itself in the ground a yard from Lister's foot.

Reketrebn started to shape-shift. The neutral form undulated into a hovering transparent curtain that wrapped itself around Lister and then hardened. Lister was forced to squat on his haunches as he found himself cocooned in a reinforced glass shell. The figures kicked the glass nut without result, before, accepting defeat, they picked it up and started to carry it back to their base.

Lister squatted inside Reketrebn and watched as he was carried down a series of cavernous passages where he was set down in front of an open fire. A figure shawled in an animal fur stood and peered down at him.

The figure was human. A human man.

Sensing Lister's mood change, Reketrebn shape-shifted into its neutral form as Lister stared into the face of another member of his species. The man held out his hand and grinned. 'Mr Lister, I presume.'

'Yes,' said Lister, dumbfounded.

'Lieutenant-Colonel Michael R. McGruder, sir,' said Lieutenant Colonel Michael R. McGruder, still holding out his hand. 'I believe you know my father.'

'Your father? No, I don't think so.' Lister shook his head. 'Who is he?'

'He's one of the greatest soldiers ever to serve the Star Fleet, sir, a man of such bravery and resourcefulness that he alone was revived by the on-board computer to protect your life. My father, sir, is Arnold J. Rimmer.'

Lister groped for some means of support to keep his balance. Finding nothing, he slowly concertinaed down on to his knees.

CHAPTER 10

Kryten gazed through the binocular eyepiece of the virion microscope in the middle of the sea of vials as the Cat and Kochanski staggered into the chamber carrying two large oxygen tanks and clanged them noisily on to the floor under the hatchway.

'We've got enough oxygen for a month and the Cat's even sniffed out some more battery back–up for Rimmer.'

A smile of relief slalomed down Rimmer's face.

'We've found something rather interesting too.'

Kryten looked up from the microscope. 'We've found some more ident coded vials, and their contents have turned out to be quite extraordinary.'

Kochanski took off her boots and tiptoed across the carpet of glass tubes as Kryten began to outline the discovery. 'One of the side-bars of the DNA research was the discovery that all viruses fall into two categories: negative and positive. The negative we're very much aware of.'

The Cat craned over his shoulder, trying to get a view down the microscope. 'What? Like smallpox, flu, measles, rabies, that stuff?'

Kryten nodded. 'But they also discovered that there

were positive viruses. Viral infections that actually improve the human condition.'

'Such as?'

'Well, at the very basic level, they predicted a kind of reverse flu, a strain of virus that promotes a feeling of unaccountable well-being and euphoria and can last for years. According to these notes, twentieth-century DJs were constant sufferers.'

The Cat inspected the tray of vials. 'So what's in the tubes?'

'Isolated strains of positive viruses that cause retro-infections.' He picked a blue vial and held it to the light. 'Inspiration.' They cooed appreciatively. He held up another. 'Sexual magnetism.'

The Cat's eyebrows crash-landed into the bridge of his nose. 'Sexual magnetism is a virus? Get me to a hospital – I'm a terminal case!'

Kryten held up a third vial. 'But perhaps this is the most intriguing of all. This vial contains the positive virus they named *felicitus populi*. More commonly known as Luck.'

'Luck is a virus?' asked Kochanski.

Kryten poured a minute amount of the liquid into a neck-blast syringe. 'A positive virus which most humans contract at some point in their lives. Usually the period of infection ends all too quickly. And here it is: Lady Luck, in liquid form. Want to try some?'

Kochanski said, 'Is it safe?'

'Perfectly. And this is such a minute dosage, it shouldn't last more than a few minutes.' Kochanski pulled her collar aside and the syringe hissed into her neck.

She rotated her head and straightened. 'So, what now?'

Kryten handed her a pack of cards. 'Shuffle these cards and then pick out the four aces.'

She shuffled, cut, re-cut, shuffled again and laid the cards on the lab bench and fanned them out, face down.

Her hand moved along the line and flicked over a card. The ace of hearts.

'The odds of you picking out that card correctly,' Kryten informed her, 'are thirteen to one.'

Kochanski's hand went down the line again and picked out a second card. She turned it over. Ace of diamonds.

'221 to one.'

Kochanski turned over a third card. It was a club. The ace.

'5,525 to one.'

The fourth card. Ace again. This times in spades.

'The odds on you picking out four aces from a pack of unmarked cards are 270,725 to one.'

They stood in a semi-circle, gawping. Kryten flipped over the other cards, to prove the pack wasn't fixed. 'Have you any conception of what this means?' he said quietly.

Kochanski nodded. 'It means we're playing poker, that's what it means. OK, twenty dollar-pounds a stake, dukes are wild.'

Rimmer chipped in. 'I don't think that's exactly what Kryten had in mind, actually.'

'Gin rummy?'

Kryten interjected. 'I mean, ma'am, that if you've contracted the luck virus, it may be possible to detect

the terra-forming viruses out of the hundreds of thousands of samples that are strewn around the chamber.'

Kochanski nodded. 'OK, but then we play poker.'

For several minutes she strolled across the lab, carefully
studying the floor. She stopped and thrust her hand into
a mountain of tiny vials and emerged with one.

'That one?'

'I think so.'

'Has it got a number.'

She rotated the vial and read off the viral ident code.
'ZCSBFD6577GJG93857JJJJJ43767737837FHDK
WOPIW53.'

Rimmer smiled. 'That's the first virus. That's it.
You've done it.'

Kochanski grinned. 'Luck be a lady tonight.' She
waded into another mound of vials, thrust her hand into
a stack and pulled out three more. 'OK, I'll put money
that the second virus we need is this one. Here we go:
KDNIUJVIURNVOENV984398404IUFN98HR9
98SSC.'

Kryten gasped in dismay. 'It's not "C", it's "J".'

Kochanski grinned. 'Just joshing. "J" it is.'

'What about the other two, why did you choose them?'

'I'm pretty sure this one is another vial of the luck virus.'

Kryten examined the serial number and nodded.

'And this one,' Kochanski held it up to the light, 'is
going to help me sometime, but I don't know how.' She
read out the serial number.

Ninety seconds later the computer flashed 'Trace complete', and a description of the vial punched up on to the
screen.

'Name: Brassica 2. Function: creates fast-growing broccoli.' Kochanski shrugged. 'Don't ask me.'

Two hours later they released the virus into the molten lava and watched anxiously for signs of cell corruption in the magma. Thirty minutes into the vigil they received a positive analysis from the Mayflower's mainframe. The report anticipated mulch within five days and predicted it would be possible to drive through the mixture of thinning lava and half-formed mulch within thirty-six hours.

Rimmer glanced at his watch. 'We haven't got much time to complete the salvage operation. I suggest we get cracking.'

Six hours later, after three muscle-pummelling round-trips from Starbug to the Mayflower and back again, Kochanski's body hit the springs of her bunk. She was asleep in seconds. Noiselessly, Kryten slipped on his diving suit and set the air-lock for remote. Within minutes he was striding back across the ocean bed in the direction of the Mayflower.

He passed under a lead archway and stepped into a large horseshoe-shaped crypt. He knew how to operate the DNA modifier now, the operation was really quite simple. He punched in the pattern of the new gene formation and a glass cylinder wooshed down from the ceiling. The modification began, and the cylinder whited out. When it rose back into the roof and the smoke had cleared, Kryten was no longer there. Instead there was a man.

A naked man.

A *Homo sapiens*.

CHAPTER 11

'What did you say your name was?'

'McGruder, sir.'

Lister's brow knitted in concentration. 'McGruder – your mother must have been Yvonne McGruder.'

A white smile neoned across McGruder's face. 'Ever since I was a small child she's regaled me with tales of his astounding feats. She said I'd probably never meet him because his ship was lost in Deep Space. Then the ship's black box touched down in the Pacific and I just knew he was still around. I also knew I had to find him and I've kind of built my career around that search. Was he really as truly astonishing as my mother made out?'

'Well,' said Lister, uncertain how to answer. 'Uh . . . obviously, uh . . . you know . . . uh.'

McGruder looked at him expectantly. 'Was he really the greatest soldier who ever lived, sir? Better than Patton, better than anyone? All those tales of sacrifice and valour. Sometimes, I have to confess, I wondered if my mother wasn't exaggerating, just a little. Tell me, what was he really like?'

Lister paced around the cave, his back to McGruder. Then he turned, his face sheathed in seriousness. 'What was he like?'

'Yes, sir.'

'He was . . . he was . . . a truly great man.'

McGruder melted. 'I knew it.'

'A fine soldier, a good friend – and a hell of a great man.'

'I just knew it,' McGruder sparkled. 'Is it true, that story about how he saved six officers when they were trapped inside the hold and he . . .'

'It's true,' Lister interrupted. 'It's *all* true.'

McGruder's eyes lit up, like two star clusters. 'And what about the time he . . .'

'That's true too. Everything's true. It's just a crying damn shame you'll never get a chance to meet him.'

'The last I heard was he was a hologram. What became of him?'

'We got split up. He's with my girlfriend and a mechanoid and this guy who evolved from cats. They could be in one of a gazillion realities.' A sad smile pinched at Lister's mouth. 'We won't find them now even if we spend the rest of eternity looking.'

Suddenly, there was a flurry of activity and a party of volunteers entered the cave. 'Nwaki, sire, the Rage is coming.'

McGruder nodded. 'Split into three groups as always. Divide the men.'

The Gelf turned quickly and left.

'The Rage? Is that what destroys the land?'

'It's a gestalt that was created by using the DNA of innocent penal colony internees.'

'I know. But why do you call it the Rage?'

'The Rage of innocence. All those internees imprisoned unfairly were forced to sacrifice their lives to help create the gestalt. All those entities, railing against the injustice of their punishment, furious at the inequity and corruption of the system, were then thrown together and moulded into one giant organism, a seething tornado of fury. That's why it attacks the lush green planet it created – it wants to make it uninhabitable for the Gelfs. So they can't use it to traverse the Omni-zone.'

Lister nodded.

McGruder continued. 'Its fury is contagious. All who inhale its wind become consumed with such wrath, such bilious resentment, they destroy one another – husband kills wife, brother kills brother, parent kills child.'

Lister remembered the snarling bodies twisted in combat in the carcass of the volunteer ship. 'And this makes the planet totally uninhabitable?'

'The Dingotangs put me on the first volunteer ship. Two thousand of us. Now there are scarcely forty left.'

'How come you guys made it?'

'We discovered a way of surviving the wind. All those who hate come together in a Circle of Sacer Facere and one must be sacrificed. The full fury of the Rage enters one of the group and he is immolated on the spot. But the others live.'

A Gelf stood in the entrance to the cave. 'Nwaki, sire, it is time. You must delay no more.'

McGruder nodded.

'Come, Mr Lister, you will travel with me. You can tell me more stories of my father's remarkable deeds.'

'Yeah,' said Lister uncertainly. 'Uh, sure thing.'

Lister, Reketrebn, McGruder and the party of Gelfs

headed south towards a fan of mountains, while the other two groups headed west and east. The Rage swept in from the north. The direction each party had taken had been decided by drawing straws and it became clear to Lister two hours later, as his group navigated its way along a mountain pathway thick with sludge, that it was their group that was going to be hit.

He stared into the valley below and watched as the electric orange twister scythed its way across the countryside, devouring the land like a greedy bird eating a line of grain. Three times the party changed tack and three times the Rage changed with them. It was moving at a speed close to four hundred miles an hour, roaring a demonic seal bark.

There was no place to hide on the mountain pathway, no place of protection. McGruder signalled in dumb show for them to stop and make their preparations. The party divided into three groups, each bound together by a rope that was secured to the rock face with climbing hooks.

Then they waited.

Less than five minutes later it was upon them.

Lister buried his head in the side of the mountain and hung on to his climbing rope as the Rage scoured the mountainside, stripping it of its plant life and vegetation. He watched helplessly as the power of the gestalt hauled the hooks out of the rock face and tossed one of the other two parties off the mountain.

Then the Rage entered him.

Its warm, nauseating breath reached inside him and started to explore his being. A tidal wave of anger thrashed through him. Pure, mindless, undiluted fury. It made him feel powerful. He had been wronged. Terribly wronged. Wronged by someone or something he couldn't quite recall. But that didn't matter, what did matter was that he had been dreadfully betrayed by someone or something and that was why this foaming lather of anger was gushing about inside him. And it felt good. So good. This anger, this fury was a great gift.

Suddenly he had something he could believe in, something that couldn't be challenged, something that was pure and true, something he would gladly have died to defend, because this anger was the fury of the right- eous, it was the fury of the wronged, the fury of the indignant, the fury of the innocent and they must have their revenge. Then the Rage passed over them and the funnel-shaped winds spiralled off into the distance, leav- ing the denuded rock face behind.

Lister watched it go. All that remained was his hatred. His hatred of some formless adversary.

Why had McGruder led them here, why had they not stayed in the valley? Why had he trusted him? He wanted to kill him. He wanted to rip off his face and stamp on it.

And the Gelfs, he loathed the Gelfs too. Why had they not warned him? Why?

McGruder untied himself from the climbing hooks, his lips drought-thin and humourless, his eyes black and dead.

Lister picked up a climbing hook and launched himself at him; the marine slammed him to the ground and stamped his foot down hard on Lister's throat. 'We have to form the Circle of Sacer Facere to banish the Rage. One of us will die.'

The eight survivors sat in the Circle of Sacer Facere and joined hands. Seconds passed before slowly, quietly, but growing in volume, a sound like ten thousand dying locusts started to vibrate into existence. And then a howling red wind, patterned with the faces of demons, came into being and rotated around the group, entering each of them by mouth or ear and exiting by the same. And the sound grew as the wind sluiced through them.

Round and round it went. Faster and faster. Louder and louder. Each time the Rage passed through Lister his whole body became energized. Even though it possessed him for scarcely a nano-second, every nerve-ending in his being pleaded for more; more of the fury, more of the power, more of the undiluted pure-white rage that lifted him beyond himself and made him a God.

Round and round it went.

All he wanted was for it to possess him so that for one brief second of time he would have the fury all deliriously, blissfully to himself. That it would take his life as a consequence was a price he would have paid tenfold.

He screamed out and begged it to destroy him. He implored it to possess him. And soon they were all shouting, all pleading, all screaming, and the red wind bansheed through them before gradually, almost unnoticeably, it began to slow down. Round it went, through Reketrebn, through McGruder, through the Gelfs, through Lister. Slower and slower. It was stopping. Through Reketrebn, through McGruder, through the

Gelfs. Then it stopped, teetering between Lister and the last Gelf. Both were screaming for it to possess them, both crying helplessly for it make them Gods for just a tiny fraction of a fraction of a fraction of time; back and forth it rocked between them before it paused over Lister and then returned to the Gelf. The Gelf's body was consumed with the full impact of the Rage. He screamed out in ecstasy before his flesh aged in an instant and fell off his bones in a curtain of dust.

Lister wept helplessly. It was over.

For now at least.

CHAPTER 12

Kochanski opened her eyes and stared at the man standing at the end of her bunk. Somehow this man had stolen Kryten's voice and was imparting an urgent message to her, using precisely the mechanoid's tones. Was she dreaming? Was this some kind of surreal nightmare?

Gradually, her ears tuned into what the figure was saying.

'. . . and now I'm human.'

'What?' said Kochanski. 'You did what?'

Kryten beamed. 'I haven't felt this good since I accidentally welded my groinal socket to a front-loading washing machine. I just wanted you to be the first to know . . .' A blush pinked his new human face. '. . . Kriss.' He chuckled like a naughty school-boy. 'See you in the morning.'

She let him get halfway down the staircase before she called him back. 'Kryten.'

'Yes, Kriss?'

'Now you're a human,' she smiled amiably, 'I want to give you a bit of advice.'

'Yes?'

'Wear clothes.'

Kryten looked down at his naked body. 'I completely

forgot. You humans, how on earth do you do it?' He cradled his temples with the flats of his hands. 'There's just so much to remember.'

At first light the Cat slunk into Starbug's mid-section and sat next to Rimmer, who was logging their current supply inventory in a dizzyingly complex array of colour codes, in preparation for their flight through the mulch. Next to him, eating breakfast, was a man the Cat had never seen before.

'Ah! Fellow humanoid! Greetings!' The man pointed to his breakfast plate. 'My very first meal. Boiled chicken ovulations! Dee-licious.'

The Cat sat down at the flatbed scanner and poured himself a glass of milk. 'Kryten, bud, is that you?'

'Isn't it wonderful?'

'What the hell happened, guy?'

'I went back to the DNA modifier and made myself human.'

'You *chose* that face?'

'I think it's rather a nice face.'

The Cat studied it carefully. 'You sure it's not inside out?'

'So how's the new human?' Kochanski trotted down the spiral staircase in a long T-shirt.

'Most excellent, Kriss. Although I must confess I have a number of questions about my new physique. I made a little list, if you'll indulge me.' He took a piece of paper from his dressing-gown pocket and scanned its contents. 'First, my optical system doesn't appear to have a zoom function.'

'Human eyes don't have a zoom function,' said Rimmer, peering up from his inventory.

A tiny fold of skin cleavaged together on Kryten's forehead. 'Then how do you bring a small object into sharp focus?'

Kochanski grimaced before she was able to reply. 'Well, you ... uh, you just move your head closer to the object.'

He eyed her, as if she were a dubious secondhand car dealer who'd just made some patently absurd claim. 'You move your head closer to the object?'

'Yeah.'

He held his list out in front of him and moved his head back and forth, testing the human zoom function. 'What about other optical effects, like split-screen, slow-motion, quantel, flips, strobing?'

Kochanski buttered some toast. 'We don't have them.'

'You don't have them. Just the zoom feature.' He zoomed in to his list again and tried to appear enthusiastic. 'Great. Well, that's ... great. That's really great. What a tricksy piece of software.' He consulted his list again. 'Next, oh yes – my nipples don't work.'

'In what way "don't work"?' asked Rimmer.

'Well, when I was a mechanoid, twisting the right nipple nut was the way we regulated body temperature, while the left nipple was mainly used to pick up short-wave radio transmissions. What I'm saying is, no matter how hard I twiddle them, I still can't seem to pick up Jazz FM.'

'Human nipples don't do that.'

'What do they do?'

'They're just there for decoration.'

'They don't perform any snazzy functions at all?'

'Sorry.'

Kryten tried to remain cheerful. 'Recharging,' he said, and picked up a brutal-looking electrical lead. 'I presume when humans want to recharge they do it in much the same way as mechanoids. Indeed, I've located what I presume to be the recharging socket, but for some strange reason it doesn't appear to have a standard three-pin connection. Do I have to use some kind of special adapter, because no matter what I seem to do, the lead keeps falling out?'

'We sleep, bud. That's our way of recharging.'

Kryten crumpled his list and began to roll it around in his hands, as if to relieve some form of embarrassment. 'Now, uh, something, well, something.' He cleared his throat. 'Something I wanted to talk to you about . . . something about . . . something I know we humans get a little embarrassed about. I understand it's a little taboo. Not something you generally sit around and chat about in polite conversation.'

Kochanski slipped the thick rubber band from Rimmer's supply log over her wrist and played with it distractedly. 'Get to it, Kryten.'

'Well, I wanted to talk to you about my penis.'

Kochanski couldn't help herself. A tiny tic of amusement crinkled across her face.

'I knew it! You've gone straight into snigger mode. Aren't we human adults? Can't we discuss our reproductive systems in a mature adult fashion without degenerating into adolescent snickering?'

Kochanski censored her expression. 'Yes. Of course we can.'

'Thank you.'

Kryten reached into his pyjama pocket, pulled out a Polaroid and handed it to her. Slowly, reluctantly, Kochanski took it and looked at it.

'Well?'

'Well what?'

'What do you think?'

'I'm not quite with you, Kryten. I mean – what am I supposed to say?'

'I want to know, is that normal?'

'Taking photographs of it and showing your friends – it's not, no.'

'No. I mean – is it supposed to look like that?'

She nodded. 'Yep.'

'But it's hideous! Is that the best design they could come up with? Are you seriously telling me there were choices, and someone said, "There – that's it – that's the shape we're looking for! The last chicken in the shop look!"? Shakespeare had one? Einstein? Perry Como sang "Memories are Made of This" with one of those stashed in his slacks?'

Kochanski hid her tears of laughter in a mug of tea.

Kryten shook his head. 'I think I understand now why humans don't have a zoom mode.' He handed her another Polaroid. 'Take a look at this.'

She blew her nose to compose herself and then peered at the new image, completely baffled.

Kryten handed her a third Polaroid. 'And this.'

She put the two snaps together, one above the other. Her mouth dropped open so wide it could have garaged a Buick.

'Now, why do you suppose that happened?'

'What were you thinking about at the time?'

'Nothing special. I was just idly flicking through an electrical-appliance catalogue. I came to this section on super-deluxe vacuum cleaners and suddenly my under-pant elastic was catapulting across my quarters.'

'You see? You're neither one thing nor the other. You're human on the outside, but you're still a mecha-noid on the inside. You shouldn't be getting a double Polaroid about electrical equipment.'

'But it was a triple sac, easy-glide vac with turbo suction and a self-emptying dustbag!'

'I don't care what model it was. Don't you see, it just means you're not truly human. You're still a mechanoid, whether you like it or not.'

'I think you should change back,' said Rimmer, com-pleting his inventory.

'What? Become one of those poor, sappy, sad-act mechanoids again? But this is my dream.'

Kochanski got up from the scanner table and started putting on her diving suit. 'Sometimes having your dreams come true can be the worst thing that can ever happen to you.'

'What do you mean?'

'I read an article once about people who were blind from childhood who'd had their sight restored. All their lives they'd dreamt about being able to see, but after they'd had the operation you know what a lot of them did?'

'What?'

'They committed suicide.'

'Oh, nice story. Walt Disney could have used a story like that.'

'The point I'm making, Kryten, is that restoring their

sight wasn't the panacea for all their problems. And becoming human isn't going to solve all yours. You're still the same person, with the same hang-ups. Inside nothing has changed.'

'But I don't have any hang-ups. Not now.'

The anxiety melted from her face and she hugged him. 'I hope you're right. I really do.'

She walked to the hatchway and picked up two oxy-tanks. 'We better get back to the Mayflower and pick up the rest of the salvage.'

Rimmer nodded. 'We want to be out of here in eight hours.'

Kryten's three Spareheads sat on the shelf in Starbug's pump room alongside his two spare arms, and his three spare hands. The door opened and all three flicked on-line. They'd expected to see Kryten, who usually came to visit at least once a day, duties permitting, but it wasn't Kryten at all. It was someone they'd never seen before – a human. He started to explain what had happened.

'What's it like?'

'It's indescribable, Sparehead One. True, I'm having a few problems coping with the human emotions, and there's no zoom, the nipples don't work and I could show you a couple of Polaroids that would make your eyes spin like fruit machines, but that aside I've never been happier.'

'This is all well and good,' said Sparehead Two, 'but what about me? It was my turn to be Main Head next month.'

'Well, sadly, that's no longer possible.'

'So what do I do now?'

'Well, you'll just have to retire from the Sparehead business. Find some other line of work.'

'What about Sparehead Three? You can't just abandon him – he's got droid rot.'

Sparehead Three chipped in with his malfunctioning voice-unit, which for reasons no one could now recall had a broad Lancastrian accent. 'I don't need no bugger to look after me. I may be 'alf-raddled with silicon rickets, me voice units may be shot to buggery, but I don't need no sympathy from the likes of 'im.'

Kryten held out his hands in pacification. 'Just because I'm a superior life form now doesn't mean I'll forget you. I'll still come and visit, I swear.'

'He won't be back, you mark my words. He'll be too busy swanking around with his new central nervous system, and his poncy new eight-valve heart, lah-de-dah-ing it with his fancy new humanoid friends . . .'

'Oh, Sparehead Three, you're so out of touch. You don't understand me or my world. All you know about is this shelf. And I don't want to stay here and end up a sad, embittered old substitute cranium like you.'

Sparehead Three gurned back at him. 'I may be half raddled, and me circuit boards may have gone bandy, but I'll tell you this for nowt: you came into this world as a mechanoid, and a mechanoid you'll always be.'

Kryten's lip reared like a bucking horse. 'In my idiotic way, I actually thought you might be pleased for me. I should have known better.' He strode across to the pump-room door and slammed closed the hatchway. 'Mechanoids – they're so absurd.'

CHAPTER 13

For most of their existence, *Homo sapiens* had lived on the fifth smallest of nine planets which revolved around a tiny dwarf star, in a solar system, which they called 'the' solar system, in a disk-shaped galaxy, which they called 'the' galaxy, which was one hundred light years long and one thousand light years deep. They called their solar system 'the' solar system and referred to their galaxy as 'the' galaxy because, although they were aware that there were trillions of other solar systems and billions of other galaxies, they felt that their solar system and their galaxy were the only ones that really counted, because they contained the most important creation in the entire Universe – them.

Homo sapiens didn't get to the top of the evolutionary tree by being modest – they got there by killing other life forms better than anyone else. Or so it seemed to Kryten. It also seemed to Kryten that for most of their existence *Homo sapiens* had been in a quite astonishingly bad mood. A feeling he was beginning to experience first hand.

The reason for his poor humour was largely due to something called Death.

Humans didn't like death. And now Kryten was

human he wasn't mad about it either. In fact, there were a whole bunch of things Kryten had suddenly taken a dislike to: he didn't like people who left sales leaflets under car windscreens advertising dodgy plumbing companies, he didn't like having to empty Starbug's dishwasher after it had completed its wash programme and return all the plates to the galley cupboards. This task used to delight him; now he was human he thought it was dull and tiresome and something to be avoided along with all the other domestic chores. In fact, the more Kryten thought about it, a lot of things made him angry now he was one of them'. But nothing made him more angry than death.

Someone should have told him. He had had no idea he was going to feel this way. When he was a mechanoid the fact that he had a termination date had never bothered him. He was created to serve and it was only logical that he had an expiry date to allow models that were technically superior to him to take over his tasks. But now it was different. Now he was human and he possessed a human's arrogance. He deserved to live for ever. Why? Because he just deserved to, that's why.

What was death? How did it happen? Kryten became consumed with the subject. It seemed to him death happened something like this: someone – say a man – would be having breakfast with some other *Homo sapieney* colleagues. He would be absently buttering a piece of toast, perhaps, and musing about the day ahead. He might be wondering whether to re-tile his bathroom, and if so what kind of tile would best suit. A plain white tile maybe, or perhaps a rather risqué and slightly more unusual champagne motif? He might also be ruminating

as to whether he needed another bucket of tile adhesive
or could he make do with the tile adhesive he had from
the time he'd done the kitchen, three years previously.
The one he kept under the stairs. He might be thinking
all these things when, all of a sudden, without any
warning whatsoever, he would be removed from existence. He would cease to belong to that particular plane
of reality. No advance notice, no opportunity to make
any preparations, the man was no longer the owner of
living molecules. His ability to inhale oxygen had been
confiscated. He would never have another thought. His
bucket of tile adhesive would remain untouched and he
would never grout again.

This made Kryten furious.

Could it be that this man had just been totally erased,
that he had been totally oblivionized? What had he done
to deserve that? All he wanted to do was tile his damn
bathroom, for God's sake. Where had he gone? No one
knew. No wonder *Homo sapiens* were largely very
grumpy. Here they were, the smartest species that nature
had ever created; they had gone to all the trouble of
obeying Darwin's theory of evolution, and out-evolving
everything in sight, and for what? So they could be
removed from existence at the whim of some invisible
force called fate.

It was a sick joke. He felt betrayed. He wanted to
complain to the management.

Being human was hard.

The afternoon began quietly enough. It started with a
blazing row, which turned into a fight to the death.
Then things got very much worse.

Kochanski, Cat, Rimmer and Kryten staggered down the thin metal staircase carrying the ten-foot-long oxygen tank like a roll of carpet. An hour remained before the mulch would be ready for penetration, and already they'd successfully completed four salvage missions.

As they rounded a tight bend in the stairwell the Cat suddenly felt his grip on the smooth black cylinder begin to loosen. 'I'm going to drop it!' Kryten started to lower his end to the floor as Kochanski and Rimmer, supporting the middle, helped him steer it groundwards. The Cat changed his mind. 'No, it's OK, I've got it again, everything's cool.'

Kochanski leaned against the stairs' metal rail. 'Are you sure?'

'Sure I'm . . .' The tank slithered from the Cat's grip and the momentum took it clean through Rimmer and Kochanski's arms. Kryten found himself falling backwards down the staircase pursued by a four-hundred-pound lead tank packed with compressed air.

Once, twice, three times the back of his head smacked against the metal railings, once, twice, three times his right elbow clunked against the sharp edging on the corner of the steps as he somersaulted boot over shoulders down the staircase. Finally he landed in a forlorn heap on the landing and began experiencing a series of human emotions he'd never felt before: pain, fury, frustration and loss of pride were among the first four. Then something else happened. Something rather unfortunate. The oxygen tank tobogganed down the final flight of steps and hit him straight in the solar plexus at a speed of just under four miles an hour. It felt to Kryten as if every molecule of oxygen had been ripped from his body. He lurched forward, breathless, and the impact forced his teeth to snap closed on his tongue. He howled plaintively. Then, still groaning, he rolled to his right and caught his testicles on the nozzle end of the tank. He pulled his body into a tight ball and sobbed softly to himself, rolling over and over on the stairwell landing. Suddenly he was in mid-air. He'd rolled under the rail at the halfway landing and was now making the final part of the journey to the bottom of the stairs in the most direct way possible. He hit the top of the packing cases with a soft thud and waited for the next terrible thing to happen to him.

Nothing did.

For almost four seconds.

Then the loose piece of railing the tank had dislodged from the stairwell slithered free of its support post and clipped him across the back of the head with an echoey clank.

His introduction to physical pain was complete.

Groggily he sat up and looked around to see the others clambering down the staircase. He gazed down at his leg, happily pumping blood from an ugly grin in his thigh. He glowered at the Cat. 'Look what you've done to my new body. I've not even had it one day, and it's a write-off.'

'Sorry, bud, I just lost my grip.'

'My whole left leg is completely ruined. It'll need stitches.'

Kochanski stepped in. 'Kryte, calm down, you'll be OK. You're suffering from "new car owner" syndrome.'

'But it was perfect, and now because of that idiot feline I'm going to have a scar the width of the Ursa major constellation!'

Kryten scrambled off the packing case and swung a right upper cut which took the Cat unawares and planted him on his back in the middle of some freeze-dried food supplies.

Kochanski and Rimmer stood bewildered, watching as the Cat somersaulted upright, and rained a series of lightning blows to Kryten's face and stomach.

Kryten staggered around doubled in two from the Cat's savaging. 'Now look what you've done, you've made me go purple.'

'You started it, First Time on the Clay-Wheel Head – you crinkled my suit.'

Kochanski bear-hugged Kryten from behind and dragged him to one side. 'OK, you and me are going to take a little walk.' She pushed him through the hatchway and they started down the corridor. She pressed a door release and a second hatchway squished open. A series of dim blue lights illuminated the room in sombre lines as they made their way to the far wall and found a pump housing to sit on.

Kochanski took out a handkerchief and handed it to Kryten to mop the blood from his mouth while she dressed his leg with bandages ripped from her blouse.

Finally, Kryten spoke. 'You don't think I should stay human, do you? You think I can't cope.'

Kochanski shrugged. 'Only you know that.'

'I'm not going to change back. I'm not. Not ever.'

She nodded and said nothing. She was looking at the nest of three stasis pods that lined the far wall.

They all bore the same name: Professor Michael Long-man. She flicked on her torch and circled the names with the beam. 'How do you get these things to activate?'

Kryten looked down at the floor and kicked at the light pattern that shone down from the grilled ceiling. 'I'm human now. I don't have all those gigabytes of Ram any more. How the smegging hell do I know?' He sighed. 'I'm sorry. I'm sorry.'

She scanned the complex display of commands and finally pressed a combination of four. Smoke hissed into the chamber and the three pods began to slide out of the wall. When they had extended to their full length, a high-pitched wheezing sound signalled that one of the lids was sliding open. Almost imperceptibly the two of them backed off across the deck.

A voice spoke from inside the stasis pod. 'Thank you.'

She pointed her torch light into the gloom. 'We didn't know anyone was alive. We thought everyone was dead.'

The voice again. 'I'm not alive.'

She didn't know how to reply to this so she just said, 'Oh, bad luck.'

Spirals of smoke swirled out of the lead-lined casket but the voice still refused to reveal itself. 'Our cells just gave up. They wouldn't be modified any more, and we were left like this.'

Now a man with watery brown eyes and a little black beard loomed into an upright position. His face was covered in yellow weeping buboes and half of his bottom lip was eaten away. He leapt out of the pod and stood on the metal grilling of the chamber floor. Kochanski gazed down at his feet. His legs belonged to a goat. He threw back his head and emitted a yowl that was on loan from Hell. Another figure slithered out of the second stasis pod and grinned manically at the two fear-frozen humans. He also had watery brown eyes and a little black beard, but his body was the body of a black-necked spitting cobra. It sizzled loathing. There was a pause and they were joined by the third Professor Michael Longman. Again, his face and brain remained intact, but this time his body had been borrowed from a leopard.

Kochanski's boots scudded across the grilled metal flooring and out into the corridor, quickly followed by Kryten. The two of them hammered down the aisle back towards the Cat.

He was leaning against the wall feeling guilty about what had happened with Kryten. He was especially guilty about creasing his sequinned jacket, and the self-reproach for marking his white stretch PVC body suit was nearly too much to bear. He glanced up and saw his two crew mates belting towards him pursued by a holo-goat, a leopard with a man's head and another man slithering along the ground with the body of a black-necked spitting cobra. His first reaction was that Kryten had gone off to enlist some serious help to get even for his nose, but after Kochanski and Kryten had screamed past him, leaving him leaning casually against the wall and quite alone, he began to change his mind.

The Cat started to run. They picked up Rimmer and the four of them pounded down the corridor and fell into the lift as the Longman-leopard flung itself against the closing doors.

Kochanski punched the button for basement and slid down the wall, sucking in air.

A flash of panic flitted across Kryten's features. 'What about the supplies?'

Kochanski looked baffled. 'The hell with the supplies. We've got plenty. Let's just get out of here.'

'You mean, we're going to leave here for keeps?'

'What do you recommend? A final touristy stroll round, followed by a cream tea?' asked Rimmer.

'I don't want to go.'

The Cat's two eyebrows did simultaneous press-ups. 'What?'

'I mean, I have to change back to what I truly am. I'm a mechanoid. I don't want to be human.'

Kochanski closed her eyes and cradled her forehead between her knees. 'What are you telling me, Kryten?'

'I want to return to the DNA suite and change back.' A grin illuminated his face, and for the first time since he'd become human he looked happy. 'I'm saying, I suppose, I just gotta be me. Naturally, I don't expect you to come with me. Just send back the sea buggy on the remote when you get back to Starbug.'

'We're not splitting up,' said Kochanski. 'We're in this together.'

'Except for me,' said Rimmer.

'And me,' said the Cat.

'All of us,' Kochanski snapped.

'Look, I can't risk dying in this outfit. This suit and rigor mortis just won't work. I need to be in something blue.'

'All of us.'

The Cat shook his head sadly. 'Don't you hate it

when she gets brave? It's her most nauseating feature, if you don't count stealing my earrings.'

They left the lift at deck four and let it continue down to the basement, hoping the Longmans would be fooled into thinking they'd headed for the airlock and fled the ship.

Kochanski elbowed in a glass cabinet and picked out a fire axe amid the shattered glass. Then, softly, they padded their way up the stairs and entered the DNA suite.

'Make it quick,' Rimmer hissed. Kryten nodded, then went over to the matrix and started scrolling through the system lists to retrieve his digitized original body data.

It wasn't there.

He double-checked. Still nothing. He decided to find it another way. He typed in 'Mechanoid Cell Template' and stabbed 'find'. The matrix sped through its data lists and came back with the results: 'No such data stored'.

A wave of panic sucked the colour from his face. 'My genome isn't here. It doesn't make sense.'

'Yes, it does,' said a voice. 'It makes perfect sense.' A mechanoid stepped out of the half-gloom. The mechanoid had watery brown eyes and a little black beard. 'Thank you for your body, Kryten. Now we want the bodies of your crew mates. We want your itsy-bitsy double helixies.'

CHAPTER 14

The Longman-leopard, its eyes blacker than a Mimiam night, rose from its sitting position, and started to stalk them on their left side. The cobra slithered into a strike position on their right and hissed a glop of venom that sizzled past the Cat's ear. The Longman-mechanoid, still smiling, edged closer, all the while speaking in his hypnotically soothing tones. 'You don't need to die, you can exist in another form. You can be anything, anything you want, if you just give us the cells that make you human.'

They stalked, they slithered, and edged, all the time getting closer. Halfway across the suite Kryten struck. His body swivelled and his fingers started hammering the command matrix.

Glass cylinders squished down from the ceiling. Five, ten, fifteen of them cannoned into the ground. The cobra was caught. So were Rimmer and the Cat. The Longman mechanoid shimmied right to avoid one, threw itself left to avoid a second, then, just as its eye-line was taken in avoiding a third, it ran straight into a fourth, which swooshed down from above.

Only the Longman-leopard was left.

It launched itself at Kochanski. Its claws, sharp as

lemon dropped in an open wound, razored towards her, ready to pluck her face off, as if it were a Hallowe'en mask. She opened her mouth and screamed as its paws landed firmly on her shoulders and sent her reeling backwards into a set of data banks. The creature arced down on top of her, its breath rabbiting down her throat. Then she felt its claws rip through her leather flight suit and slice into her skin with gut-sickening ease. She staggered backwards, momentarily dazed, almost relaxed, ready to submit to death.

Then the adrenalin poured into her brain, like the cavalry arriving.

For five years she'd trained in jujitsu and judo and now it all came down to whether she could execute one single throw.

A sacrifice throw, a sumigaeshi. It was her tokui – her favourite throw. Kochanski, the tori, swept her right leg inside the uke's left foreleg and fell backwards using her full body weight to sweep the leopard on to its back. She scrambled backwards on her bottom and clambered to her feet by the wall.

A waza-ari!

The Longman-leopard prepared to launch again. But she'd bought herself some time.

Kryten continued to pummel the keypads and a rain of glass cylinders squished down and then up and then down again as they negotiated their way across the floor.

Squish.

She moved right.

Squish.

The leopard moved left.

Squish.

The leopard seared through the air for a second time, its open claws sharking once more towards her face. She tried to move backwards and slipped. The creature swept down on top of her. She screamed as its claws clattered into the outside of the glass cylinder that had dropped on top of her. The cylinder squished back into the ceiling as she half-staggered, half fell into the middle of the suite.

The Longman-leopard swivelled and again started to move towards her.

A warm trickle of liquid dribbled between her breasts. Without taking her eyes off the leopard she ran her finger down her chest and tasted it. Blood? No, it had a warm glucose taste.

The luck virus.

She'd forgotten all about it. The leopard must have broken the glass vial. She dipped her finger into the tiny rivulet and drank some more. All she had to do now was persuade the leopard to have a game of poker with dukes wild and she'd be fine.

But what if this was the broccoli tube? Maybe they tasted similar. There was no way of telling.

She'd find out soon enough. Distractedly, she scratched her wrist and backed off around the chamber. There was something there. A rubber band; the chunky thick rubber band she'd absently taken from Rimmer's supply inventory. Things were looking up already – now she was armed.

In the right hands a rubber band could be a lethal weapon.

She laced it on to her second finger and wrapped it

around her thumb before lacing it back again on to her first finger. As a kid at school in Perth she'd been pretty good with rubber-band guns – she could usually hit a classmate's neck ten desks away.

The leopard launched itself through the air. She aimed, fired and flung herself left. The band ripped through the air, passed silently between the leopard's front legs and pinged its mighty right testicle. She watched as the leopard's expression shifted from snarling attack to puzzlement and then to intense pain. It lost interest in its prey, hit the floor, folded in two and started groaning quietly to itself.

That sure as hell wasn't down to any fast-growing broccoli virus. 'Squish it, Kryte.'

The glass cylinder swooped down and trapped the yammering creature in a prison of glass. Kochanski got to her feet. 'OK, do what you've gotta do and let's get the smeg out of here.'

Starbug purred through the mix of lava and mulch and broke the ocean surface in an explosion of foam. The Cat flicked the craft on to auto-pilot and joined the others in the mid-section.

Rimmer sat in front of the mainframe and closed down the com channel. 'That was the Head of Records in Cyberia. Seems Listy was sentenced to eighteen years' hard thought for leading the break-in.'

'And?' said Kryten, knowing from the tone of Rimmer's voice the news wasn't good.

'And he's no longer there. He escaped three weeks ago with some kind of morph; a symbiote or something. The point is that no one's got the faintest clue where he is now, although there's a substantial reward for his recovery.'

'He could be anywhere in the belt,' Kryten sighed. 'He could even have gone back through the Omni-zone. That's presumably where Mr Lister believed we were heading.'

Rimmer shook his head. 'Finding him is going to be next to impossible.'

Kochanski looped the vial of luck virus off her neck and held it up to the light. The liquid had clotted over the crack in the tube and a quarter remained. 'We've got to be able to use this somehow.' She pointed at the tube. 'The answer's in there somewhere.'

They stared at it – thinking.

Kryten began. 'What is luck? When a person is lucky – "on a roll" I believe is the vernacular – it seems to me they have the ability to influence and manipulate the physical environment. They're able to make a roulette wheel stop on a certain number, persuade others to do their bidding, browbeat fate into giving them what they most desire. How? There's only one explanation: if luck is some kind of positive infection then it must somehow enhance the individual's sixth sense, imbue them with new powers. After all, stopping a roulette wheel is a form of telekinesis.'

Kochanski nodded. 'If that's true, there are no boundaries to what this stuff can do. The only limitation will be our own imaginations.'

'OK, how about this?' said Rimmer. 'It breaks every known law of the universe, and some that are unknown too, but if Kryten's theory is right and seeing as we've got zero options – what the hell.'

'Go on,' said Kochanski, intrigued.

'We each take a sip of the luck virus and write down the coordinates of where we believe Lister is. If that stuff really works, then by pure luck we should each write down the same correct set of coordinates. Then we set a course.'

Kryten beamed. 'Bravo, Mr Rimmer, sir. A most meritorious scheme.'

The vial was passed around the table, and one by one they imbibed its contents.

Kochanski took the almost empty tube and hung it back around her neck. 'Poles: north is positive, south is negative. We should each have six figures with degrees and minutes. Good luck.'

They each wrote down a set of coordinates, folded the paper and placed it in a pile in the middle of the scanner table.

Rimmer opened the first. '25°, 46′ − 80°, 12′ − 34°, 54′.'

He opened the second piece of paper. '25°, 46′ − 80°, 12′ − 34°, 54′.'

The third. '25°, 46′ − 80°, 12′ − 34°, 54′.'

Finally he opened the last. '62°, 18′ − 21°, 37′. Whose is this?'

'Mine.' Kryten replied. 'I was using Johnstone's elliptical system. I didn't realize you'd be using the old galactic guide. Allow me to transpose the figures. First coordinate, 25°, 46′ − 80°, 12′. Third figure . . .'

They all yelled in unison: '34°, 54′.'

Kryten waddled up to the navi-comp.

Rimmer followed him. 'Where is it?'

Kryten logged in. 'According to the star charts it's a planet that's dangerously close to the event horizon of the aureole of black holes that rings the Omni-zone. In fact, it should get sucked past the event horizon any day now.'

'Then that's it. The event horizon's the point of no return. What's our ETA?'

Kryten loaded the information into the computer. 'At present speed we'll be there in . . .' A blip pinged up on to the computer screen, announcing the computer had finished computing the mathematics, '. . . thirty-two weeks.'

'Thirty-two weeks? That's way too late.'

The Cat picked up a pen and started to scribble furiously. 'Wait a minute, I'm getting an idea. OK, here it is. I'm just going to take a shot at guessing a new system of transport. I'm going to call it a hyper-drive. And it works like this – first you punch a hole in space, then you bend time and leap into the tenth dimension, harnessing something I'm going to call superstring. Here's the first bit of it: "$SD^{10} \times\ <Y^{\star}Y^{\star}Y = 2 \ldots$"

'What do you think?'

'Extraordinary. You've just correctly guessed the equation for hyper-space. What an astonishing piece of luck. Sir, I implore you, keep going. We need to know how we can produce the almost infinite amount of energy that's required to puncture the space/time continuum.'

'Lemme see,' said the Cat, licking the point of his pencil. 'Puncture the space/time continuum, eh? Create the required energy. Okey-dokey, here we gokey.' The

Cat started to scribble furiously again, covering the paper with his childlike scrawl.

Rimmer squinted down over his shoulder. 'Does this make sense? Can we use it?'

'The first part, the theoretical equation for hyper-space, is absolutely correct, sir. However, the computations after that will be a stroll into the unknown with a white cane. I suggest we log it into the computer and see what happens.'

CHAPTER 15

The small emerald planet teetered on the brink of the event horizon of the ambit of collapsed stars that acted as a protective membrane around the Omni-zone.

Down on the surface, gravity gales swept across a mackerel sky, as slowly, almost indiscernibly, the planet engaged in the final leg of a losing battle to remain in its own Universe.

Lister, Reketrebn, McGruder and the rest of the survivors huddled around a sad-looking fire, sipping the last of the soup supplies and staring down the massive canyon that looked as if it had been gouged out of the desert rock by a gigantic ice-cream scoop. In the distance, in front of a sky ripped through with fashionable cloud tears, the Rage patrolled the entrance to the underground caverns half a day's walk away. These were the planet's only safe houses when it finally lost its battle with gravity and was sucked through the aureole of black holes into the Omni-zone.

The Rage had won. It had successfully defended its planet from all comers. No one could survive here. No one could live on its surface. And now, vindictive to the end, it shielded the caverns from the survivors, ensuring their destruction when the planet passed through the ring of black holes.

Lister swirled a piece of bread around in his soup. They had to kill the Rage. It was their only hope.

But how? It was an entity composed of pure emotion, a force, an energy, something without conventional form or content, something without a heart or brain, something that was just a mass of seething resentment. Out of control. And determined to defend the planet from life, any life. A tiny smile jogged across his face as he watched Reketrebn, sitting opposite him, suddenly shape-shift into a variety of forms to lift him from his black dog. Henry VIII, Laurel and Hardy, Queen Victoria, Albert Einstein and various famous newscasters all morphed before him; all naked. This was Reketrebn's idea of a joke. It knew naked people always got a reaction. Finally, it shape-shifted back into its neutral form and smiled at Lister. 'There is not much time now. Half a day, maybe less.'

'We'll figure out a way. It's just we ain't thought of it yet.'

'That is not how you feel. You feel there is no way. You say these things to make me happy when I should feel afraid. Why?'

'I thought you could read my mind.'

'Sometimes. Other times I have to guess and I am wrong.'

'Guess anyway.'

'You lie because you care.'

'You think?'

'Yes. But when you don't lie does that mean you don't care?'

'You know what I'm thinking now?'

Reketrebn nodded. 'You're thinking, "Shut up, Reke-trebn, you're really beginning to get on my pecks."'

'You got it.'

As Reketrebn made to reply a noise of landing retros cut across him and the clay ceiling of the cave started to crumble. It was almost as if a spacecraft was trying to land on top of them.

Lister rushed outside on to the precipice overlooking the canyon and looked up at the roof. Tilting at a ridiculous angle was a small green craft lodged precariously in the foliage of the mountainside. The hatch door hinged open and a girl with lagoon-blue eyes and a pinball smile strode down the landing ramp.

A smile sawed Lister's face in half. 'Hey!'

'Hey!' She threw herself off the cave roof and landed on top of him. They hit the ground hard and rolled over and over in the dirt. They kissed: small and big. They devoured one another, they hugged, they laughed, they cried, they hugged some more, then they just looked at one another, holding hands and grinning like puppies. After that, to the distress of everyone watching, they started all over again from the top. Many minutes later, far more than it's interesting to recount, they emerged with kiss-smudged faces, grinning and breathless.

The Starbug crew stood in a horseshoe alongside Reketrebn, McGruder and the assortment of Gelfs. Lister grabbed its hand. 'Come on, you've got to meet the posse.'

Reketrebn stood in its neutral form. 'This is Reke-trebn, it's a symbi-morph, saved my life at least ten times, this is Mike McGruder.' McGruder smiled amiably and shook Kochanski's hand.

Then Lister remembered. 'Where is he?' He gazed around, looking for Rimmer. 'Man, come here, there's someone you've got to meet.' He beckoned him forward. 'Rim– uh, I mean, uh, Arn– uh, sir, uh. Over here.'

Rimmer stepped through the pack. Lister brought the two men together. 'I want you to meet Lieutenant-Colonel Michael R. McGruder.'

'Pleased to meet you, Lieutenant-Colonel,' Rimmer smiled courteously.

'And, Mike,' said Lister, pulling McGruder closer, 'this is Arnold J. Rimmer.' McGruder blinked twice, smiled sweetly, then six foot two inches of solid marine hit the dirt in a dead faint.

Rimmer smirked down at the pole-axed figure. 'Supposed to be a marine and he's fainted like a bloody girl guide. Who did you say he was?'

'His name is Michael McGruder. He's your son.'

'Pardon me?'

'I said, he's your son.'

'My *son*?'

'Yes.'

'*My* son?'

'Yes.'

'*My son*???'

'Yes.'

Rimmer cleared his throat and kicked some dirt about with his right foot. Then looked up again. 'Who is he?'

'He's your son, Rimmer.'

Rimmer looked at Lister, his head angled in bemusement. 'My son?'

'Yes.'

'That man there. The one who just fainted?'

'The one who's your son, yes. That one. He's your son.'

'Wait. It's terribly important that I get this clear in my head. Let me tell you what I think you're saying.' Rimmer tried to cough away a dry throat. 'You're saying that this man, this man, here, who is my son, is in fact, my son.'

There was a cloud of dust and Rimmer joined Mc-Gruder, belly up in the dirt.

CHAPTER 16

Rimmer watched Lister's face as his mouth opened and closed, garbling his version of what had happened.

He heard hardly a thing he said.

He was a father.

Him.

It was too bizarre for words. His son was almost the same age as he was; he'd had his ageing gene removed and appeared just a couple of years younger.

He had a son.

He hadn't even known he existed. He could have spent his whole life in ignorance.

He was lobotomized with shock. Yvonne McGruder had decided to have his child. If it hadn't been for the radiation leak and Red Dwarf having to be jettisoned off into the wastes of space, perhaps she might have tried to contact him. Maybe they would even have got together again.

Yvonne McGruder. She was really together and attractive and she'd had *his* son.

Lister's voice dragged him from his musings. 'Look, man, listen to me, this bit's important.'

'What bit?'

'Yvonne McGruder – she's been bottle-feeding him warm bull since the day he was born.'

'What do you mean? She's done a fantastic job. He's a space corps marine, an *SCM* – there isn't a finer soldier.'

'No, I mean about you. She's sort of given him the impression that you're some sort of . . . hero. He's kind of modelled his life on this father figure who's a mix of Patton, Nelson and Ulysses, all rolled into one. I've played along with it. Seemed no point in telling him. But now you're here. He'll know in two seconds you've got less backbone than custard. I think you've got to come clean with him before he works it out for himself.'

'Why would Yvonne tell him stuff like that?'

'What do you expect her to say? She'd just been let out of the concussion ward and got herself up the duff by a bloke who cleaned out chicken-soup dispensers?'

'She wasn't concussed,' Rimmer said emphatically.

'The point is that she left the ship at Miranda. As far as she knew the ship was lost and who was going to contradict her story?'

Rimmer nodded. He didn't blame Yvonne. Who wanted a father as ordinary as he was? After the ship was lost in Deep Space she could create anything she wanted and there was no one around to tell Michael any different.

For ten minutes Rimmer considered trying to keep up the pretence; perhaps he could pull it off. Arnold J. Rimmer – swashbuckling space adventurer. But the more he thought about it the more he knew it was an absurd idea and someone, if not him, would reveal the truth at some point. He had to face up to his first duty as a father. He had to go and tell his son that he was a worthless piece of crap.

★

'Damn it.' Kochanski hit the console with the palm of her hand and tried again. 'Come on, you son of a bitch, start.' She opened up the retros and listened to a sharp metallic clicking sound as the starter motor failed to ignite the engines.

Lister shook his head. 'They're dead. No charge. Same thing happened to the Volunteer ship. Some kind of pulse hit us shortly after we landed and knocked out all the power. It's something to do with the Rage; it's able to detect and neuter large electrical power sources.'

'What about Kryten and Rimmer? They're both part electrical.'

'I suppose their power sources are too small to detect.'

Kochanski tried the engines again, this time trying a mix of words cooed in encouragement before giving in to shouted obscenities. All to no avail.

Lister continued. 'If it's anything like last time, the Rage will make a move any moment. It'll want to total the ship before we're able to salvage too many supplies.'

Kryten stood in the open hatchway and gazed through a pair of unoculars across the plain. 'I believe it's started to make its move already, sir. At present speed it should be here within the hour.'

Lister turned and addressed the Cat and Reketrebn. 'Guys, get the others and start up the mountain with the heavy stuff. We'll catch you up. We'll be twenty minutes behind you, OK?'

The Cat and Reketrebn nodded and disappeared down the landing-ramp carrying a large wooden food crate. Lister and Kochanski started ransacking the galley while Kryten made a start on the obs deck.

No one had worked it out yet, and Kryten was thankful.

It gave him more time to make his preparations undisturbed. He climbed the steps up to the obs deck and got started.

With luck, he'd be far away and unstoppable before anyone even knew what he was up to.

The time had come.

CHAPTER 17

Rimmer found McGruder sitting on a rock staring across the canyon at the out-of-control gravity gales. For some time he just stood there, unsure how to open the conversation. Finally, it was McGruder who detected his presence and turned to face him. 'Beautiful view, isn't it? Or is that sort of thing, beautiful views I mean, not really of much interest to someone like you?'

Rimmer's weight shifted from foot to foot. 'No, it's uh, beautiful, yes.'

'Made a bit of an ass of myself back there. Fainting and what have you. Needed to be alone to sort of try and regain my composure.'

Rimmer studied some dirt on the ground and was lost for something to say.

'Don't suppose you've ever fainted, sir? Not really on, is it, for a man?'

Rimmer changed the subject with a grating of gears. 'Understand you're a SCM.'

'Yes, sir. West Point, sir. Fought on Hyperion in the Saturn war.'

Rimmer shook his head in amiable disbelief. 'A Space Corps Marine. You're the guys who say: "Smoke me a kipper, I'll be back for breakfast," before embarking on some damn fool mission to save the solar system.'

'It's just space-jock banter, sir.'

'And I understand you were decorated?'

'You've been an inspiration to me, sir. Always gave me something to look up to.'

'Yes, right.' For a second Rimmer was silent. 'Look, there's things we should talk about. Things you've been told which aren't true.'

'Sir?'

'Your mother, uh, she was a woman. A very remarkable woman. It can't have been easy bringing up a boy on geo-mapper's wages, getting you through college and into the Academy. Some people, and I used to count myself among them, believe there's a class system and someone like you – who doesn't have a completely pukka background – would never be admitted into such high-ranking company. That's bullshit. Your mother went out and proved that. She got you through college, she got you through the Star Fleet and now here you are, an SCM. She's a remarkable woman, a truly courageous, remarkable woman.'

'It's you who were my inspiration, sir.'

Rimmer shook his head. 'You owe everything to her. Everything. She really made you into something. Something you should be proud of.' Rimmer looked out over the canyon. 'When I tell you what she had to do, to make you into that something, I don't want to hear you feel let down or resentful.' Rimmer rubbed his eye-socket and continued. 'I'm not going to lie to you, uh, do you mind if I call you Michael?'

'I'd be honoured, sir.'

'You can call me, uh, you know, if you want.'

'Sir?'

'Father, or Dad, or whatever.'

'Really, sir?'

'Anyway, where was I? Oh, yes, your mother. The thing is, I never really knew your mother. It was . . .' Rimmer was going to say 'a one-night stand', but suddenly the phrase stuck in his throat, like a second adam's apple. He couldn't say that to his son. 'What I'm saying is, I'm not who you think I am. I'm not special. In fact, *you* are everything I ever aspired to.' Rimmer looked into his son's clear green eyes. 'I'm nobody, Michael. I could have been, even should have been, but I blamed all my failings and shortcomings on my parents, and that's a well that never runs dry.'

'She always said you were fantastically modest.'

Rimmer shook his head. 'I'm not modest. I'm not an officer, either. It was always my great passion, but I never made it. Not good enough. I'm sorry, but your mother invented a father figure for you – to give you something to live up to. I'm just a technician. I never even managed to pass the astro-engineering exam. Didn't have the right stuff. In fact, coming here today and telling you this is the only gutsy thing I've ever done in my whole life.'

An alloy of emotions passed across McGruder's face, an ugly mixture of disbelief, betrayal and contempt.

'You're a technician?'

'Yes.'

'What class?'

'Third,' Rimmer mumbled quietly.

'That's beverage maintenance.'

Rimmer stood straight-backed. 'Yes.'

McGruder savaged him with a look of utter disparagement and stomped off back to the caves.

Kryten glanced over his shoulder as he shuffled down the Starbug's storage deck. He was alone. Excellent. He reached the far wall and stood before a multi-coloured facia. He typed an override code on to the keypad and the door to the vault opened with a smoky sigh. Again, he checked he was alone, then he entered the vault.

His olfactory system went into a system–alert mode. He didn't know what was wrong with it just lately. It had constantly been alerting him for no reason at all; possibly he had mechaneumonia. He'd have to replace the whole unit the first chance he got. He opened his chest plate and closed the system down.

The storage vault was a circuit board of tall thin corridors. He followed the alphabetically marked floor-to-ceiling expanse of storage drawers, making numerous lefts and rights before he reached the letter 'O'. A mechanoid bray of triumph breezed out of his voice unit. He pulled the sliding tubular aluminium stepladder underneath the storage box he desired and swiftly climbed the steps. Again he typed in a pass–code. A box zinged out of the wall. He typed in a second pass–code and the box opened silently. He reached in and took hold of a vacuum flask, spun off the top and took out a tiny pink disk. He hurried down the stepladder and made his way to the exit.

All he had to do now was feed the oblivion virus into his own network and walk across the canyon and meet the Rage. When the gestalt entered him, it too would become contaminated, its energy force would be neutered by the electric-killing virus and, although he would be terminated, the Rage would be slain. That was why his plan had to remain a secret. If he'd suggested it to Lister and the others they would have forbidden it and then his CPU wouldn't have allowed him to carry it out. However, if he didn't tell them he could loophole his way around his programming. This was clearly the only solution to their dilemma; resisting his scheme would simply result in everyone winding up dead; it was his role as the least important member of the crew to make the obvious sacrifice.

He hurried down the aisle and walked into a bank of storage units. A dead end. In his musings he'd missed a turn. He started to retrace his steps. He'd never noticed before how dark it was in the storage vaults, just the low neons casting sober orange fingers over the floors and walls. Left, right, left. Again he walked into a dead end. Did this have something to do with his olfactory system? He decided to turn it back on. He opened his chest plate and flicked it back on-line. The system-alert mode was still engaged. It was telling him there was code 0089/2 in the local vicinity. Kryten searched through his long-term memory banks to discover what a 0089/2 was – he had a feeling it was either the sweet fragrance of a blossoming peach tree or a decomposing body. His long-term memory informed him that he could rule out the blossoming-peach-tree possibility. In a way that made quite a lot of sense to Kryten, in that blossoming peach trees were generally thin on the ground in storage vaults. This left him with the second possibility.

How could it be true? Apart from anything else, there wasn't anyone around who could be dead. Everyone was alive and accounted for.

It must be his olfactory system that was faulty. He made a right and saw two feet sticking out behind a bale of storage drawers. Two feet; whose, it was impossible to tell. What sex or species was also impossible to guess. Kryten began the very long walk up to them. As he walked he started to eliminate all the people those feet couldn't belong to. Long before he reached them he knew whose they were. A stalactite of panic sliced through his being. Then a high-pitched squeaking noise made him spin round. It was the sound of the giant wheel on the reinforced steel doors being spun shut as the storage vault was locked from the outside.

CHAPTER 18

The bottom, sides and top had fallen out of Michael McGruder's world. He sat huddled in front of an unnecessarily chirpy fire and tried to sift through the events of this quite unbelievable day. All his life he'd believed in this God-like father figure: all through his childhood, all through Cadet school, all through the Star Fleet he'd been plutonium driven to succeed, to live up to the unattainable. Now it turned out his father was nothing more than a chicken-soup-machine mainten-ance repairman.

A third technician, for God's sake. A zero. A nobody. Images from his past flicked into his mind, like shots from a slide show. Had he ever been more completely betrayed? He saw his girlfriend, Mercedes, still-framed, clutching the corner of the sheet and holding it up against her naked body; his eyes panned right, almost in slow-motion, and there was his best friend, Ben. Their Star Fleet apartment, their bed. He felt worse now. At least Mercedes and Ben weren't a lifetime of betrayal, not like his father.

He started to choke, dry-retching, gasping for air. He couldn't breathe.

The garrotte flashed over his head and dragged him

backwards along the cave floor. He kicked helplessly, vainly trying to get his hands between the thin metal wire and the soft skin of his throat. Suddenly, gaffer tape was wrapped expertly across his mouth and round his head; then he was rolled on to his front and the tape was round his wrists, and then on his back again and he could see his attacker.

It was Lister.

At least, it looked like Lister.

Rimmer stood in the mouth of the cave and watched bewildered as the two men rolled around in the dirt. Suddenly, the man sitting astride his son turned and saw him.

Lister's other self: he was still alive.

Alive? But how? It wasn't possible. He'd been taken by the Kinitawowis.

Lister's other self regarded him through hooded eyes as a smile as thin as melba toast edged across his lips. 'Hi, there.'

'You.'

Lister's other self sprayed a staccato snigger into the chilling afternoon air. 'You just can't keep a bad guy down.'

A twinkle of gun-metal grey flecked into Rimmer's peripheral vision. Four feet to his right lay Lister's other self's IR pistol. All he had to do was make two strides, bend and pick it up.

This was his moment.

Four feet away. Two strides. Pick up the pistol and point it at Lister's head. Bark out an order to get the hell off his goddamned son and march the punk out of the cave. He would still be a third technician, he'd still be a nobody who had never navigated his way up the ziggurat of command, but at least in some small way he'd have proved himself in front of Michael.

Rimmer watched as Lister's face etiolated with shock as he realized the rad pistol was nearer Rimmer than him.

Rimmer grinned. This was his moment. All he had to do was pick up the rad gun, stick it in his ear and march him out of the cave. He'd be a hero. He'd have saved the day. And wouldn't that be sweet.

Then a voice. Somewhere inside Rimmer's head.

Hero? Who the hell was he kidding? Any jerk could do what he was about to do. He was just lucky enough to chance along at the right time and find himself standing next to the pistol. It was hardly the stuff of the SMCs; he wasn't exactly uzi-ing the door in and walking behind a blazing bazookoid.

Then he would have been a hero.

But this? This was kiddy stuff. And anyway, why should he have to prove himself to Michael? His son would have to learn that there's more to life than being a great soldier. If they were to have any kind of relationship he'd have to learn to care for Rimmer for what he was, with all his failings. And if he couldn't do that unless his old man turned out to be Tommy Testosterone, Space Marine, that was just tough.

Lister's other self's foot lanced into Rimmer's solar plexus and he hammered backwards into the cave wall, still enraptured by his own thoughts. A punch sent him caroming sideways and a second kick to his temple forced him backwards on to the hard stone floor. Lister's doppelgänger picked up the rad pistol, twirled the rad setting to neuter and pointed it at Rimmer's groin. 'On your feet.' He jabbed a look at McGruder. 'You too.' The two men got to their feet.

McGruder's eyes stood on tiptoe above an oblong of masking tape and drilled into Rimmer. Why hadn't he grabbed the gun? He'd had a chance to take the guy out and he'd botched it. What the hell else could you expect from a mookle who fixed chicken-soup machines for a living?

He'd botched it.

His bloody father had botched it.

Kryten stared down at the four dead Kinitawowi tribes-people. They'd never left the ship. Lister's other self had regained consciousness at some point during the walk through the decom chamber and had managed to over-power all four of them. Now he was out there some-where and the Rage was only fifteen – perhaps twenty – minutes away. He tapped the pink disk of the oblivion virus on his open palm, the disk that was utterly useless while he was still locked in here.

A syringe of air signalled the wheel on the vault door was being spun open. The door yawned wide and Rimmer was shoved inside. It closed again.

Rimmer started to explain. 'He didn't leave . . .'

Kryten stopped him with a nod of the head. 'I know. I found the Kinitawowis.'

'He's got Michael.'

Kryten's eyes closed softly in sympathy.

'And I had a chance to nail the son of a bitch and I blew it. It was all there – the pistol, my moment to make everything OK – and I blew it.'

Kryten knelt by his side and patted him softly on the back.

'I blew it.'

'Sir, I . . .'

'I blew it, Kryten.'

'Sir, it's imperative we get out of here. I suggest we cover every inch of the storage vault to see if there's any possible escape route.'

'Haven't you already done that?'

'Twice, sir.' Kryten shrugged. What else was there to do?

Rimmer mopped his face with the flat of his hand and nodded.

They began their search, first examining the locking mechanism on the vault door and then following the walls round the room, looking for air vents.

'I'm a father, you know. I still can't believe it.'

'I heard, sir.' Pause. 'You must be very proud.'

'He's not. He's about as thrilled as Edward II when they started to heat up the poker. Understood I was some kind of one-man army.'

'Resenting their parents is the human way, sir. Black widow spiders eat their mates after sex, humans blame their parents for all their failings. It's the characteristic which makes you lovably idiotic to all the other species.'

'What are you saying, Kryten?'

'I'm saying, why are you surprised your son resents you, sir? He can't help it, he's a human.'

'But I don't want him to resent me, I want him to think I'm OK. I've missed the first forty years of his life. Now I want him to . . . like me.'

'Look!'

'Yes?' Rimmer waited for him to make his next point.

'Look!' Kryten repeated. Rimmer swivelled. Kryten was pointing to the four-inch-wide oxygeneration outlet pipe that surfaced by the pump-housing in the corner of the vault.

'It's an oxygeneration outlet pipe – so what?'

'Sir, if I turned your light bee off and set it to delay-timer mode, then brought it back on-line again, say sixty seconds later, we could push your light bee down the outlet pipe and it'd drop through to the quarters below.'

'Or, alternatively, it could wind up in the oxygeneration unit itself.'

'That is a possibility.'

'Where I'd get minced.'

'The plan does have a down side, I must confess.'

'A down side? Is that what it is?'

'However, if the scheme were to succeed, you'd re-materialize on the deck below and be able to sound the alarm. We could attempt to rescue your son Michael.'

'No. I'm sorry. It's too risky.'

'Very well, sir.'

'And don't try and change my mind. It won't work.'

'No, sir.'

They walked along in silence for almost twenty seconds. 'You're doing it on purpose, aren't you?'

'Sir?'

'Creating this incriminating silence. Stop it.'

'Sir?'

'I'm warning you, Kryten, if you continue this voice-less, unspoken disapproval, you're on charge.'

'Sir?'

'You know what I'm talking about; now just quit it. Talk, or hum, or whistle, or something. But no more accusing silences. Got it?'

'Yes, sir.'

Pause.

'You're doing it again!'

'I can't think of anything to say, sir.'

'Hum, then.'

'Yes, sir. Permission to hum, sir?'

'Granted.' Rimmer sighed impatiently.

Kryten began humming a plaintive version of 'Danny Boy'.

Eventually Rimmer caught on.

'"Oh Dannyboy, the pipes the pipes are calling . . ." I've seen mud guards on boy racer Mustangs that weren't as low as you.' He exhaled and contemplated the floor. After several seconds he looked up. 'Right, very well, OK. I must have less brains than the offspring of a village idiot and a TV weathergirl – I'll do it.'

Kryten beamed munificently. 'Good decision, sir.' He clicked on the pressure point at the back of Rimmer's neck and turned off his hard-light drive. His form faded away with an electronic sigh and all that was left of Red Dwarf's third technician was his light bee, which hovered three feet off the ground, moving in tiny unsteady circles. Kryten took hold of the bee, flipped open its top and started to examine its workings.

Several minutes later he unscrewed the outlet pipe's gauze cover and dropped the delay-timered bee down the tube.

The bee clanged down the pipe, slaloming round

corners, ricocheting down the colon of tubing, pinging back and forth across the narrow passageways as it fell through the oxygeneration system until, almost forty seconds later, it bounced out of an outlet valve and rolled across the grilled flooring of E-deck's gantry. It rolled across the five-foot walk-way before plummeting over the edge and smacking on to D-deck's gantry one hundred feet below. Again it rolled across the walkway and teetered on the edge of the grille overlooking the small sewage plant on C-deck. Spinning like a drunken room, it hugged the very edge of the walkway before it waltzed back into the middle of the gantry and slowly spun to a halt. Finally the light bee toppled on to its side and rocked back and forth on its axis. Seconds later Rimmer burgeoned back into existence, and found himself on the paint-shop gantry on D-deck. He went to find the others.

Kochanski and Lister piled the palettes of freeze-dried fruits on to the loading truck. She was just finishing her account of what had happened on the Mayflower: the Longmans, discovering the vials of the luck virus, when she heard the soft hum of ionizing radiation being pumped into an IR pistol's discharge tube. They looked up.

Lister's other self gestured for them to drop the peaches as he yanked McGruder on a wire garrotte across F-deck. 'Better put me back on your Christmas-card list, kids.'

Lister frowned disbelievingly. 'You left the ship with the Kinitawowis. Kryten saw you.'

'No, he saw me enter the decom-chamber.'

'You've been around since then?' asked Kochanski. 'When we were on the Mayflower? All that time?'

Lister's other self cheesed a grin. 'Got a mite messed up when I had my altercation with the Kinitawowis. Couldn't make my comeback until I'd healed up a little.'

Lister's other self ripped the gaffer tape off McGruder's mouth and yanked the garrotte around his neck. 'Tell them what I want.'

'He wants the escape pod,' McGruder wheezed through the choking wire noose.

'What escape pod?' asked Kochanski, deadpan.

Lister's other self tightened the noose around McGruder's neck. 'Back in the days when I had a craft our Starbug had an escape pod.'

'Yeah?' said Lister.

'Powered by solar energy. I don't suppose you guys'd possess such a thing? No point in all of us dying. You got one?'

They said 'no' in unison.

'Thought so. Used to be on C-deck. Grab the supplies and let's take a look.'

'Look, you want to take it,' Kochanski spat, 'go and take it. There's no time to screw around. The gestalt is going to be here in less than fifteen minutes and if that doesn't wipe us out, the crossing into the Omni-zone will. Take the damned pod and get the hell out of here, and let us get the hell out of here too.'

Lister's other self grinned. '*You* can come with me, doll. Plenty of room for you if we scrunch up.'

'Thanks for the offer, but sadly I'm sane.'

He tugged again on McGruder's garrotte. 'I'm serious.'

'So am I.'

'Stay here, sweetheart, and you're going to get wiped.'

Lister interjected, 'Take the EP and vamoose, OK?'

His other self continued, 'And if you get wiped, what happens to the human race?'

Kochanski eyed him narrowly. 'I wouldn't go with you if you were the last guy in the Universe.'

'I'm going to be.' Lister's other self smiled. 'Certainly the last guy around here who can have children.' Without warning he pointed the rad pistol at Lister's crotch and fired a volley of radiation into his groin. Lister folded like an origami figure and hit the floor, clutching himself.

'Because from this moment on your boyfriend's as sterile as a surgeon's scalpel.'

Kochanski fell by his side.

'Bambinos for you guys? Sadly, no longer possible.' Lister's other self tugged McGruder over to the moaning Lister who was now gently being comforted by Kochanski. 'So how about it? Me and you – what do you say?'

Slowly, Kochanski clambered to her feet and ran at him, screaming. He spun the rad setting and put two volleys of laser into her: one in her shoulder, the other in her left knee. She stumbled but didn't fall as she staggered towards him, vainly trying to get within kicking distance of his head. A third beam struck her left thigh and she flailed and fell.

Lister's other self stood over her and pointed the rad pistol into the middle of her forehead. 'I'm going to ask you one last time for a date. If the answer's still no, something really tragic is going to happen. So whaddayasay? Want to be my Eve? I'll buy you a fig leaf.'

'Go screw a dog.'

Lister's other self shook his head sadly as he re-cocked the pistol.

Kochanski sucked her right index finger. 'You evil bastard,' she said quietly.

'Say "hi" to Jesus for me.' He pulled the trigger.

Rimmer hurried along the paint-shop gantry, past the shelves stacked with giant cans of green emulsion lined with river drips of dried paint and moved towards the bulkhead wall. Several floors above he could make out a vague mix of voices.

He reached the hatchway and discovered it was locked. He doubled back and tried the hatchway at the opposite end of the gantry. That was locked too.

He was trapped.

He spun round, looking for another exit point. There wasn't one. He was a prisoner.

For several minutes he ransacked the shelves of equipment looking for help. Then he turned up one of the Mayflower's old astro-strippers Kryten had bought from the Kinitawowis. He unhooked it from the shelf and laid it out on the floor. Astro-strippers were used for mining ore and burning old paint off ships or research centres before they were repainted. The harness was intended to be worn over the shoulders; the front had a brutal-looking torch-gun funnel that jetted flame sixty feet, while the back had a second funnel that threw out a power jet so the pilot could transport himself around the outside of the ship when preparing the metal for new paintwork. Rimmer checked the tanks: both booster and flame tank were a quarter full, more than enough for him to torch his way through the hatchway lock. He hauled the harness over his head and tried to click the buckles closed.

The harness webbing wouldn't reach. Five, maybe six inches short. Who'd last worn this? A hugely overweight pigmy? He adjusted the straps to their maximum length and tried again. Still he couldn't press the stud key into its buckle. Maybe if he did just the top one that would hold it.

It did. Just.

He looked for the control stick; it was behind his back, near the booster funnel. Why put it there?

Who had designed this thing?

He twisted to examine the facia. He'd seen Lister use one once when he'd been put on punishment detail and had to strip and paint a hundred-yard section of Red Dwarf's hull.

He swivelled the joystick and clicked on the stripper flame, but instead of a controlled jet of flame pouring out of the funnel on his chest plate his rear booster flared into life and propelled him twenty feet backwards across the gantry corridor, over the railing and into the 300-yard drop before it politely clicked off, leaving him to plummet groundwards.

He had the damned thing on backwards. That's why the straps were so tight. As he plunged towards the sewage tank below he swivelled and tried desperately to refire the booster jet. His fingers groped blindly across the controls before he engaged the twin stripper/booster auto switch whereupon both funnels flared into life.

Three feet from the sewage tank the flame hit the methane of the raw sewage and powered him back into the air like an old Apollo space rocket. Blindly · he groped and fumbled about with the joystick, trying to guide the human fireball he'd now become as he ricocheted off the hull walls and powered upwards.

Lister's other self stood over the motionless body of Kristine Kochanski as she lay on the floor. Her lagoon-blue eyes were open, wide and defiant. She licked her right index finger, called him a bastard and watched him pull the trigger. Lister was helpless, nauseated and feeble from his radiation blast, and McGruder, his hands bound and his neck leaking blood from the garrotte, was equally powerless.

The barrel of the gun rested on a cobbled street of perspiration that ran across Kochanski's brow. Lister's other self pulled the trigger. There was a hollow click as the rad pistol's chamber jammed.

Kochanski stroked the neck of the tube that hung around her neck and licked her finger again.

He fired. Hollow click. Jammed again. He fired a third time. Same. And again and again. Each time his pistol jammed.

She licked her finger and looked up at him, almost smiling. Then he realized. He'd heard them talk about the luck virus as he crawled about the vent shafts waiting to heal, but he'd never seen it. That's why she kept licking her finger. The bitch was taking the luck virus and making the pistol jam. He held her hand down by her side. 'No luck virus this time, sweet pea.'

He started to squeeze the trigger again. Inch by inch

he pulled it back until one inch away from discharging the deadly bolt of radiation into Kochanski's head – something happened.

A noise. A strange roaring noise that distracted him from his task. Lister's doppelgänger swivelled left and looked out over the gantry rail. The sound grew louder until suddenly, in a roasting typhoon of dust, a mighty bird rose, phoenix-like, into view, vomiting flame.

Lister's doppelgänger shielded his eyes from the light and peered into the blinding dust storm as the twin jets of flame powered over the group in a sting of singed hair. The phoenix screamed off along the length of the gantry before it turned and, to the accompaniment of a screaming man, strafed them a second time. Lister's other self dived headlong behind a pile of freeze-dried almond crates, dragging McGruder with him.

Once again the fireball dressed in an impenetrable coat of smoke and flame ping-ponged down the length of the deck. Lister's other self watched it go. 'What the hell is that?'

McGruder turned to look at his captor. 'What the hell is that? I'll tell you what the hell that is – that's my Pop.'

'Your what?'

'And you better look out, Mister,' said McGruder in his best western drawl, 'because he's come for his boy.'

Rimmer's wails of terror were buried under the booster's roar as he ricocheted off three cargo-bay walls, flattened out and scorched the gantry floor with a new orange carpet of fire.

A banshee wail, a deafening whoosh and the four

almond crates imploded in a series of pretty blue-and-red mushrooms. McGruder whooped in delight. Lister's doppelgänger dropped the garrotte and dived for cover.

Rimmer cannoned down the deck, smacked into the far wall, scraped a ceiling joist and started to make the return journey.

Lister's other self walked to the middle of the gantry floor. He placed both his hands on the butt of his pistol to steady it and took careful aim. The Rimmerteer powered towards him.

He squeezed the trigger and two rad bolts sizzled past the astro-stripper and exploded in muffled yelps in the far hull wall.

Twenty yards away Kochanski huddled with Lister behind a forklift truck. 'He's aiming for his light bee,' Lister croaked. 'If he hits it, it's curtains.'

Two more radiation bolts flared towards the advancing phoenix. Rimmer fumbled behind his back and angled left to avoid the first one and right to avoid the second; slowly but surely he was mastering the controls of the backward astro-stripper. Hell, he was almost beginning to enjoy it.

Almost.

He looked down at Michael, who stood behind a crate of burning almonds, his face blackened like a Caribbean red snapper, gazing adoringly up at him. Two more rad bolts hissed towards him; again he dodged left and right.

Lister's other self watched him bearing down. He steadied the pistol on the side of a crate and waited until Rimmer was almost on top of him.

Rimmer groped behind his back and searched for the flame control. He intended to increase it to maximum just as he passed overhead. That would give his jet another ten feet of flame and hopefully persuade Lister's doppelgänger to call it a day. He powered down once more and squeezed off the extra jet.

Lister's other self released his next two bolts; the first missed, the second hawked into Rimmer's shoulder, disrupting his hard-light transmission and causing his body to go into an electric spasm of blue light that ripped around his body like a frightened angel fish. Seconds later it fizzled out as the light bee fought to restore normal transmission.

When it cleared Lister's other self was crumpled on the floor, his rad pistol abandoned as he tried to put out the blaze that was engulfing his right arm. Rimmer had scored a direct hit.

He peered down and saw Michael standing in an aisle of flaming grates, waving up at him, wearing a giant grin. An avalanche of joy poured through him.

He'd done it. He'd damn well done it. He scorched around the cargo bay once more, banking right around a tight corner before loop-de-looping and levelling out again.

Three decades of misery were banished. The creature that had roamed the plains of his soul, devouring his confidence, paralysing his initiative and poisoning his self-esteem, was slain. His neuroses crumbled like banks of sugar candy as self-confidence began to drip-feed into his psyche.

At last he'd done something right. He was OK. He was an OK guy. Okaaaaaaaaaaaaaaayyyyyyyyyyyyyyyyyyyy.

That's what he was. He was Okaaaaaaaaaaaaaaaaaaa-aaaaaaaaaaaaayyyyyyyyyyyyyyyyyyyy. And not only he thought so; his son Michael thought so too.

He caromed around the cargo bay a final time as Lister and Kochanski hollered up at him, jumping and waving.

Another flaming loop-de-loop. He could really drive this thing.

Crrrrrrrkkkkkk. He glanced at his shoulder, the shoulder the rad bolt had impacted against. The frazzled belt buckle had started to shear.

Crrrrrrrrrkkkkkk. Again. Now it was only hanging to his body by five thin strands of cotton and he was sixty feet from the ground, screaming round the cargo bay at sixty miles an hour. Crrrrrrkkkkkkkkkkkkkkk. The astro-stripper slipped off his left shoulder. He dropped thirty feet before he managed to haul the shoulder harness back on again.

Crrrrrrkkkkkkkkkkkkkkkkkkkkkkkk. Three strands.

He had to land. He swivelled and managed to flick the boosters on to hover mode, but he couldn't land and hold the harness simultaneously.

Lister's other self sculled along the floor on his one good arm and grabbed hold of the discarded rad pistol. He balanced the barrel of the gun on the side of a crate and pointed it at his target hovering helplessly thirty feet off the ground.

There was no time to use the escape pod now. He needed that astro-stripper. It was the only means of escape.

He squeezed the trigger. The rad bolt hummed through the air and hit the light bee full on. It erupted in a sad blue flare. Rimmer's image corrupted and shut down, and what remained of the carcass of his bee fell to the ground with a hollow clunk.

McGruder staggered across to where Lister's other self was slumped against the crate and hit him over the head with his two bound hands. He sat on him; demonized by fury, he started to bang his head against the floor. His screams and sobs swirled around the cargo bay before they were drowned by a new sound.

The sound of the Rage. It was upon them. Its wind seared though the cargo decks and began to engulf them.

They huddled behind the crates, which offered scant protection as the Rage bathed them in its waves of rancorous bile. Minutes later they were all baptized in hatred, saturated with the gestalt's malevolence, pulverized by a fury that whispered to each of them of some dreadful, intangible injustice that was never made clear. Then it was gone, swirling off the ship and continuing its cattle drive of virulence across the planet's surface.

Lister stood. 'We have to form a Circle of Sacer Facere.' His face was grey and hollowed, his mouth drained of all saliva, while a new set of facial expressions, driven by his darkest emotions, changed the character of his face. 'We have to form a circle. One of us will die.'

Kochanski, her eyes stabbed through with scintillas of fury, her lips bubbling spittle, said, 'No. There has to be another way. There has to be.'

'There is no other way,' McGruder thundered above the arguing voices. 'We're possessed by the Rage. It's only by channelling its poison into someone, and inviting it to consume them, that any of us will survive.'

Something caught Kochanski's eye. She turned to see Lister's other self making off across the deck, nursing his wounded arm. She stumbled after him, dragging her injured knee across the charred deck, and finally brought him down with a flying body check. She stood over him, her face engorged with venom. 'You caused this, you piece of scum. Without you we'd be out of here. History.' She started to pummel his chest with her white-knuckled fists until she was restrained by Lister. 'We've got to form the circle of Sacer Facere, before we all kill each other,' he said again.

The four of them sat in a tight circle and held hands. Lister gazed across at Kochanski and she returned his scared smile. One of the four would die, one of them would be taken by the Rage, one of them would be devoured by its fury.

Lister felt the clamminess of his other self's palm, straining to be released, straining to be no part of the circle. He held him on one side while McGruder held him on the other.

Then there was a sound. Almost indiscernible. But growing. Getting louder and louder until finally the banshee shriek of a plague of dying locusts emerged from within them. A chill wind riddled with the faces of demons started to swirl through the circle, entering their bodies by mouth or ear and leaving them in the same way.

Round it went. Faster and faster.

Lister's other self gazed at Kochanski; amused by her fear. His eyes dropped down her body, drawn by two small test tubes hanging round her neck.

The luck virus.

He thrust himself backwards to create some slack and then yanked himself forward; his tongue flicked over her skin before he scooped the tubes into his mouth and ripped the chain from around her neck. His teeth crunched triumphantly through the tube into the sweet tasting liquid.

The glucose gushed over his tongue. He had taken the luck virus. He felt its sparkling force twinkle through his body. Now he was safe. The Rage would choose another.

The Rage entered him, but he wasn't concerned, he knew it would pass him by. And so it did, as round it went; faster and faster, growing in power, growing in strength.

Now it was in McGruder and then Kochanski and then Lister and then back again.

It was in him once more. He felt its power, and tasted its awesome promises. Then it left him and entered McGruder. But he wanted it to stay, to possess him, to engorge him with its power.

He wanted the Rage.

They all wanted the Rage. Soon they were all screaming, pleading with it to choose them, to apotheosize them.

But only one of them had taken the luck virus.

And the luck virus made your dreams come true. The Rage chose him.

He let out a sob of ecstasy and felt the full onslaught of its power before his body was seared by an acid wind that cleaned him of his flesh. His bones tumbled to the ground.

CHAPTER 19

Lister watched as McGruder stooped and picked up his father's devastated light bee. The minute holographic projection device rolled across his open palm, mutilated and corrupted beyond repair. He could tell from the way McGruder's face had surrendered into an expressionless grey mask, punctured by two tiny, hopeless eyes ringed with tear skids, what was going through his mind. He knew he was thinking he would have given anything to bring Rimmer back. He knew he was thinking he would have given anything to have had a few precious minutes with him to make his peace. Now it was too late. He was gone. Lister knew all this because he was thinking exactly the same thing.

He pulled himself upright. The pain in his groin had faded into a bearable ache. But he'd never have children now.

Never. His lungs drew in a huge breath of air as the shock of the news filtered into his brain.

Never.

It had always struck him as deeply ironic that someone who had specialized in dodging responsibility – someone who'd left his job as a Megamart shopping-trolley collector because he wanted to get off the career-rung rat-race – should wind up having the greatest responsibility of all: safeguarding the future of his species. In his early twenties he found it tough to write and post a letter. He'd ridden around on his first 250 cc motorbike and never even bothered to get a licence. Too much hassle. Strings would break on his guitar and he'd make do without them. Ironed shirts were for snobs. He had the drive and ambition of a sleeping hippy. He'd borrowed a book from the library called *How to Get Your Life Together*, forgotten to read it and didn't take it back for three whole years. And when he finally did he had to explain to the chief librarian why there was a piece of fossilized popadom preserved between pages forty-two and forty-three. A together guy he was not.

But whether he liked it or not, fate had chosen him.

He was the one. The last human.

He had to change. He had to get his smeg together. And with Rimmer's bureaucratic cajoling, somehow he did. He smiled. Rimmer's micro-minded mentality and love of order and routine had actually helped him. Forced him to grow up.

They'd headed back towards Earth.

Along the way they'd located Kochanski's ashes and her life was resurrected in a backwards reality. For a while he had thought he was going to pull it off. He thought, maybe he could do this, somehow, somewhere, bring about the restoration of the human race. Now that hope was dead.

The dull burn in his crotch told him that.

He'd failed. He'd blown it. He could feel the swamp of depression ready to engulf him.

Suddenly, the ground shook as a massive tremor

ripped the planet and roused him from his dark brood-
ings. Now was not the time to think about this.

The next ten minutes seemed to go in slow-motion.
Slurred by grief and self-recrimination, he and Mc-
Gruder hauled down the spare astro-strippers from the
paint shop while Kochanski ran off in search of
Kryten.

A second tremor rifled through the ship. The planet
was minutes away from the event horizon. The gravitational allure of the ring of black holes was now close to
irresistible.

They ran down the gantry refuelling the spare strip-
pers and grabbing any supplies they could carry as
Kochanski emerged with Kryten.

Minutes later they scrambled down the disembarkation ramp, cranked on the astro-stripper's back-boosters
and were soon speeding across the planet's surface in
search of the Cat, Reketrebn and the others.

They found them negotiating a mountain precipice,
making their way down the valley towards the sanctuary
of the caverns. The Cat scanned the group of three.
'Where's Goalpost head?' Lister placed a hand on the
Cat's shoulder and shook his head. The Cat frowned,
not understanding. McGruder held out Rimmer's
broken light bee.

'Man,' was all the Cat was able to say. 'Oh, man.'

The night sky was ravaged by glowering thunder clouds
driven across a whisky-sodden moon by the merciless
gravity storm. Lister took out his unoculars and studied
the entrance to the limestone caverns six hundred feet
below. Above the entrance, like a guard dog, the Rage

swirled in a tight protective circle. It was back in position.

Kryten checked the geiger reading on his psi-scan. 'According to the radiation read-out, we're six minutes, twenty seconds away from the event horizon.

'If we're not 1,500 feet below in five minutes' time we're all going to wind up with less life than a Cornish discothèque.'

'But how do we navigate our way past the Rage?' asked the Cat.

Kryten slipped off his backpack and started to unload a computer. 'I anticipated this, sir. Indeed, I intended to engage the Rage earlier but your other self locked me in the storage vault.' He unscrewed a vacuum-sealed flask and took out a small pink disk.

'The oblivion virus?'

'The Rage is an electrical energy force. In theory, the oblivion virus has the capability to disarm its electrical charge.'

'So if we can infect the Rage, we can incapacitate the gestalt . . .'

'Theoretically.'

'But how?' asked Kochanski. 'Someone would have to . . .'

'I volunteer, ma'am.'

'No way, Kryten,' said Lister.

'Then we will all die, sir.'

'No.'

'There are no alternatives, bud.'

'I don't care, man. We've already lost Rimmer. We're not losing Kryten too.'

'Sir, listen to me, I implore you. If you do not allow

me to do this then all of us will be lost. My death will allow you to enter the caverns, where you have an eleven to four chance of survival.'

'What's that?' asked Reketrebn.

Lister shook his head. 'I don't care that it's illogical. I don't give a toss that it doesn't make sense. I'm not giving you permission to over-ride your programming and do this. We'll stay on the surface and take our chances.'

'What's that?' Reketrebn repeated.

'What's what?' asked Kochanski.

Reketrebn pointed to McGruder's pocket, where a tiny, faint orange glow was permeating the cloth. McGruder hauled the light bee from his pocket. A tired glow emanated from the bee in a series of flashes. Flash, flash, flash, flash, pause, flash flash, and again. Flash, flash, flash, flash, pause, flash flash.

'What's it doing?' asked McGruder.

Flash, flash, flash, flash, pause, flash flash.

'I don't know.'

Again. Flash, flash, flash, flash, pause, flash flash.

'My God,' said Kochanski. 'He's talking to us in Morse code.'

Flash, flash, flash, flash, pause, flash flash.

'She's right,' said McGruder. 'Look . . . Dah, dah, dah, dah, space dah dah. Four dashes followed by a space and two dashes. Four dashes is "H" followed by a space which means new letter, then two dashes, "I". H. I. Hi.'

The light bee started to flash again. Dot, dash, dash . . .

'W . . .'

Dot . . .

'E . . .'

Dot, dash . . .

'A . . .'

Dash, dot, dash . . .

'K . . . W.E.A.K. Weak.'

Dash, dot . . .

'N . . .'

Dash, dash dash . . .

'O . . .'

Dash.

'N.O.T. Not . . .'

Dash, dash . . .

'M . . .'

Dash, dot, dot, dash . . .

'U . . .'

Dash, dot, dash, dot . . .

'C . . .'

Dot, dot, dot, dot.

'H . . . Much. Not much . . .'

Dash . . .

'T . . .'

Dot, dot . . .

'I . . .'

Dash, dash . . .

'M . . . Not much time . . .'

Dot . . .

'E . . . Right, not much time.'

Dash, dash, dot . . .

'G . . .'

Dot, dot . . .

'I . . .'

Dot, dot, dot, dash . . .

'V...'

Dot.

'E... Give...'

Dash, dash...

'M...'

Dot...

'Give me...'

'Give you what?' asked Lister.

Kochanski blinked away a lens of tears. 'I know what he's going to say.'

Rimmer's light bee, weakening by the second, stumbled on. Dot, dot, dot, dash...

'V...'

Dot, dot...

'I...'

Dot, dash, dot...

'R...'

Dot, dot, dash...

'U...'

Dot, dot, dot...

'S...'

The light bee's projection beam flicked off. 'What's happened?' asked the Cat. 'It's stopped.'

'The power it needed to Morse code all that stuff must have been too much for it,' said Lister, pulling up the collar of his jacket to screen off the gravity storm.

Suddenly Rimmer's light bee fluttered unsteadily off McGruder's hand and buzzed into the air. A little shakily, almost as if it were being driven by a drunken driver, the bee chugged around their faces as it tried to demonstrate it could transfer the oblivion virus into the gestalt.

'It's transferred all its power to its flight programme,' said Kryten. 'It's proposing we use it to transfer the virus.'

The light bee did a tired little loop-deloop to signify that was exactly what it was proposing.

The virus was loaded into the computer and transferred into the bee. It hummed and squeaked as the deadly programme flooded into its system. Kryten explained to Rimmer that he'd stored the virus in his data base in a muffle programme. Once he accessed it it would destroy him and anything he came into contact with, but until that moment it was perfectly safe. 'Do you understand, sir?'

'Dash, dot, dash, dash.'

'Yes . . .'

Kryten held the bee in his hand. 'There's nothing more we can do now, sir.' He threw the bee into the air. 'God speed.'

The bee floated around in an unsteady circle before it straightened and headed off across the plain towards the malevolent gestalt.

They stood and watched as the light bee wended its way shakily across the tract of gnarled plain, over the blackened, holocaustic stumps of petrified woodlands, over the desiccated fingers of dead riverbeds, over a landscape that had once been lush and joyous but was now a shrivelled, embittered wasteland. Finally the bee hovered before the orange twister that spun in spiteful circles over the caverns, protecting them like a lioness might protect her cubs. The bee stopped, teetering on the edge of the Rage's bitter winds, almost as if it were having a change of heart.

Lister aimed the unoculars across the canyon. 'He's stopped. He can't go through with it.'

The gravity gale howled through their guts as the light bee paused and then started to flash a new message. Dot, dot, dot.

'S . . .'

Dash, dash . . .

'M . . .'

Dot, dash . . .

'A . . .'

Dash, dot, dash . . .

'K . . .'

Dot, dot . . .

'I . . .'

Dash, dot, dot, dot . . .

'B . . .'

Dash, dot, dot, dot . . .

'B . . . again.'

Dot, dot, dash, dot . . .

'F . . .'

Dash, dot, dot, dot.

'B . . .'

The bee clicked off.

'S.M.A.K.I.B.B.F.B?'

'Smakibbfb? What does that mean?' asked the Cat.

'Maybe the muffle programme's poisoned his system too early,' said Kochanski.

Lister shook his head. 'S.M.A.K.I.B.B.F.B. Smoke me a kipper, I'll be back for breakfast.'

McGruder smiled.

The bee transferred back to its flight programme and powered into the heart of the Rage.

Nothing happened.

They watched in silence.

Nothing.

Silence.

Then the Rage erupted in an extended volley of blood black explosions that lacerated the plain. Gargantuan lightbulbs of fire plumed skyward, accompanied by the agonized screechings of a million dying creatures; all the Gelfs who'd been forced to surrender their lives and their identities to create the gestalt, all had been poisoned by recrimination and resentment, all had vented their spleen through the power of the gestalt, but now their fury was over. Their pain had ended. They were free to die.

The Rage was dead.

The gravity winds smashed Lister and the others against the rock face as they ran along the mountain pathway towards the sanctuary of the caverns. Once in, they ran past falling boulders and schisming floors, past breaking stalactites and flooding underground rivers, deeper and deeper, farther and farther into the ground. Finally, the planet was hauled into the aureole of black holes and a series of tremors hurtled through the subterranean chambers sending massive chasms zigzagging towards them. Leaping left and right and left again they continued their flight into the planet's core until the gravitational pummelling the planet was receiving from the Omni-zone was nothing but a distant rumbling.

CHAPTER 20

It took them three weeks to burrow their way to the surface. Surviving on subterranean fauna, they bored through fallen boulders, dug their way past mudslides and avalanches of clay, until finally, having navigated their way round countless flooded chambers and fled from more disintegrating ceilings than anyone could remember, they chiselled away a final piece of rock and staggered into daylight.

Lister gazed skyward. A bashful sun hung back behind a gang of cloud. He filled his lungs with air. It smelt as fresh as ice. They had made the crossing into a new dimension; which dimension it was impossible to tell.

'Look.'

Kochanski pointed down the length of the canyon. Rivers crossed and skipped along its length like playful children. The first signs of a new, greener kind of vegetation were beginning to peek through the sandy soil.

They staggered around in groups of two and threes, holding on to one another and grinning. Finally they broke apart.

Kryten pulled the healer disk from his belt pocket and tapped it quizzically against his chest plate. Then, word-

307

lessly he started towards the caverns that the Rage had once guarded with such venom, trailed by the Cat, McGruder and Reketrebn. Their heads stooped low, brows furrowed, they scoured the ground looking for a small dead light bee.

Lister looked at Kochanski through panda eyes. 'We're home.'

She kissed him. 'I know.'

They clambered down the canyon and started to walk alongside a chirpy flood river that gambolled across the valley. Past the purple flowers of meadow saffron. It felt like it was spring.

She looked at him. And squeezed his hand.

'Don't think that.'

'Think what?'

'That we've got all this and what's the point if we can't have kids.'

He smiled a heavy smile.

'We don't need kids to make us happy, hon. We're not incomplete without them. We've got us.'

He smiled. 'I know.'

'But?'

'But I just feel I screwed it up. I had a responsibility to restart the human race and I blew it.'

'Let me show you something.' She tugged off her loosely buttoned mauve shirt and pulled her T-shirt over her head until she was down to just her jogging bra. 'You know you never plan ahead. You live for now and hope everything works itself out. Personally, I think that's kind of cute but then I have major character flaws of my own.'

'What are you talking about?'

'Planning ahead. You never do.' She grinned. 'Lucky then you got yourself entangled with a gal who does.' She slipped her hand into her bra cup and pulled out a small, one-inch vial. 'You've also got a memory like a sieve. I took a second vial of luck virus, remember?'

A slow smile started to break across Lister's face.

'I can see you're ahead of me.' She took a swig and handed it to Lister. 'Here's the deal.' She picked up two flat stones and handed one to him. 'If we can both skim these two stones down the river so that they each bounce seven times and wind up in that little ox-bow pond over there, it means . . .' She pointed to the edge of the canyon where a skirt of sorghum grass was swaying in the breeze. 'When we hit the long grass over there we're going to wind up making the first of our many children.'

Lister swigged from the luck virus.

'You ready?'

He nodded. 'I'm ready.'

They took aim and fired. The pebbles landed simultaneously and perfectly on the surface of the river. They bounced once, twice, three times, two feet apart and still in perfect unison.

Four times, five times, still together.

Six times, still in absolute synchronicity, almost as if they were bound together by some invisible cord.

Seven times. Still as one.

Up they went a final time before they touched down in the little ox-bow pond in a harmonious chord of simultaneous plops.

Lister and Kochanski swivelled and looked at one another, wearing monkey grins that were almost too big to fit on their faces. They hugged and screamed and yelled and hollered. Then gradually the grin faded from Lister's face. He picked her up in his arms and stared into her eyes. He was disembowelled by her diamond brightness, he was mesmerized by her beauty.

She kissed him on his bottom lip.

He started to carry her across the canyon towards the leaning choirs of tall grass. He carried her over the streams, over the sand estuary, past the meadow saffron until finally they were there, walking through the yellow blades of maize. They melted down into the sorghum grass and disappeared from view.

Slowly, gently, almost imperceptibly, the grass began to sway.